William Chaffers

The Keramic Gallery

Vol. 1

Anatipos

William Chaffers

The Keramic Gallery

Vol. 1

Reprint of the original, first published in 1872.

1st Edition 2023 | ISBN: 978-3-38213-047-3

Anatiposi Verlag is an imprint of Outlook Verlagsgesellschaft mbH.

Verlag (Publisher): Outlook Verlag GmbH, Zeilweg 44, 60439 Frankfurt, Deutschland
Vertretungsberechtigt (Authorized to represent): E. Roepke, Zeilweg 44, 60439 Frankfurt, Deutschland
Druck (Print): Books on Demand GmbH, In de Tarpen 42, 22848 Norderstedt, Deutschland

THE

KERAMIC GALLERY

CONTAINING

SEVERAL HUNDRED ILLUSTRATIONS OF RARE CURIOUS AND CHOICE EXAMPLES OF POTTERY AND PORCELAIN

From the Earliest Times to the beginning of the Present Century.

WITH

HISTORICAL NOTICES AND DESCRIPTIONS.

BY

WILLIAM CHAFFERS,

AUTHOR OF "MARKS AND MONOGRAMS ON POTTERY AND PORCELAIN," "HALL MARKS ON PLATE," ETC.

In Two Volumes.

VOLUME I.

LONDON:
CHAPMAN & HALL, 193, PICCADILLY.

1872.

INTRODUCTION.

A FEW remarks may be considered necessary in bringing this illustrated work before the notice of the Public. It originated in a course of Lectures on Pottery and Porcelain, delivered by me at the Society of Arts, in 1867, which I had frequently been solicited to publish. A recent invention in photography having been submitted to me by Mr. Cundall as a desirable and comparatively economical means of illustrating these Lectures, I resolved to adopt the Woodbury process of printing the plates in permanent ink from metal *clichés*, transferred from photographic negatives. These have been taken under my superintendence, expressly for this work, from examples in well-known collections, thus securing in every instance absolutely faithful copies of the originals.

It is important to notice that the "KERAMIC GALLERY" does not supersede my original work, entitled "MARKS AND MONOGRAMS ON POTTERY AND PORCELAIN," but forms a Pictorial Supplement to it; and those readers who desire a more detailed account of the various *fabriques*, and a more extended list of their marks, should consult that volume, which has been so favorably received by the Public both at home and abroad.

W. CHAFFERS.

19, FITZROY SQUARE,
December, 1871.

List of Illustrations.

NOTE.—The references are to "MARKS AND MONOGRAMS ON POTTERY AND PORCELAIN, by W. CHAFFERS." 3rd edition, 1870.

ANCIENT POTTERY.

EGYPT.

GREECE.

ITALY—MAIOLICA.

PERUGIA.

FAENZA.

GUBBIO.

DERUTA.

FERRARA.

NOVE.

VENICE.

SAVONA.

MONTE-LUPO.

GENOA.

LORETO.

CASTELLI.

TURIN.

MILAN.

FLORENCE.

SPAIN—MAIOLICA.

HISPANO-MORESQUE.

TALAVERA.

TRIANA.

92 Costume Figure, temp. Louis XIV, forming a bottle, with inscription. *Lady C. Schreiber.*

93 Dish, landscape and figures. Dated 1774. *Lady C. Schreiber.*

ALCORA.

94 Plaque, painted with scriptural subject. 18th century. (Chaffers, p. 232). *Mr. C. W. Reynolds.*

95 Plate, painted with landscape and ruins. 18th century. *Lady C. Schreiber.*

PERSIA—FAYENCE.

96 Tile. Flowers in relief, coloured. *S. K. Museum.*

97 Tile. Horsemen in relief, coloured. *S. K. Museum.*

98, 99 Two Plates, painted with scrolls. *S. K. Museum.*

FRANCE—FAYENCE.

OIRON (Henri II. Ware.)

100 Candlestick, cream coloured ware, inlaid with arabesques and other patterns in dark brown and reddish brown, with reliefs of three boys, tragic masks and shields of arms of France and cipher of Henri II., and above three terminal figures of Satyrs. About 1540. (Chaffers, p. 157). *S. K. Museum.*

101 Biberon, interlaced with bands, scrolls and masks. *Mr. Andrew Fountaine.*

APT.

102 Yellow Vase with masks. 18th century. *Lady C. Schreiber.*

BLOIS.

103 Pair of Candlesticks, painted with mermen, masks, &c., in colours. Marked "Blois 66." 19th century. *S. K. Museum.*

PALISSY.

104 Ewer, dark blue ground with masks, cartouches and scroll foliage in various colours; the handle of scroll form, decorated with a nude female figure in high relief holding a cornucopia. 16th century. (Soulages Coll.) *S. K. Museum.*

105 Plateau. "La belle Jardinière." In the centre a figure of Flora, at her feet gardening implements, the border decorated with an embossed arabesque design. 16th century. (Soulages Coll.) *S. K. Museum.*

106 DISH with reptiles, fish, shells, plants, &c., in proper colours in relief, on deep blue ground. 16th century. (Soulages Coll.) *S. K. Museum.*

107 PLATE, round the edge daisies in relief, floral medallions in the centre upon a perforated ground. 16th century. (Pourtalès Coll.) *S. K. Museum.*

NEVERS.

108 PILGRIM'S BOTTLE, *bleu de Perse* ground, birds and flowers. 1650 to 1680. *S. K. Museum.*

109 EWER, Chinese figures in a landscape. 1650 to 1750. *S. K. Museum.*

110 VASE, boys on dolphins and marine animals *S. K. Museum.*

111 CUP, double spout, and small handles. 1640 to 1700. *S. K. Museum.*

112 PILGRIM'S BOTTLE. Apollo and Daphne and Bacchanalian Scene. *S. K. Museum.*

ROUEN.

113 LARGE EWER, coloured landscapes. Temp. Louis XIV. *S. K. Museum.*

114 PLATE, figures in blue in the centre, surrounded by scrolls, garlands, &c. in polychrome. Temp. Louis XV. *S. K. Museum.*

115 PLATE, octagonal, rosette in centre, border of scrolls and medallions. *S. K. Museum.*

116 EWER. Helmet shaped, painted with foliage and scrolls. Temp. Louis XIV. *S. K. Museum.*

117 COMPOTIER, with rosette, garlands, &c. Louis XIV. *S. K. Museum.*

118 SUGAR CASTOR, ornamented with foliage and scrolls. Temp. Louis XIV. *S. K. Museum.*

119 DISH, octagonal, subject after Klingstedt, polychrome border. Temp. Louis XIV. *S. K. Museum.*

120 COMPOTIER, *à la corne*, flowers, &c. Temp. Louis XIV. *S. K. Museum.*

121 COMPOTIER, painted with Chinese figures and landscape. Temp. Louis XIV. *S. K. Museum.*

122 DISH, painted with a shield of arms, polychrome border. Temp. Louis XV. *S. K. Museum.*

123 JUG. St. Jacques. Inscribed and dated 1737. *S. K. Museum.*

STRASBOURG.

124 LARGE FOUNTAIN, with dolphin, crocodile, &c. in relief, surmounted by a swan. Mark of Paul Hanung. *S. K. Museum.*

125 CLOCK AND BRACKET, with projecting busts, surmounted by a figure of Time. Mark of Paul Hanung 1680-1720. *S. K. Museum.*

MOUSTIERS.

126 DISH, in the Beraine style, with arabesques. *S. K. Museum.*

127 PLATEAU, pastoral group in green *camaieu.* 1720 to 1760. *S. K. Museum.*

128 PLATE. Hunting scene. 1680-1720. *S. K. Museum.*
129 PLATE, painted with flowers: Juno in the centre. 1680 to 1720. *S. K. Museum.*
130 BARBER'S BASIN, Diana and Actæon, with the mark of Olery. 1680 to 1720. *S. K. Museum.*

MARSEILLES.

131 TUREEN, cover and stand, painted with flowers. *S. K. Museum.*
132 PLATE, painted with a landscape by Veuve Perrin. *Mr. C. W. Reynolds.*

LUNEVILLE.

133 TWO STATUETTES of rustic figures, c. 1775. *S. K. Museum.*
134 DISH, painted with birds, c. 1760. *S. K. Museum.*
135 DISH, painted with birds, c. 1760. *S. K. Museum.*

APREY.

136 PLATE, painted with flowers, c. 1780. *S. K. Museum.*

ST. CLEMENT.

137 ECUELLE with gilt scrolls on white ground. *Lady C. Schreiber.*

TOULOUSE.

138 HUNTING BOTTLE, inscribed "Laurens Basso à Toulouse, 14th Maij, 1756." (Chaffers, p. 227.) *Mr. C. W. Reynolds.*

NIDERVILLER.

139 COMPOTIER, flowers, with mark of Beyerlé. *S. K. Museum.*
140 TRAY, landscape with ruins in lake *camaieu*. Inscribed "J. Deutsch del. sculpt à Niderviller 1774. *S. K. Museum.*
141 VASE, lake *camaieu* landscapes. Mark of Custine. *S. K. Museum.*

SCEAUX PENTHIÈVRE.

142 PLATE, painted with birds and trees. *Mr. C. W. Reynolds.*

CREIL.

143 PLATE, yellow border, transfer landscape. *Lady C. Schreiber.*

SWEDEN, DENMARK, &c.—FAYENCE.

RÖRSTRAND.

144 TUREEN and cover, white with coloured flowers and scroll margin, the cover surmounted by a half figure of a deer. Dated 1770. *S. K. Museum.*
145 BUTTER-BOAT, leaf shaped, painted with flowers. 1771. *Mr. C. W. Reynolds.*

MARIEBERG.

146 VASE and cover, with branches and flowers, coloured in relief; on the cover a sitting bird. About 1770. *S. K. Museum.*

147 VASE, oviform, with transfer landscape, on the pedestal a mouse creeping round. Dated 1774. *Lady C. Schreiber.*

148 PLATE, pierced border, with a shield of arms and flowers, 1768. *Mr. C. W. Reynolds.*

149 BOWL, painted with arms and flowers, satyrs' head handles, 1769. *Mr. C. W. Reynolds.*

KIEL.

150 THE BISHOP MITRE BOWL, painted with subjects. Inscribed "Kiel. Buchwald Director. Abr Leihamer fecit." (*Described in Chaffers, page* 236.) *Mr. C. W. Reynolds.*

GERMANY—GRÈS—FAYENCE.

NUREMBERG.

151 GROUP in high relief, representing a sleeping knight, by whose side is a man with winged cap holding a globe, behind a horse tied to a tree. Early 16th century. *S. K. Museum.*

152 JUG, in various colours, with figures in low relief; in front, two armed figures in full relief, on each side of a tree. Attributed to Viet Hirschvogel. Early 16th century. *S. K. Museum.*

153 DISH, painted in the centre with the Ascension. Dated 1723. Signed *Glüer.* *Mr. C. W. Reynolds.*

COLOGNE.

154 JUG, German grès or stoneware, brown glaze, with large rosettes, &c. in relief. 16th century. *Geological Museum.*

155 LARGE FOUNTAIN, purple, blue and white, the lower part gadrooned, with central band of figures in niches, and openwork wheels. Height 30 inches. 16th century. *S. K. Museum.*

156, 157 CANETTE, embossed scriptural and classical subjects, arms, &c. 16th or 17th century. (Bernal.) And another. *S. K. Museum.*

158, 159 TWO CRUCHES, blue and white ornaments in relief. 17th century. *S. K. Museum.*

HARBURG.

160 JUG, painted in grey *camaieu* with a landscape, signed "Joh. Schaper." About 1640. (Marryat Coll.) *Chaffers, page* 247. *S. K. Museum.*

GRENZHAUSEN.

161 JUG, reticulated pattern, engine turned, enriched with brilliant enamel colours, in geometrical patterns; 18th century. *S. K. Museum.*

CREUSSEN (BAVARIA).

162 TANKARD, with gilt and coloured ornaments and figures of the Electors of Germany on horseback and the Emperor. Dated 1696. *S. K. Museum.*

DRESDEN.

163 Coffee Pot, of red Böttcher ware, gold figures and arabesques. *S. K. Museum.*

TEINITZ.

164 Plate, painted with Calisto and Diana, inscribed Welby, Teinitz. (Chaffers, p. 254). *Rev. T. Staniforth.*

ARNSTADT (Gotha).

165 Jug, with St. George; signed. (Chaffers, p. 253). *Rev. T. Staniforth.*

AMSTERDAM.

166 Fruit Dish, painted in blue with a man and woman seated, marked with a cock. *Mr. C. W. Reynolds.*

ORIENTAL PORCELAIN.

CHINA.

167 Crackle Vase, ring handles. *S. K. Museum.*
168 Vase, coloured flowers and insects. *S. K. Museum.*
169 Plate, egg-shell porcelain, painted with two cocks and flowers, pink flowered margin, rose coloured border under. (Bernal Coll.) *S. K. Museum.*
170 Plate, white ground, painted with two quails and chrysanthemums, border of opaque white flowers. (Bernal Coll.) *S. K. Museum.*

JAPAN.

171 Bottle (Satsuma ware). 19th century. *S. K. Museum.*
172 Bowl (Satsuma ware). 19th century. *S. K. Museum.*

ITALY—PORCELAIN.

FLORENCE.

173 Plate, deep centre, painted in blue with flowers; flowers also on the reverse, and a device of a ball with three flaming rays and short spikes between. Marked at the bottom in blue with the cathedral of Florence and the letter F. About 1600. (Chaffers, p. 311). *S. K. Museum.*
174 Bowl, painted inside and out with blue flowers. Marked with the cathedral and the letter F. About 1600. *S. K. Museum.*
175 Cruet for oil and vinegar, scroll ornament in blue; on each spout A and O (Aceto and Oleo). About 1600. *S. K. Museum.*

DOCCIA.

176 Tea Pot, painted with flowers, purple border. *Lady C. Schreiber.*

NAPLES. CAPO DI MONTE.

178 Cup and Saucer, painted with the signs of the Zodiac, blue and gold borders, on the saucer a figure of Time. *Rev. T. Staniforth.*

179 VASE, green ornaments on gold ground and medallions of figures; one of a pair in the possession of *Mr. Chas. Dickins.*
180 SAUCER, with portrait of King Ferdinand IV. Mark *N.* crowned. *Lady C Schreiber.*
181 CUP (cream coloured). Mark *F. R.* crowned. *Rev. T. Staniforth.*
182 CUP AND SAUCER, landscape and figures. Mark *N.* crowned. *Mr. C. W. Reynolds.*
183 COFFEE POT, painted with classical subjects. *Mr. Walker Joy.*
184 MILK POT, lake *camaieu* landscapes. *Mr. Walker Joy.*
185 CUP AND SAUCER, Bay of Naples. *Mr. Walker Joy.*

TREVISO.

186 ECUELLE, blue ground, painted with buildings and figures; marked *F. F.* "Fratelli Fontebasso Treviso, 1799." *Rev. T. Staniforth.*
187 CUP AND SAUCER, painted with figures, by Fontebasso. (Chaffers, p. 319). *Mr. C. W. Reynolds.*

TURIN (VINEUF).

188 ECUELLE, ornamented in gold with initials and Royal Arms. *Mr. C. W. Reynolds.*

VENICE.

189 SAUCER, lake *camaieu*, "Autumn," by L. Ortolani. *Mr. C. W. Reynolds.*
190 VASE, (centre) painted with flowers (Cozzi period). *Lady C. Schreiber.*
191 CUP AND SAUCER, painted with fruit. *Mr. Walker Joy.*
192 PAIR OF FIGURES of the Seasons. *Lady C Schreiber.*
193 VASE AND COVER, painted in lake *camaieu* with landscape and figures. *Mr. W. Chaffers.*

NOVE.

194 BOTTLE, St. Roch, in lake *camaieu.* *Lady C. Schreiber.*
195 MILK POT, painted with landscapes. *Lady C. Schreiber.*
196 OVAL JARDINIÈRE, painted with landscapes and figures in four medallions. Inscribed "Nove. Gio Marcone pinx.t" (Chaffers, p. 330). *Mr. C. W. Reynolds.*
197 VASE, female figure handles, painted with classical subjects. *Mr. C. W. Reynolds.*

SPAIN—PORCELAIN.

MADRID (BUEN RETIRO).

198 GROUP OF TWO CHILDREN with a goat; coloured; height 14 in. *Sig. Donna Emilia de Riaño.*
199 VASE, with scenes from Don Quixote; height 17 in.; one of a pair in the possession of *Sig. Donna Emilia de Riaño.*

200 VASE, painted with children; height 22 in.; one of a pair in the possession of *Sig. Donna Emilia de Riaño.*

201 GROUPS (a pair) of Boy Bachanals seated on wine casks. *Mr. C. W. Reynolds.*

ALCORA.

202 PLAQUE, with figures at a fountain in conversation. (Chaffers, p. 333). *Mr. C. W. Reynolds.*

GERMANY—PORCELAIN.

DRESDEN.

203 to 205 SUCRIER, dish, and cup and saucer, of Dresden porcelain, engraved with a diamond, by Baron Busch; signed. (*Chaffers, p.* 339). *Lady C. Schreiber.*

206 FIGURE of a man in theatrical dress; signed J. F. 1738. *Lady C. Schreiber.*

207 VASE (lofty white Dresden) with flowers and birds in full relief; height 20 in. *Lady C. Schreiber.*

208 VASE and cover, tureen shaped, perforated and gilt, raised cartouches and cupids; painted with views of public buildings in Dresden, the cover surmounted by a crown. *S. K. Museum.*

209, 210 BUSTS of a boy and girl in white porcelain. *S. K. Museum.*

211, 212 TEA POT, cup and saucer, pink ground, landscapes and figures. *Mr. Walker Joy.*

213 CUP AND SAUCER, the outlines of the flowers forming profile portraits of celebrated men. *Rev. T. Staniforth.*

SCHLAKENWALD.

214 CUP AND SAUCER, painted with costume figures. *Mr. Walker Joy.*

BERLIN.

215, 216 MILK POT, cup and saucer, blue and gold scale pattern and cupids in red. *Mr. Walker Joy.*

HÖCHST.

217, 218 TRAY AND SUCRIER, painted with birds, harlequin borders. *Mr. Walker Joy.*

219 SUCRIER, painted with conversation subjects. *Mr. Walker Joy.*

220 LAMP, painted in lake, with landscape, &c. *Mr. C. W. Reynolds.*

FRANKENTHAL.

221 PLATE with chronogram of 1775, and specimens of colours used in the *fabrique*, initials of Carl Theodor. (Chaffers, p. 360). *Rev. T. Staniforth.*

222 to 225 DEJEUNER, painted with Fête Champêtre Scenes, &c. *Mr. C. W. Reynolds.*

226 CUP aud saucer, painted with animals. *Mr. Walker Joy.*

VIENNA.

227 CUP and saucer, pink drapery. (*See Chaffers, p.* 347.) *Mr. Walker Joy.*

NYMPHENBURG.

228 CADDY, painted with cattle. Mark a triangle. *Mr. C. W. Reynolds.*

ANSPACH.

229 SUCRIER and cover, painted with flowers. *Mr. C. W. Reynolds.*

KRONENBURG, OR LUDWIGSBURG.

230 COFFEE POT, painted in lake *camaieu* with landscape after Claude, gilt arabesque and scroll border. (Bernal Coll.) *S. K. Museum.*

FULDA.

231 COFFEE POT, with sea view and figures. *Mr. Walker Joy.*
232 TEA POT, painted with urn and insects. *Mr. Walker Joy.*
233 CUP and saucer, painted with birds. *Mr. Walker Joy.*
234 and 235 PAIR OF FIGURES of peasants. *Mr. C. Dickins.*

VOLKSTEDT.

236 TEA POT, painted with flowers. *Mr. C. W. Reynolds.*

RUDOLSTADT.

237 MILK POT, painted with flowers. Mark, a hay fork. *Mr. Walker Joy.*
238 CUP and saucer, with pastoral figures. Mark *R.* *Mr. Walker Joy.*

REGENSBERG.

239 CUP and saucer, with sepia landscapes. *Mr. Walker Joy.*

GROSBREITENBACH.

240 CUP and saucer, painted with flowers. *Mr. Walker Joy.*

LIMBACH.

241 CUP and saucer, with sepia landscapes. *Mr. Walker Joy.*

GERA.

242 CUP and saucer, with black profile portrait. *Mr. Walker Joy.*

GOTHA.

243 CUP and saucer, painted with a view of Gotha. *Mr. C. W. Reynolds.*

WALLENDORF.

244 TEA POT, painted with blue sprigs. *Mr. Walker Joy.*

SWITZERLAND—HOLLAND—PORCELAIN.

NYONS.

245 Cup, with two handles, portrait in the centre. *Rev. T. Staniforth.*

ZURICH.

246 Cup and Saucer, painted with fruit. *Mr. Walker Joy.*
247 Group of a soldier trampling on a Turk, unveiling a lady, martial and love trophies on the ground. *Mr. C. W. Reynolds.*

WEESP.

248 Large Ewer, painted with a basket of flowers. Mark *W.* *Mr. C. W. Reynolds.*
249 Coffee Pot, figures after Teniers. Mark, cross and dots. *Mr. Walker Joy.*

LOOSDRECHT.

250 Vase, perforated, painted with birds. *S. K. Museum.*

AMSTERDAM.

251 Pair of Bottles, painted in lake with birds. Mark, a lion rampant. *Mr. Reynolds.*

AMSTEL.

252 and 253 Tea Pot and sucrier, Views in Holland. *Mr. Walker Joy.*
254 Sucrier, painted with birds. *Mr. Walker Joy.*

HAGUE.

255 Milk Jug, painted with flowers. *Rev. T. Staniforth.*

LILLE.

256 Cup and Cover, with landscapes in indian ink. Inscribed "Fait par Le Brun à Lille." *Mr. C. W. Reynolds.*

TOURNAY.

257 Cup and saucer, painted with animals and birds, illustrating "Fontaine's Fables." Marked with a gold kiln. (Chaffers, p. 387). *Rev. T. Staniforth.*
258 Basin, lake camaieu landscapes and figures. Mark, cross swords and crosses. *Mr. Walker Joy.*

BRUSSELS.

259 Milk Pot (portion of a service) with the name L. Cretté. (Chaffers 388). *Rev. T. Staniforth.*
260 Tea Pot, painted with roses, &c., gilt borders. Mark *B* impressed. *Mr. C. W. Reynolds.*

LUXEMBURG.

261 to 264 Four Figures, by Boch, of Luxemburg. *Mr. Chas. Dickins.*

RUSSIA.

ST. PETERSBURG.

265 CUP and saucer, with Imperial Arms. Mark of Emperor Paul. *Mr. C. W. Reynolds.*

266 VERRIÈRE, band of roses on gold, and views of buildings. *Mr. C. W. Reynolds.*

MOSCOW.

267 CUP and saucer, painted with a view of Moscow, bearing the mark AП (A. Popoff). *S. K. Museum.*

KORZEC.

268 CUP and saucer. (Chaffers, p. 394) *Rev. T. Staniforth.*

COPENHAGEN.

269 SERVICE (portion of a) with portraits of painters. (Chaffers, 397). *Rev. T. Staniforth.*

270 CABARET, with medallions of landscapes. *Mr. Walker Joy.*

FRANCE—PORCELAIN.

ST. CLOUD.

271, 272 TWO JUGS and covers of quilted china. *S. K. Museum.*

273 STATUETTE of Astronomy, seated, holding the sun. *Lady C. Schreiber.*

CHANTILLY.

274 CUP and saucer. Chinese flowers. *S. K. Museum.*

MENEÇY.

275 SUGAR BASIN, stand, and spoon. Flowers. *S. K. Museum.*

276 BASKET and cover with flowers in relief. *Lady C. Schreiber.*

277 VASES (pair of white), flowers in relief. *Mr. C. W. Reynolds.*

SCEAUX.

278 CUP and saucer, flowers. Anchor mark. *Mr. C. W. Reynolds.*

279 MILK POT, painted with poultry. Mark *S.X.* *Mr. C. W. Reynolds.*

ARRAS.

280 SEAU, painted with flowers. *S. K. Museum.*

BOULOGNE.

281 PLAQUE of a dead bird, executed in biscuit (modern). *Lady C. Schreiber.*

282 BISCUIT SUCRIER, with relievi of cupids (modern). (Chaffers, p. 411). *Lady C. Schreiber.*

CLIGNANCOURT.

283 Milk Pot, gold flowers. Mark, a windmill. *Mr. C. W. Reynolds.*
284 Dish and cup, painted with flowers. *Mr. C. W. Reynolds.*
285 Milk Pot, painted with figures. *Mr. C. W. Reynolds.*
285* Milk Pot and stand, with floral initials. *Mr. Walker Joy.*

ORLEANS.

286 Sucrier, with medallions of roses. *Mr. Walker Joy.*

NIDERVILLER.

287 Cup and saucer, painted with birds. Count Custine's initials. *Mr. Walker Joy.*

BOISSETTE.

288 Tea Pot, painted with flowers. *Mr. C. W. Reynolds.*

CAEN.

289 Tea Cup and saucer, painted with green and gold festoons, and medallions of landscapes. *Rev. Thomas Staniforth.*

STRASBOURG.

290 Milk Pot, with landscape and figures. *Mr. C. W. Reynolds.*

PARIS.

291 Tea Pot, gold border and festoons, by Veuve, M. & Co. *Mr. Walker Joy.*
292 De la Reine.—Sucrier, with festoons of flowers. Mark *A.* crowned. *Mr. Walker Joy.*
293 Angoulême.—Cup and saucer. Sprig pattern. *Mr. Walker Joy.*
294 De la Courtille.—Tea Set. *S. K. Museum.*
295 Pont aux Choux.—Tea Pot, painted with sprigs and flowers. *Rev. T. Staniforth.*
296 Rue de Crussol.—Cup and saucer (canary coloured), painted with flowers and butterflies, by Potter. *Rev. T. Staniforth.*

SÈVRES.

297 Ecuelle, 1771. (Bernal Coll.) *S. K. Museum.*
298 Biscuit Group. Cupid and Psyche. *S. K. Museum.*
299 Vase, boat shaped, painted with cupids. *H.M. The Queen.*
300 Vaisseau à Mat, landscapes and figures. *H.M. The Queen.*

ENGLAND.

STAFFORDSHIRE.

301 Tyg with four handles, 1621. *Geological Museum.*
302 Mug with two handles, 1682. *Geological Museum.*
303 Tea Pot, of mottled open work. *Geological Museum.*

LEEDS POTTERY.

349 CHESNUT BOWL and cover, pierced. *Geological Museum.*
350 PLATE, painted with a portrait. *Geological Museum.*

CASTLEFORD.

351 TEA POT, ornaments in relief and blue lines. (D. D. & Co.) *Geological Museum.*
352 CANDLESTICK. Similar. *Geological Museum.*

YARMOUTH.

353 PLATE, painted with flowers. *Geological Museum.*

NEWCASTLE.

353* MUG, with toad inside, and printed Monument of Nelson, by "Fell & Co., Newcastle pottery." *Geological Museum.*
354 DISH (Queen's ware). Fruit in relief, by "Fell, Newcastle." *Geological Museum.*

ST. ANTHONY'S.

355 JUG with lustre and subjects in relief. "Sewell." *Geological Museum.*

NOTTINGHAM.

356 MUG, of brown ware. "Made at Nottingham the 17th August, 1771." *Geological Museum.*
357 BROWN BEAR, forming a jug. *Geological Museum.*

CADBOROUGH, NEAR RYE.

358 and 359 SUSSEX PIG, and small green vase. *Geological Museum.*

LOWESBY.

360 and 361 GARDEN POT (brown) and a small vase of green glaze. *Geological Museum.*

PORCELAIN.

WORCESTER.

362 CHAMBERLAIN'S PLATE, blue and gold. *Geological Museum.*
363 MUG, printed. King of Prussia. *Geological Museum.*
364 SUCRIER and milk jug. Garden Scenes. *Geological Museum.*
365 LARGE JUG, blue and medallions of birds and flowers. *Geological Museum.*
366 CUP and saucer, dragon pattern. *S. K. Museum.*
366A PART OF A TEA SET, transfer printed ruins, painted and gilt. *Mr. W. Chaffers.*
366B PART OF A TEA SET, painted with blue, red and gold, Japanese pattern. *Mr. W. Chaffers.*

SWINTON (ROCKINGHAM).

367 PATTERN PLATE. Service of William IV. *Geological Museum.*
368 VASE, or centre piece of a dessert service made for William IV., with paintings of *The Tight Shoe*, &c. Height 14 in. *Mr. Emerson Norman.*

DERBY.

369 SCENT VASE, with flowers in full relief. "Crown." *Geological Museum.*
370 PLATE, painted with flowers, by Billingsley. *Geological Museum.*
371 CUP (two handled), cover and saucer. "Crown." *Geological Museum.*
372 VASE, with painted medallions. Chelsea Derby. *Lady C. Schreiber.*
373 GROUPS (pair of)—Lovers in alcoves. Chelsea Derby. *Lady C. Schreiber.*
374 CUP of china, with the letter R, attributed to the early Cock Pit Hill Works. *Mr. Alfred. Wallis.*
375 PAIR OF CHELSEA-DERBY VASES, views in Derbyshire. *Lord Scarsdale.*
376 to 378 THREE CUPS and a saucer. *Lord Scarsdale.*
379 THE DERBY "PRENTICE PLATE," painted by Billingsley about 1785, kept for 60 years at the works as a copy. *Mr. J. Haslem.*
380 THE "THISTLE PLATE," painted by W. Pegg about 1800. *Mr. J. Haslem.*
381 THE "RODNEY JUG," painted by E. Withers about 1782. *Miss Ward.*
382 PAIR OF CHOCOLATE CUPS, views in Derbyshire. *Mr. J. Haslem.*
383 CHELSEA-DERBY TEA POT, dish, cup and saucer. *Mrs. Nixon.*
384 CHOCOLATE CUP, cover and stand. *Major John Evans.*
385 CHOCOLATE CUP, cover and stand. *The Earl of Chesterfield.*
386 CUP and saucer, blue and gold, jewelled. *Captain F. N. Smith.*
387 CROWN-DERBY CUP, cover and stand, painted with "The Smugglers" and flowers, on gold ground. *Mr. Jas. Sanders.*

BURTON-ON-TRENT.

388 COMPORT OF PORCELAIN, painted with flowers and fruit, attributed to this place. *Mr. W. Bemrose, Jun.*

WIRKSWORTH.

389 CUP and cover, raised scale pattern. *Mr. W. Bemrose, Jun.*

PINXTON.

390 FLOWER POT, French sprig pattern. *Mr. W. Bemrose, Jun.*
391 ICE PAILS (pair of porcelain) primrose ground, with deep border of flowers, painted by Billingsley. Early 19th century. *S. K. Museum.*
392 SUGAR BOWL and cover, painted with a landscape. *Mr. J. Hawkins.*
393 JARDINIÈRE, views in Derbyshire, Dovedale, &c. *Mr. J. Haslem.*

LOWESTOFT.

394 to 395 PLATE, cup and cover, with views and birds, elaborately gilt. *Mr. Walker Joy.*
396 CUP and saucer. Crest of an owl, and initials of W. Woodley. *Mr. Walker Joy.*
397 to 401 COFFEE POT, and four cups various. *Mr. Emerson Norman.*

PLYMOUTH.

402 Coffee Pot, blue ground and panels of flowers. *Lady C. Schreiber.*
403 Beaker and cover, painted with flowers. *Lady C. Schreiber.*
404 White Bird. *Lady C. Schreiber.*
405 Statuette of Woodward the actor, with the Plymouth mark. *Mr. W. Edkins.*
406 Pair of Figures, shepherd and shepherdess. *Mr. W. Edkins.*
407 Sweetmeat Stand, in form of shells and rockwork. *Mr. W. Edkins.*
408 Lofty Centre Piece of shells and rockwork. *Mr. W. Edkins.*

BRISTOL.

409 Dish, painted with flowers, presented by Mr. Cookworthy to the *Geological Museum.*
410 and 411 Bowl and cover, cup and inkstand. *Geological Museum.*
412 Tea Pot with flowers *Lady C. Schreiber.*
413 Tea Pot with flowers. *Lady C. Schreiber.*
414 Dish with flowers and ribbons. *Lady C. Schreiber.*
415 Tripod (white), supported by griffins. *Lady C. Schreiber.*
416 Salt Cellar, in form of a shell. *Lady C. Schreiber.*

CAUGHLEY.

417 Jug, painted in blue, "James Kennedy, 1778." *Geological Museum.*
418 Mug, painted in blue with birds and fruit. *Geological Museum.*
419 Plate, blue Chinese landscape and figures. *Geological Museum.*

COLEBROOK DALE (COALPORT).

420 Pattern Plate of a service, given by Her Majesty to the Emperor of Russia. *Geological Museum.*

BOW.

421 Salts (pair of), kneeling figures holding shells, (see fragment found at Bow, *Chaffers, p.* 699). *Mr. John. J. Bagshawe.*
422 Statuette of Mrs. Clive, the Actress. *Mr. John J. Bagshawe.*
423 Milk Pot, goats and bee in relief, painted. *Geological Museum.*
424 Tea Pot, flowers and insects, embossed and coloured. *Geological Museum.*
425 Salt Cellar, shells in relief. *Geological Museum.*
426 Bowl on foot, with insects. *Geological Museum.*
427 "New Canton" Inkstand, 1751. *Geological Museum.*
428 Plate, painted flowers and hawthorn relief border. *Geological Museum.*
429, 430 Two Cups, one flowers, the other hawthorn pattern. *Geological Museum.*
431 Tea Pot, printed with Frederick the Great, King of Prussia. *Lady C. Schreiber.*
432 Plate, printed with Æneas and Anchises. *Lady C. Schreiber.*

433, 434 BOWL, painted by Thomas Craft in 1760, and the inscription on the box which contained it. *British Museum.*

435 PORCELAIN figure, a coloured model of the Farnese Flora at Naples, ascribed to John Bacon, R.A. Late 18th century. *S. K. Museum.*

436 VASE with scrolls and cover, with flowers and birds in full relief, at top a woman and poultry. *Lady C. Schreiber.*

437 BASKET VASE, supported by two cupids, flowers in relief. *Lady C. Schreiber.*

438 SAUCE BOAT, flowers, &c. in relief. Mark a triangle. *Lady C. Schreiber.*

439 PUG DOG, of white china. Caduceus mark. *Lady C. Schreiber.*

440 SPHINX, of white china. *Lady C. Schreiber.*

441 BUST in white porcelain of George II. Height 17 in. *Lady C. Schreiber.*

441A GROUP of the Seasons, in white porcelain. *Mr. Jas. Sanders.*

441B GROUP of the Tea Party, slightly damaged. *Mr. Jas. Sanders.*

CHELSEA.

442 STATUETTE of Marshal Conway. Height 13 in. *Lady C. Schreiber.*

443 STATUETTE of Wilkes. Height 13 in. *Lady C. Schreiber.*

444, 445 SHEPHERD and Shepherdess. Height 12½ in. *Lady C. Schreiber.*

446 to 451 SIX BIRDS, some with raised anchor. *Lady C. Schreiber.*

452 VASE (large Chelsea). "Death of Cleopatra." *British Museum.*

453 VASE, supported by three caryatids, morone ground. *Lady C. Schreiber.*

454, 455 FIGURES (pair of). Pedlar and his Wife. *Lady C. Schreiber.*

456 STATUETTE of Diana with a dog. *Miss Hartley.*

457 VASE, in imitation of wicker work, scroll stand and birds. *Miss Hartley.*

458 PLATE, with rose bud and leaves in relief, coloured. *Miss Hartley.*

459 DISH for fruit, painted with flowers. *Miss Hartley.*

460 GROUP of the Three Maries before the Cross. Height 10½ in. *Lady C. Schreiber.*

460A PAIR OF STATUETTES, Euterpe and Melpomene. *Mr. Chas. Dickins.*

SWANSEA.

461, 462 Two PLATES, with flowers and birds. *Geological Museum.*

NANTGARW.

463, 464 Two PLATES. Basket of flowers, and group of flowers. *Geological Museum.*

465 CUP and saucer, scale pattern, birds and flowers. *S. K. Museum.*

466 VASE, painted with flowers; Welsh harp handles. *Mr. W. Bemrose, Jun.*

467 VASE, with flowers and gilt scrolls. *Mr. W. Bemrose, Jun.*

468 VASE, painted with flowers, gilt vine ornament in relief. *Mr. W. Bemrose, Jun.*

THE KERAMIC GALLERY.

Ancient Pottery.

IT would be a vain attempt to endeavour to particularize any country or race of people, from whence the art of making pottery took its rise. It is one of the oldest branches of human industry, and sprang from the requirements of man, desirous of finding a convenient mode of conveying the fruits of the earth to his mouth; that the appetite might be appeased and life sustained: one of the first laws of nature. Earth the commonest of materials was ready to his hand; he could not fail to observe that the rain falling upon the clay, would soften and render it plastic; while the influences of the sun and air, would dry and harden it. It is therefore reasonable to suppose, that the primeval races of man would naturally fashion the soft clay into rude cups or bowls and dry them in the heat of the sun. Subsequently, as the human race became dispersed over the face of the globe, either by conquest, colonization or other causes, peculiar methods of mixing the clays, conventional forms and ornamentation, would be manifested by each, and we are thus enabled to trace most of the vessels to their source and appropriate the varied productions of keramic artists with some degree of certainty.

The potter's wheel was an early invention and a great improvement upon the methods previously adopted in fashioning the rude sun-dried vessels by the hand alone. It enabled the potter to make symmetrically a great variety of forms and every combination of circular, spherical and cylindrical shapes, in true proportions. Its origin is unknown, although it has been ascribed to several nations, where excellence in the potter's art has been attained; thus Athens, Corynth and Sicyon, the three great rivals in the keramic art, have all been mentioned as inventors of this simple machine, but we must look to a still more remote period for its origin.

M. Brongniart assigns it to the Chinese, and infers that after leaving China where it had been long known, it passed into Egypt, thence into Scythia, and nearly at the same time into Greece and its colonies in Southern Italy, reaching Etruria at a later date, and that it then penetrated the whole of Southern Europe, Rome and its colonies, Spain &c.; as these countries became civilized and acquainted with the arts of the East, stopping at the southern part of Germany and only partially entering it, and that while penetrating into Gaul it remained unknown among the ancient Scandinavian nations. All the early vases of Greece bear traces of the lines of the wheel, except in some later specimens where moulds alone were used. The representations of the potter's wheel in the tombs at Thebes show, that the general method of using it in ancient times was much the same as at the present day.

Modelling by the hand and moulding were both frequently employed for raised ornaments, and bronze or baked terra cotta stamps for impressing devices and patterns have been discovered. These ornaments were moulded or stamped on round or square cakes of clay, and applied while moist to the terminations of the handles or lips of the vases. Borders and zones of small patterns in relief were impressed by cylindrical stamps revolving in a frame or handle and passed round the vessel.

We will first briefly advert to the nature of clay as regards the change it undergoes in the process of manufacture

Suppose we take a lump of clay or earth, soaked in water sufficiently to render it plastic, and then form it into a brick or tile, and lay it in the sun to dry; as the moisture evaporates the brick hardens and the particles adhere slightly together; but we have produced simply a brick of desiccated clay, which may, by adding the quantity of water taken from it, be again converted to its original state. But if we place this brick in a kiln, the nature of the clay is altogether changed; the high temperature melts all the parts and cements them together, effecting a great chemical change, the substance being so altered from its original state, that water could never mix with it, so as again to form clay.

During this operation of baking the clay in the kiln, the object into which it is made decreases materially in bulk; this is termed the *shrinkage*, and arises, first from the drying up of the moisture, amounting to even 15 per cent. or more; and secondly by the fusion of the substances, the component particles draw closer together, causing a considerable diminution in size. To illustrate this, let us suppose the potter wishes to make a bust or statuette in earthenware. The original model is placed in his hand, which he proceeds to mould in plaster; into this hollow mould he presses the clay, which shortly contracts itself so as to become detached from the sides; he then dries it in the air, and again its size diminishes and one hardly understands how it can be a strict reproduction of the original. Another ordeal follows, it is subjected to the high temperature of the kiln, and it is still more sensibly reduced.

A beautiful exposition of the *shrinkage* of clay, is exemplified in the modern Dresden and other china figures, which are veiled with a fine keramic net work in close imitation of lace. The process, however, is simple when the method of performing it is known. A piece of lace is steeped in diluted clay or slip, termed by the French *barbotine*, thus prepared it is thrown over the statuette, when dried in the air the bulk of the keramic coating decreases; but it is in the kiln the magic effect is accomplished, the great heat entirely destroys the vegetable fibre, which formed the net work and flowers; the paste thus freed from its nucleus is contracted to such a degree that the outer covering becomes more delicate than the thread which it surrounded.

The proper selection of clays for making pottery is a most important matter, as some contain a greater proportion of moisture, or more fusible materials than others; it is therefore evident, that if the clays are not all of the same composition, or not well kneaded and mixed together, the shrinkage of the vessel in baking will be irregular, and cause it to be distorted or cracked. While speaking of the nature of clay and its fitness to be moulded or fashioned into form and to receive impressions, we may mention one or two curious facts in connexion therewith.

In London and various other parts of England, on the sites of ancient Roman buildings, there are frequently found Roman tiles with foot prints of dogs, wolves, and other animals, the feet and claws of monstrous birds and various creatures which inhabited this island nearly two thousand years since, many of which are now extinct; these impressions were made when the tiles were in a plastic state and placed out in the fields to dry, by animals prowling about at night and trampling over them in search of their prey. In some instances also the perfect impression of a man's *caliga* or nailed shoe, is discovered; these tiles being subsequently baked, the imprints were indelibly marked upon their surfaces.

A curious property in clay is that when a potter commences to work the clay into the desired form, it may happen that during the operation, by some accident the surface of the vessel comes in contact with a seal, a figured button, or perchance a piece of money; the workman to efface the defect, presses the impression inwards, and smoothes it over with his hands. The heat of the kiln brings again to the surface the figure it had before received. Hence Roman vessels have been discovered bearing the impress of a medal or a coin, with which it had inadvertently come in contact.

The most extraordinary fact connected with the keramic

art is—that notwithstanding the fragility of the specimens and their liability to injury by damp or friction, our museums throughout Europe abound with perfect and uninjured examples of ancient art, not only of pottery, but of the still more fragile material—glass. These have not been handed down to our times from generation to generation by hand, subject to the incessant care and anxiety of the persons from time to time in charge of them; such a thing would be next to impossible, considering the chances of utter demolition which would necessarily attend them. We are indebted for the preservation of all these fragile and elaborate works of art to the simple piety of the ancients, for we learn from various authorities, as well as from actual observation, that it was customary, according to their rites of burial, to place in the grave those objects which the deceased esteemed most during his lifetime; thus we find, by the side of the skeleton, in the simple tumulus of earth, or in the stone sarcophagus, and (when cremation has been adopted) by the side of the cinerary urn—gold and silver personal ornaments, fictile vases, and other keramic remains, glass vessels, weapons, &c. And this is the source of our possession of such valuable testimonies of the habits and customs of the ancients; for without exception all the relics preserved to us, have been discovered either in places of sepulture, or in the exhumation of long buried cities, devastated by conquest or overwhelmed by volcanic eruptions.

In our endeavours to trace the earliest examples of the potter's art, we must necessarily consult ancient histories of Oriental countries, but these are so mixed up with traditions and fables, that it is extremely difficult to elicit the truth; and it is only by comparing such statements with actual discoveries on the sites of cities coeval with them, that we can verify the assertions of ancient writers. For instance, it is related by Herodotus that the city of Ecbatana, the capital of Media, was surrounded by seven walls, painted in seven different colours; the first and largest of a white colour, was nearly equal in extent to the city of Athens; the second was black; the third purple; the fourth blue; the fifth orange; and the two innermost in different colours, the battlements of the one being plated with silver, the other with gold. If there be any truth in this relation, the walls were probably of brick, the surfaces being enamelled in colours, a custom adopted in many towns of China and India.

A building of similar character is described by Sir Henry Rawlinson, as still existing in Chaldæa, called Birs Nimrùd, which from the custom of placing cylinders in the corners of the stories is ascertained to have been restored by Nebuchadnezzar the King, (605 B.C.) who designates it, "The stages of the seven spheres of Borsippa." This structure consisted of six distinct platforms or terraces, each about 20 feet high and receding 42 feet towards the summit, so arranged as to form an oblique pyramid, and upon the top a vitrified mass which has caused much discussion. Each story was dedicated to a particular planet, and vitrified or glazed with the colour attributed to it by astrologers in this order. The lowest stage, 1st, was *black* for Saturn; 2nd, *orange* for Jupiter; 3rd, *red* for Mars; 4th, *yellow* for the Sun; 5th, *green* for Venus; 6th, *blue*, for Mercury; and the temple on the summit probably *white* for the moon.

Recent investigations on the site of another celebrated city of old, Babylon, have brought to light bricks covered with enamel glazes of different colours, showing that the use of oxides of copper, antimony and tin in producing their colours, was known as early as the eighth or seventh century before our era, and proves that the opaque white stanniferous enamel was used at that early period, although generally supposed to be a comparatively recent invention, and ascribed to Luca della Robbia in the fifteenth century. The glazed Babylonian bricks formed the innermost coatings of walls, and the patterns upon them are rosettes, palmette ornaments, circles, trellis work, men, animals, trees, &c.

Mr. W. Kennett Loftus (*Travels and Researches in Chaldæa*, &c.), gives us an interesting account of a ruined city, called Warka, in Mesopotamia, which had been a cemetery of the

Chaldæans; he found quantities of enamelled earthenware lamps, cups, jugs and figures (some of good work); but, he says, all these relics sink into insignificance, when compared with the glazed earthen coffins heaped, piles upon piles, to the depth of 45 feet in the mounds at Warka, proofs of successive generations by whom this method of burial was adopted from its foundation, until the place was abandoned by the Parthians; a period probably of more than 2000 years.

These remarkable coffins are slipper-shaped, like a covered bath, with a large oval aperture at its widest part by which the body was admitted, a lid was placed upon it and cemented down; at the lower extremity a small semi-circular hole was pierced, to allow the condensed gases to escape and prevent the bursting of the coffin; the upper surface was covered with elevated ridges forming square panels, each containing an embossed figure of a warrior, with an enormous head-dress of very curious appearance, bearing a striking resemblance to the heads on the coins of the Parthian and Sassanian periods. The whole visible surface of the coffin is covered with a thick glazing of rich green enamel on the exterior, and of blue within the oval aperture; it is made of yellow clay mixed with straw and half baked. Three of these are now in the British Museum. Mr. Loftus remarks, it would be too much to say positively that Chaldæa was the necropolis of Assyria, but it is by no means improbable. The two great rivers, the Tigris and Euphrates, would afford an admirable conveyance from a distance, even from the upper plains of Assyria.

Pottery was an important branch of the domestic arts in Egypt, in which the potters displayed great skill. Coptus was the chief seat of this manufacture; vessels were made to hold the waters of the Nile and for numerous household purposes, also to hold mummies of sacred animals. Earthenware deities and emblems were made in immense quantities; their composition being a sort of silicious earth or frit covered with a greenish blue glaze. These small objects were frequently made of steatite dipped in blue glaze, which substance withstood the heat required for its fusion. The forms of their vases are well known by the representations on the catacombs and monuments; the favorite ornamentation being derived from the sacred flower of the Nile, the Lotus, its buds and flowers; the borders and details being derived from the petals, stems and divisions of the calix. The material of which the earliest specimens were made, was a sort of stone ware or frit, resembling porcelain biscuit, and has therefore been called *Egyptian porcelain*, these were covered by a thin glaze. Some of the small deities must have been made at a very remote date. On good authority, as well as from the sacred writings, we learn that the most flourishing period of Egyptian art goes back as far as 2000 years before our Era. The period of the Ptolemies is known by a marked influence of Greek artists: the silicious frit gives place to a pottery, coarse and soft, sometimes painted on the plain surface, and sometimes glazed; this was continued down to the second and third centuries of our era, when Egypt was under Roman domination.

Figs. 1 and 2 represent two examples of early Egyptian vessels in the British Museum: a vase of light coloured clay, with three handles, pencilled in black with deities, &c.; and a bottle of red terra cotta, glazed, in the form of a female playing on a guitar. It is ascribed to the XIXth dynasty, and was found at Thebes.

The Greek fictile vases found in large quantities in the sepulchres of Etruria during the last century, were erroneously called Etruscan, and continued to be so called, even after they were discovered still more abundantly, in the sepulchres of Magna Græcia, Sicily, Attica, and in the Islands of the Ægean. It is indisputable that the vases found in Etruria are the productions of Greek artists, and the style of painting as well as the designs, completely Greek; and it has been observed that although the Etruscans have inscribed every work of art with their own peculiar characters, no *painted* vase has yet been found with any other than a Greek inscription. So also the Greek vases found in Campania and

Sicily, and the south of Italy: they invariably came from Greece and are the works of Greek artists. They are the earliest monuments of Greek civilization, ranging from the eighth or tenth century to the second century before our era.

For the purpose of classifying these vases according to the styles of decoration, we may divide them into five periods, assigning approximate dates of their antiquity:—

1st. Archaic period, previous to the VIIIth Century, B.C.
2nd. Archaic period, from the VIIIth to the VIIth Century, B.C.
3rd. Archaic period, from the VIIth to the VIth Century, B.C.
4th. The finest period, from the VIth to the IVth Century, B.C.
5th. The Decadence, from the IVth to the IInd Century, B.C.

1st. *Archaic period, previous to the VIIIth Century*, B.C.

The earliest specimens of Greek fictile art, are those discovered at Athens, Corinth, Melos, and other parts of Greece, Camirus in Rhodes, and some from Etruria. Most of these are exceedingly rude, painted in brown or black on ash coloured ground, with chevrons, concentric circles, meanders, stars, chequers, &c., and primitive representations of men and animals. The shapes of the vases are peculiar and differ materially from those of the later periods. A very interesting and probably unique specimen discovered at Camirus, is a terra cotta coffin of oblong quadrangular form, painted round the margin with lions and bulls and a helmeted head; now in the British Museum.

2nd. *Archaic period, from the VIIIth to the VIIth Century*, B.C.

The vases abundantly supplied from Camirus in Rhodes, show a great improvement in the drawing of the figures; they are usually of cream coloured clay, painted with crimson and white, sometimes black and crimson, and red on black, the details being scratched with a point. The forms are still peculiar, but approaching to the best period: the Amphora, Œnochoe, and small vessels like the Alabastron, Bombylios, &c. The style of ornamentation being composed of two or more rows of animals (real and imaginary), birds, harpies, &c.

Fig. 3 represents a Hydria of the Archaic period, found

at Camirus, now in the British Museum, painted with two rows of animals, and above is another row of birds. On a *pinax* of this class, in the British Museum, is represented a combat between Menelaus and Hector over the wounded Euphorbos, with their names inscribed in Greek characters: this is the earliest vase from Camirus in which writing is introduced.

3rd. Archaic period, from the VIIth to the VIth Century, B.C.

The next period is still of a very severe style of art, but more artistic than those which precede it; the figures are in *black on a red* ground, heightened with a reddish violet, and the flesh of the females painted white to distinguish them from the men; the outlines of these figures are usually graved with a point and present *silhouette* sort of divinities, mythological and heroic subjects.

These are among the most valuable of the Greek vases, and the patterns on the necks, handles and borders, are very elegant and characteristic. The designs are not painted all over the vase, but are confined to a tablet between the handles, the rest of it being painted with a lustrous black varnish; more complicated subjects are found—quadrigæ and chariots and groups of figures; symbols are introduced in the field, such as a dolphin to indicate the presence of water, and a flower or tree to represent land. Inscriptions in Archaic Greek letters are traced in the same colour; the white was not used for inscriptions until about the middle of the IVth Century, B.C.

Fig. 4 represents a Hydria, with black figures on a red ground, on which is depicted the quarrel of Agamemnon and Achilles; it is a very fine specimen of the third period. (British Museum).

4th. Period, from the VIth to the IVth Century, B.C.

We come now to the best period of Greek art. In criticising these beautiful productions, we must bear in mind the fact, that all these drawings were executed on the moist clay before the vessel was baked, so that great freedom of touch and unhesitating decision, as regards the object to be represented was essential, for the mark of the pencil once made could not be obliterated or retouched, and a complete and perfect line was to be traced without taking the brush from the surface. The white and other colours used upon these vases are not enamels, but coloured clays, painted upon them after the design was made. The outline was first sketched upon the clay, and the black background carefully filled in, leaving the figures in red; the details of costume, features and anatomical delineations, were effected by thick or thin strokes and touches as required.

Fig. 5. As a specimen of the fourth or beautiful period, we have selected an exquisite Lekythos preserved in the British Museum. It is thus described:—a *lêkythos*, representing Aphroditê with her son Erôs seated on her shoulder. In front of her are three draped female figures bringing fruits, over whose heads are inscribed respectively their names, "Kleopatra," "Eunomia," and "Paidia." Behind Aphroditê is the goddess Peithô, decking a tripod with myrtle branches, and behind her a figure inscribed "Eudaimonia," who with her right hand holds a plate full of fruit. This composition is remarkable for grace and refinement of drawing.

Sometimes we find black subjects on red and red on black on the same vase, forming a sort of transition from the Archaic to the more artistic period.

The Panathenaic amphoræ are of great interest, being given as prizes to the victors in athletic sports. On these we usually find on one side Pallas Athênê holding a spear and shield, and on the other representations of wrestling, running, boxing, chariot racing, and other games of the circus, inscribed occasionally with the name of the artist. A very fine vase in the British Museum is inscribed ΤΟΝ ΑΘΕΝΕΘΕΝ ΑΘΛΟΝ. The prize given at Athens. The subjects on others are derived from mythology or from divine and heroic legends of the Greeks, and occasionally domestic scenes and actual life, as displayed in in-door amusements and occupations, &c.

Fig. 6, represents a Rhyton in shape of a ram's head, painted in red on black, with a winged figure on the neck, selected from a variety in the British Museum.

In Greek art, gods, heroes and mortals are constantly represented in the attire and costume of the period when the painting was executed; they all consequently more or less depict the manners and customs of the Greeks themselves. Most of the vases of this period come from Vulci, Canino, Cervetri, and other parts of Etruria. To about the same date we may refer the vases of Campania, of which so many have been discovered at Nola. These, which are distinguished by a brilliant black glaze, are also celebrated for the elegance of their forms and the beauty and finish of the subjects represented, they are in red on black ground; many being entirely covered with this black varnish, which has been conjectured to be due to volcanic ashes spread over the surface of the vessel, and then exposed to a heat sufficient to fuse it. They are frequently ribbed and impressed with elegant patterns.

The 5th Period, from the IVth to the IInd Century, B.C.

This may be called *the Decadence*, and dates from the accession of Alexander the Great, B.C. 336 to 186 B.C., when it is presumed the fabrication of painted vases altogether ceased; shortly after the edict of the Roman Senate against the celebration of the Bacchanalian festivals in that year. As we approach the IInd Century, B.C., we find less freedom of design and a certain mannerism in the drawing, as well as a greater profusion of ornament.

Fig. 7 is a grand and most elaborate specimen of this late period of Greek fictile art, preserved in the British Museum, which is thus described in the catalogue :—

"*Kratêr*. 1. The Thracian king Lykurgos destroying his family while in a state of frenzy. The composition is arranged in two rows of figures: in the centre of the lower scene is Lykurgos, about to slay his wife with a double-edged battle-axe, *pelekys*. Over this group a winged figure, probably *Lyssa*, 'Frenzy,' hovers in the air, surrounded with a triple radiated circle; with her right hand she aims a goad at the figures below, and has two snakes twined round her left arm. On her right are Apollo and Hermês, and on her left a male and female figure, probably Arês, and a local nymph. On the right of Lykurgos a male and female figure are carrying off one of his dead sons.

"2. *rev.* Interview between Pelops, Hippodameia, and Myrtilos. Above are four deities, Aphroditê (?), Pan, Erôs, and a female figure, probably a local nymph. Myrtilos stands before Pelops, as if receiving a command at the moment of his departure; in his left hand he holds a chariot wheel, the instrument of his treachery.

"The tall Ionic column, surmounted by a tripod, the prize of Agonistic victors, which is introduced in the scene, probably indicates Olympia as the place of meeting. (*Monum. dell' Inst. Arch. Rom.*, vol. V., pl. 22, 23). *Ruvo.*"

It now remains for us to notice another description of ancient pottery, in which it may be said painting gives way to sculpture, excepting in the application of simple colours to heighten the effect of the relief. These vases are of a grand and imposing character, and are modelled in a masterly manner, evidently intended from their fragile nature to be seen from an elevated position and out of reach of the ordinary spectator. These religious vases have seldom any apertures, and could not contain liquids or be used for domestic purposes. They are modelled in terra cotta, only slightly baked, and painted over with white, pink, blue, or other light colours. The usual form is a sort of Hydria or Askos, the spout rises perpendicularly from the front, and from the bottom of the neck the handle arches over the globular body and is fastened at the back; this handle on the larger specimens is surmounted by a lofty draped female figure, supported on each side by winged genii resting on the body of the vase; in front on each side of the spout, are projecting sea horses or tritons, and under the imbricated spout is placed in relief the head of Medusa surmounted by a small victory. They vary in height from 3 to 5 feet, and are discovered in Magna Græcia, especially in Apulia; at Cumæ in Campania, and other places. From being found at these places, they are sometimes called *Cumæan* and sometimes *Apulian*, but although possibly the work of Greek artists, they are of the Roman era, that is about 200 B.C., and succeeded the painted vases, a branch of art which was never cultivated by them. We give representations of two found in Magna Græcia, preserved in the British Museum (figs. 8 and 9); the lower parts are in form of female heads, above, each vase has a long neck and handle, on which are terra cotta figures.

We next furnish an illustration of the Macedonian period in an exquisite terra cotta vase, now in the British Museum (fig. 10), reminding us of the obverse of the Syracusan medallion, and the graceful personal ornaments which adorn the beautiful female head and bust of that well known medal. It is thus described in the catalogue:—"An *oinochoê*, in the form of a helmeted female head, probably of Athênê. The neck of the vase rises from the crown of the head. The helmet is ornamented on each side with a seated female figure in relief, and in front with a female head issuing from leaves; over the forehead is a row of rosettes; the ear-rings are in the form of winged female figures surmounted by rosettes; the necklace is formed of pendants; the whole has been coloured and the earrings gilt. The design of this vase is bold and original, the modelling excellent, and much taste is shewn in the application of the ornaments. It is further interesting from the correspondence in form of the jewels with those found in Etruscan tombs of the Macedonian period. (*Mon. d. Inst. Arch. Rom.*, vol. V., pl. 48.) *Vulci.*"

Within the sepulchral chambers of Etruria are discovered, arranged in niches round the sides like the Roman Columbaria, small oblong quadrangular urns, about 2 feet long, and about the same height, including the cover, used to contain the ashes of the dead. In places where stone was abundant, they were of stone or of tufa, which from its soft nature was easily carved, sometimes of alabaster, but most frequently of terra cotta. In the front of these sarcophagi, is generally carved in relief an allegorical subject, such as a mortal conflict, with winged genii bearing torches, and on the cover a recumbent figure of the deceased, her head resting on her left hand; most of these earthenware urns bear traces of colour, especially blue, brown, and pink, and frequently have Etruscan inscriptions.

In many of the sepulchres of Etruria, bronze specula or mirrors are found in juxta-position with the Greek vases. They are doubtless the work of Etruscan artists and not Greek. They are circular discs of bronze with long handles of the same metal, terminating usually in animals' heads; one side is polished, the other engraved with mythological or heroic scenes. These hand mirrors formed a real part of the toilet of the ladies of Etruria, and according to ancient custom, having been constant and valued objects during life, were consigned as companions in death. Fibulæ, hair pins, gold wreaths and other articles of female ornament are also frequently discovered.

ARRETIUM, in Italy, is one of the towns mentioned by Pliny, who wrote in the Ist Century, as being celebrated for the finer description of earthenware, and the manufacture was frequently extolled by ancient writers. Dr. Fabroni has published a work descriptive of this ware (*Storia degli Antichi vasi Fittili Aretini. Arezzo*, 1840). It is quite a distinct ware from the Samian, differing both in colour and execution. The patterns and the figures are elegantly designed in low relief, the artists being evidently influenced by the study of Greek models, exhibiting the higher style of art employed in ornamenting vases in Roman Italy. They are moulded in the same manner as the Samian ware, the clay being pressed into a mould of the desired form with incuse patterns on the inside. Dr. Fabroni discovered some fragments of bowls still remaining in their moulds, as placed in the kiln for baking by the Roman potters. They are made of a fine compact clay, and frequently have the potter's name impressed at the bottom or on the side of the vase. The forms are usually bowls, cups or pateræ, and were intended for domestic use.

fig. 11.

fig. 11*a*.

Evidence of Roman occupation is always manifested in excavations, by the discovery of numerous fragments of vessels of a beautiful coralline red ware, commonly known as Samian. From the quantity of this lustrous red ware, which has been observed on the sites of Roman cities, it has been conjectured that it is the identical Samian spoken of by Pliny and other ancient authors as having been used by the Romans at their meals, and for other domestic purposes. Pliny, indeed, expressly states that the ware made of Samian earth, and which came from the island of Samos, was much esteemed by them to eat their meals out of and to display upon the board. He says the Samian ware was transported into foreign countries, and that most nations under heaven used it at their tables. Martial, Persius and Lucilius, all refer to these vessels as being of a red colour.

The most remarkable fact connected with this ware is its uniform colour, whether discovered in France, Germany or England, and this circumstance has caused considerable discussion as to the locality in which it was originally made. The texture, density, and the colour are always the same, and when we consider the number of places at a great distance from each other, and the difference of soil in each, it is difficult to understand how the Roman potters could everywhere make a paste so exactly similar with materials necessarily so different. In England no kilns for making it have been discovered, but in France and Germany both kilns and moulds have been found, which were supposed to have been used for the manufacture of this particular ware. These vessels usually have the names of the makers stamped upon them, preceded by the letters OF. (officinâ), *from the workshop of*, or terminated by, M. S. F. *manû suâ fecit*. We find among the names of the potters many apparently of Gaulish origin, as Dagodubnus, Dagomarus, Cobnertus, Tasconus, &c. but the greater portion are obviously Roman, as Severus, Albinus, Cassius, Censorinus, Felix, Domitianus, Vitalis, &c.

fig. 12.

The ornamentation in relief upon these bowls was moulded in the following manner: stamps with handles either of bronze or baked clay were modelled in relief, with patterns, devices and potters' names; these were employed to impress an incuse pattern on the interior of a general mould of soft clay, capable of containing the vessel in one piece (which being usually a bowl or hemisphere could easily be accomplished) the interior being first rounded smoothly into a perfect form by the lathe. The mould thus covered with the required pattern, was fired and became perfectly hard and ready for use. The moist paste of which the vessel was to be made was then pressed into the mould by hand, so as to obtain a perfect impression of all the minute details. The irregular surface of the interior was smoothed by being turned in the lathe (for the lathe marks are always visible) while yet in a soft state and before it was removed from the mould, thus preventing any injury which might otherwise happen to the ornamental surface of the bowl by handling. Both the bowl and its mould were then placed in the kiln and baked, the latter having been already fired, would not shrink, but act as a seggar to protect the bowl from smoke and regulate the heat, but the other would be contracted and easily removed when finished, and the mould kept for future use.

Some of the patterns are exceedingly beautiful and interesting, illustrating the Roman mythology and the games they were accustomed to celebrate in the amphitheatre, gladiatorial combats, conflicts between men and beasts in the arena, hunting subjects, the pigmies armed with spears attacking their inveterate enemies the cranes, who invaded their cornfields, heathen deities, &c.

fig. 13.

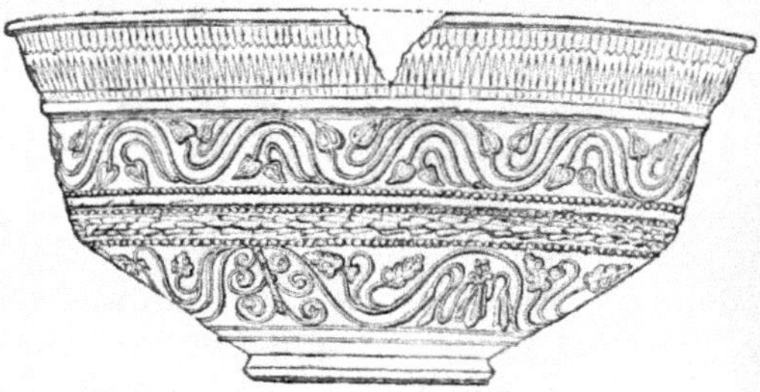

In general the ornaments are moulded, but in some few instances the figures in relief appear to have been cast in a mould and carefully finished, previously to their being affixed to the surface of the vase. Others again have incuse patterns cut into the surface with great sharpness and skill, evidently by the lathe, and many are ornamented with engine-turned patterns.

The general forms of the Samian ware are bowls and pateræ of considerable thickness, to bear the constant wear to which it was subjected in being moved on and off the board at meals. Drinking cups of the red ware are less common; they are frequently surrounded by birds and leaves in relief in a slip of the same coloured paste trailed over the surface. These bowls and pateræ were intended to contain the viands and substantial part of the repast, while the small plain cups of the same red ware are those described by ancient writers as the salinum or salt cellar, and the acetabulum or vinegar cup.

fig. 14.

Another curious ware is found in various parts of England and Germany, especially at Castor in Northamptonshire, where the late Mr. E. T. Artis discovered some kilns, in which these vessels remained as placed by the Roman potters for baking; they are therefore called for the sake of distinction, Castor ware, although they were made doubtless in other parts of Northern Gaul. The forms are usually drinking cups ornamented in relief with men and animals, hunting subjects,

fig. 15.

fig. 16.

scrolls and foliage. This ornamentation consists of a sort of diluted clay, technically termed *slip*, which is trailed over the surface by a potter's implement, like a long-pointed spoon with a groove in its centre; this operation requires great care and skill, as each line, however long, must be completed with one stroke of the tool in a simple off-hand manner, and there is no retouching after the slip has been applied; the vessel is afterwards covered with a brownish black metallic glaze. Sometimes the relief is of a different colour, as white on a light brown ground, &c.

Cups for Drinking.—The usual form of the wine cup is somewhat barrel shaped, but smaller at the bottom than at the mouth, holding about half a pint. These cups are usually glazed and variously ornamented, encircled by plain or engine-turned lines, frequently indented, and having scrolls, ivy leaves or coloured bosses; others are inscribed, in white slip with short convivial words, as IMPLE, REPLE, DA VINUM, VITA, FELIX, PIE, AMOTE, &c.

fig. 17. *fig.* 18. *fig.* 19.

Pitchers of various capacities, from half a pint to two quarts, are very common in plain unglazed cream-coloured earthenware, with one, two, and occasionally three handles; sometimes we find them of red clay, accompanied by a basin for washing the hands.

Large amphoræ, capable of holding ten or twelve gallons, for storing wine, oil and other liquids, of very thick light brown clay, have been frequently discovered. In some instances they have been found converted into a sort of tomb by being cut in half, the upper part fitting on as a cover, and containing glass cinerary urns, filled with charred bones collected from the funereal pyre. Smaller amphoræ of the same unglazed clay are commonly used for domestic purposes.

fig. 20.

Urns are also very numerous; they are hemispherical with small bases; those used for funereal purposes are generally plain, but others, although of a common and inexpensive character, have yet an elegant appearance from the simple scroll of ivy leaves which encircles them.

Among the culinary utensils used generally by the Romans was a broad shallow vessel, termed a *mortarium*, used for mixing a favourite dish called *moretum*, a salad composed

fig. 21.

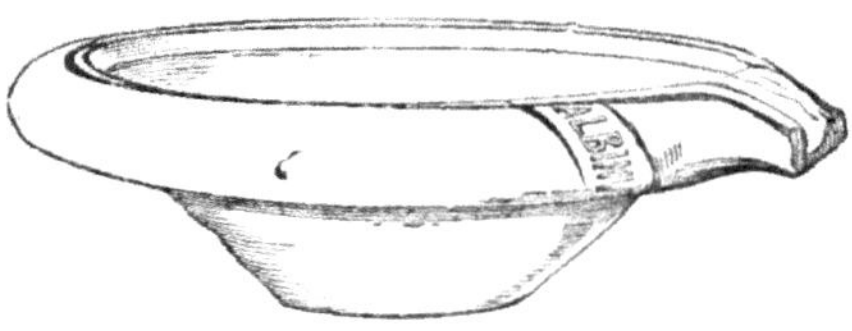

of garlic, parsley, vinegar, oil, &c. These mortars had on the inside small angular pebbles embedded in the clay to assist in triturating the vegetables, which were also occasionally cooked in them; they are provided with spouts to pour off the mixture when rubbed to the required consistency; the broad rim is turned over outwards for the purpose of concentrating the heat round the vessel when placed on the fire. These mortaria are exceedingly numerous, not only in London but wherever Roman buildings have been discovered.

LAMPS.—Lamps for ordinary use were made of earthenware, circular, with a small handle at one side and a spout or nozzle opposite to contain the wick, and a hole in the centre to admit air, and fill the lamp with oil; they are frequently ornamented with objects in relief, as masks, birds, animals, figures, and an infinity of patterns. The centres are generally concave or furnished with a rim to prevent the oil spilling when the lamp is carried in the hand, and underneath is frequently stamped the maker's name; they average about 3 to 4 inches in length and are usually of a reddish clay, unglazed. Sometimes they are found with two or more burners. When not carried about they were placed in stands, made of clay or bronze, suspended by chains singly from a bracket, or round the rim of a candelabrum with a long stem, provided with stands hanging by chains.

fig. 22.

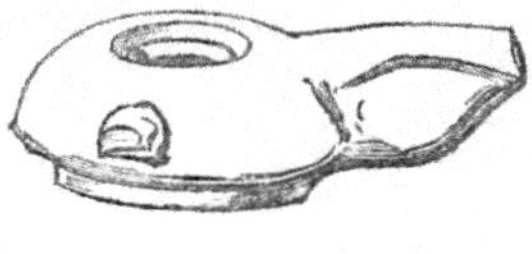

fig. 23.

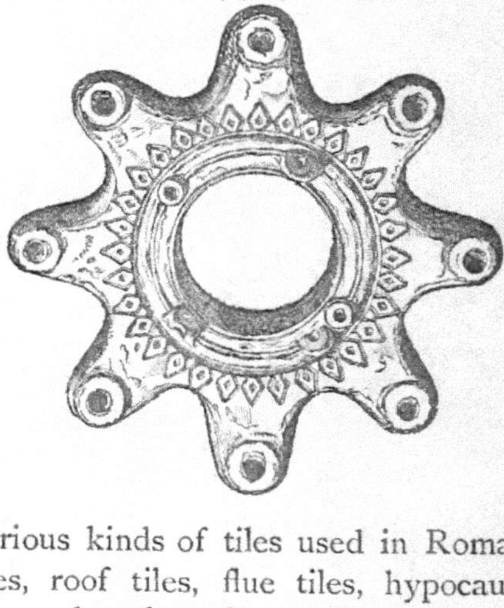

TILES.—There were various kinds of tiles used in Roman buildings, as bonding tiles, roof tiles, flue tiles, hypocaust tiles and draining tiles, made of a fine red clay, very compact and well fired, and extremely durable; for those made 1500 years since are now as firm as when they originally came from the kiln, and are in fact frequently found built up in the walls of some of the early churches as the best that could be obtained. The bonding tiles were thus employed by the Roman builders; they first laid about six courses of Kentish rag or other squared stones, on which they placed two courses of bonding tiles firmly imbedded in mortar; then stones and tiles alternately until they had reached the required height. Bonding tiles were also used for arching over doors and windows; they usually measure about 15 inches long by 12 broad.

fig. 24.

Hypocaust tiles were about 8 in. square, and were used for constructing the pillars of the hypocaust; these are interesting from being frequently stamped with the name of the cohort or legion of the Roman army, stationed at the time in the vicinity, but larger tiles were used for the bases of the columns and floors above.

Flue tiles were of various dimensions, but usually quadrilateral, long and hollow, with openings at the ends; they were built one upon another end ways, on the inside of the wall, to convey the hot air from the hypocaust to distant rooms. They are ornamented with incuse geometrical patterns and wavy lines, the object of which was to make the cement adhere more firmly.

fig. 25.

Roof tiles were flat with longitudinal edges turned upwards, these when placed side by side were fastened together by the imbrices or semi-cylindrical tiles, larger at the lower end which overlapped the narrow end of the one below it.

Tubular drain tiles were used by the Romans, fitting into each other, and cemented as at the present day.

Clay Statuettes.—The penates or household gods were generally made in bronze, but we find occasionally some small figures from 6 to 9 inches in height, made of a fine white clay, which served among the humble classes as domestic ornaments or votive offerings.

Heathen deities are common; Hercules, Pallas, Venus, Mercury, and subjects of Roman mythology; a lion and other animals and birds.

Mons. Edmond Tudot, in a pamphlet entitled "Figurines en argile," has given a very interesting account of the statuettes found in the neighbourhood of Moulins, in the valley of the Allier. This spot seems to have been the site of an ancient manufactory of pottery. In 1857 the chief explorations took place, and remains of furnaces or kilns were found arranged in groups, as many as ten and fifteen in each group; the size of them averaged 9 feet in length by 4½ feet wide. The upper parts were wanting, but the foundations and side walls were tolerably perfect. Near the kilns were the materials for fabrication, viz. clay, wood and moulds, but no tools or implements of any kind were seen. The objects discovered amounted to very large numbers, consisting of perfect figures of divinities, personages unknown, busts, medallions, grotesque figures, animals, birds, and moulds bearing the makers' names. M. Tudot mentions especially as of frequent recurrence: statuettes of Venus Anadyomene or the Venus Genetrix of the Romans, Fecunditas and Abundantia, lions and other animals, cocks, peacocks, &c.; grotesque figures and articulated children's dolls; horses in bigæ; a pack horse laden with amphoræ, illustrating the manner in which these large and footless vessels were transported to and from market when filled with wine or oil. It is difficult to fix certain dates, but many of them could not be assigned to a later time than the first half of the second century. They appear to be the work of inferior artists, in imitation of designs originally good. The manufactories of pottery extended over a large tract of country in the valley of the Allier, not only in objects of the white clay to which we have referred, but also other kinds of pottery. He is also of opinion that the red ware called Samian was made here, and gives a list of about 270 potters' names, of which more than 100 are to be found on the red ware discovered in England.

Having briefly referred to the pottery of the Greek and Roman periods, we next come to the earthenware vessels which were used in the ages subsequent to the withdrawal of the Romans from Britain, viz. from the fourth to the seventh centuries of our era. In England we designate this period Saxon, but in France and Germany it is called Frankish or Merovingian. These vessels belong to the dark ages which immediately followed the extinction of the Roman power in Gaul and Britain, and the irruptions of the Franks into the former and the Saxons into the latter country.

The records by which we can gain any information are very scanty, and in the absence of written testimony we must be content to gather our knowledge of their habits and customs from their graves, which are plentifully scattered over various parts of Europe. We have seen that the Romans universally adopted the practice of cremation or burning their dead, and gathering the charred remains into urns, which they deposited in cists or sarcophagi; but the Saxons buried them entire, clothed in the dresses they were accustomed to wear, together with the weapons which they carried in warfare, their personal ornaments, the knife with which they cut their food, and the bowl and cup from which they drank.

SAXON OR FRANKISH GRAVE.—To give some idea of the usual disposition of the various objects contained in a Saxon grave, we will briefly describe one which may be taken as the type of the greater number; it belonged to a Frankish warrior. The skeleton is placed in a natural position with the face upwards; on the right shoulder is one or more bronze fibulæ, which fastened the cloak and under garment, across his body may be seen the knife or dagger, and at his waist the large bronze buckle of the sword belt; by the side of the left arm is the pointed umbo of a shield with the metal rivets, and underneath the long two-edged sword; on the right a spear and a war axe, with here and there some small lance heads and numerous coloured glass beads. The implements being of iron (although much corroded) still retain their original form, but the wooden handles and the leather of which the shield and belt were composed, have long since perished, except some fragments which still adhere to the metal. At his feet an ornamented earthenware bowl or urn, and a glass drinking cup. These Saxon earthenware urns are sometimes profusely ornamented with diagonal lines, annulets and rosettes, the favourite pattern being a zig-zag, or what we term Vandyke, and some are more highly embellished with stamped patterns, and occasionally they have projecting bosses, formed by pressing out the sides of the urn from within while in a soft state. They are mostly of a dark brown clay, wrought by hand and slightly baked.

Maiolica.

THE painted pottery of Italy ever since its introduction into that country in the XVth Century, has been called by the Italians themselves *Maiolica*. In England it was in the last century called *Raffaelle ware*, on account of an impression which existed, that the great Raffaelle himself condescended to paint on some of this ware. This probably originated from the fact that many of his designs were reproduced on maiolica by the Keramic artists from engravings of Raffaelle and other great masters. The best period of art pottery was subsequent to his death, which took place in 1520.

The term *maiolica* appears to be derived or rather corrupted from Maiorca, one of the Balearic Islands in the Mediterranean, near the east coast of Spain, noted for its pottery from a very early period. It was in the XVIth Century called *Maiorica*, and subsequently *Maiolica*. As this word is Italian, and has not yet found its way into English dictionaries, it ought doubtless to be pronounced in the Italian manner. To call it *Madjolica* grates sadly upon the ear of a linguist, and I think it therefore better in writing to substitute the i for the j—*Maiolica.**

The distinguishing feature in the manufacture is a covering of a thick opaque milk-white glaze, resulting from the introduction of the oxide of tin, which from the dissemination of its particles when fused, imbedded uncombined amid the glass, renders the substance opaque, and not only covers the dingy colour of the clay, but forms a fine colourless ground for the painter; it is termed stanniferous enamel. The presence of tin in glaze has been detected in the bricks of Ancient Babylon; and we may infer that it was not unknown to the Arabs of Northern Africa in the VIIIth Century. It was therefore doubtlessly introduced into Europe by the Arabs and Moors during their power in Spain, and from thence into Italy, at the Conquest of Maiorca by the Pisans in 1115, and the ware which it covered was so much esteemed that discs or plates were used as decorations in the churches of Pisa and Pavia, where they still remain to attest the fact.

Another proof that the stanniferous glaze was well known at the commencement of the XIVth Century is adduced by M. Piot (*Cabinet de l'Amateur*), who quotes a receipt in the "Margarita Preciosa," written in 1330:—"Videmus cūm plumbum et stannum fuerunt calcinata et combusta quōd post ad ignem congruum convertuntur in vitrum, sicut faciunt qui vitrificant vasa figuli." "We find, when lead and tin are calcined and fused together by the fire, they are converted into a glass; as they (the potters) do when they glaze earthen vessels."

All the manufactured pieces of pottery after the first baking were covered wholly or partially with this glaze, diluted, so that the water was absorbed by the biscuit, leaving the enamel in a state of powder on the surface; on this crude and gritty surface the painting was applied, which was necessarily accomplished by single strokes of the brush, as no

* For the same reason we have in our title spelt the Greek term *Keramic* as it should be pronounced, substituting the K for C, as frequently used.

retouching or corrections were possible. It was then placed in the oven again, to melt the glaze and fix the colours.

The painting in metallic lustre colours appears to have been carried on largely at Gubbio, especially by M°. Giorgio, in beautiful gold, ruby, and other lustres ; and plates, after they had been painted at Urbino, by Xanto and others, were sent to Gubbio to be touched with lustre. The ruby lustre was doubtless a secret, known only to that botega, and was altogether lost early in the XVIth Century.

The maiolica painters frequently derived their subjects from engravings : in the MS. book written by Piccoi Passo in the XVIth Century,* now in the South Kensington Museum, is a sketch of a painting room, with designs or prints hanging upon the walls. The engravings which served as models for many of these paintings were those of J. B. del Porto, Marc Antonio, Marco di Ravenna, and others, who made known to the world the compositions of Raffaelle and other great artists.

PERUGIA OR CITTA DI CASTELLO.

To this place have been attributed the earthenware vessels with stanniferous enamel, called in Italy *sgraffiato* ware, being engraved in outline and decorated en *engobe*, that is, the object before being glazed is covered with a second coating of coloured slip or *engobe*, on which is graved the ornament or design after it has been merely dried by the air, leaving a sort of *champ lévé*, and afterwards baked in the kiln. These fayence vases are generally enamelled in yellow, green and brown. There are several specimens in the Louvre and Musée de Cluny. In the Louvre is a bowl on a triangular foot formed by three lions, and on the interior three musicians in the costume of the latter half of the XVth Century. Another, somewhat similar, is in the South Kensington Museum, (see fig. 27); round the stem, which is decorated with foliage, are three lions seated, in full relief; round the

* "*Li tre libri dell' arte dell Vasaio*," by Chevalier Piccolpasso.

bowl runs a wreath of yellow flowers; within is a man wrestling with a dragon, surrounded by a wreath; date about 1460, height 9¾ inches. A plate in the same collection (fig. 26) has in the centre a shield of arms surrounded by a border of scroll work; date about 1540, diameter 11½ inches. Among other specimens in the South Kensington Museum is a plate with the arms of Perugia. There was also a manufactory of this *sgraffiato* ware at La Fratta, near Perugia, which has been continued down to a late period. Fig. 28 represents a modern basket-shaped pot with bucket handle, in red glazed earthenware and ornaments in relief.

CAFFAGIOLO.

This *fabrique* was established towards the end of the XVth Century, and became very important, lasting probably throughout the XVIth Century. The name is spelt in different ways, but generally Chaffagiuolo, the *Ch* at the beginning, as written in the XVIth Century, may easily be mistaken for a G.

The most ancient dated pieces, are two in Baron Gustave de Rothschild's collection, 1507 and 1509, both decorated with grotesques in the style of Faenza. The latest is 1590, mentioned by Delange in his translation of Passeri. Among the ornaments on this ware are frequently tablets with SPQR and SPQF (Florentinus), and on several the motto "Semper," adopted by Pietro di Medici in 1470, and continued by Lorenzo il Magnifico. The device of a triangle and the word "Glovis," meaning when read backwards "si volge" (it turns), was used by Giuliano de Medici in 1516, alluding to his change of fortune.

Another characteristic of this *fabrique* is the dark blue backgrounds of many of the pieces, and the method in which it was coarsely applied by the brush. It has been observed that the secret of the metallic lustre was not known, but we have seen a specimen with the mark of the *fabrique* under the handle. There are several very interesting specimens of

Caffagiolo maiolica in the South Kensington Museum. The most celebrated is the interesting plate of a maiolica painter in his studio, who is occupied painting a plate, in the presence of a lady and gentleman of distinction. It was styled in the Bernal catalogue "The Raphael and Fornarina plate," assuming the seated figures to represent them; an impression seemed to be general that Raphael himself was the painter. It was purchased at the Stowe sale for £4., but the competition was so great at the Bernal sale that it brought £120.; the highest price at that time ever given for a maiolica plate. In the same collection is a large dish with Pope Leo X. seated on a throne, borne on the shoulders of the populace, composed of upwards of fifty figures; the portrait of Pietro Perugino, with a wide border of foliage and medallions of birds; a triumphal procession after Mantegna, painted in brilliant colours, dated 1514; and the St. George of Donatello, from the bronze statue in the church of "Or San Michele," at Florence, are represented in fig. 29.

The marks on this ware are a large P with a paraphe or bar through the lower part, as shown in the woodcut, the name of the *fabrique*, and sometimes the trident. The mark here given occurs on a plate in the possession of Lord Hastings, and has all the marks which appear separately on other pieces.

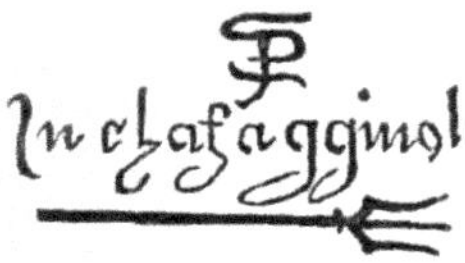

FORLI.

According to Passeri there were *fabriques* of maiolica at Forli in the XIVth Century. Its contiguity to Faenza exercised a great influence on the decoration of the ware, and the patterns on the obverses and reverses are similar; doubtless many are therefore still attributed to Faenza. We can consequently only assign those which have the name Forli written on the back of the plate. The example we have selected (fig. 30) is in the South Kensington Museum:— a plate painted in blue, relieved with white, Christ among

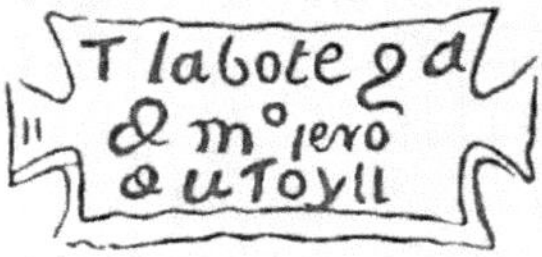

the Doctors, the edge filled up with trophies of musical instruments; XVIth Century; diam. 14 inches. It reads on the back "In la botega di M°. Jeronimo da Forli," as given in the cut.

RIMINI is only known to us by three specimens, which are actually signed, and the mention made of its *fabriques* by Piccolpasso. The pieces are dated 1535, and as late as 1635.

VITERBO, RAVENNA and TRAVISIO, are also only known as manufactories of maiolica from solitary specimens in the South Kensington Museum, and in the collections of Mr. Henderson and Mr. Addington. (See Chaffers' *Marks and Monograms*, page 99). The former is illustrated (fig. 31) by a dish in the South Kensington Museum, painted with Diana and Actæon and a border of trophies of arms; a man at bottom holds a scroll, inscribed "VITERBO DIOMED, 1544."

SIENA.

The earliest specimens known of this important manufactory are some wall or floor tiles of the commencement of the XVIth Century. They are of maiolica, ornamented with polychrome designs of chimeræ, dragons, amorini, masks, birds, &c., in brilliant colours, especially orange and yellow on black ground, beautifully painted. They vary in shape, being triangular, pentagonal or square, to suit the geometrical designs of the wall or floor they covered; the average diameter is 5 inches. Several hundreds of these tiles are preserved in the South Kensington Museum, which came from the Petrucci Palace at Siena, some are dated 1509, and have shields of arms and arabesques. A pavement of similar tiles still exists *in situ* in a chapel of the church of San Francisco, at Siena, and there is a frieze of them in the Biblioteca. All these are clearly traced to, and were doubtlessly made at Siena; Mr. Darcel, however, attributes them to Caffagiolo, and Mr. J. C. Robinson to Faenza, but no reason is given, except the similarity to works executed at those *fabriques*. That there was a manufactory there early in the XVIth Century is proved by a plate in the South Kensington Museum, representing St. Jerome in the Desert, in blue *camaieu* on white ground, highly finished, with arabesque border. It is signed on the reverse "fata in Siena da M°. Benedetto;" it has no date, but may be assigned to about 1520 (fig. 32). Many other specimens are referred to in Chaffers' *Marks and Monograms*, pages 105 to 107.

After a long interval, the name of the town again appears on maiolica of a very characteristic description, accompanied by the names of the artists: Bartolomeo Terenze (or Terche) Romano in 1727, and Ferdinando Maria Campani, 1733 to 1747, the subjects being taken from Raffaele, Annibale Caracci, and other masters. Fig. 33 is a plate, painted with a woman and two peacocks, in the back ground rustic buildings; date about 1720. Fig. 34, a plate, subject—the Vintage, signed "Ferdinando M. A. Campani, Siena 1747." Figs. 35 and 35[a] are also specimens of Siena ware of the XVIIIth Century of a very effective character: Juno soliciting Æolus to let loose the winds, and Galatea, after Annibale Caracci. All of these are in the S. K. Museum.

PISA.

This city was, about the middle of the XVIth Century, the centre of a considerable trade in the exportation of Italian fayence into Spain, and especially to Valencia, in exchange for the golden metallic lustre ware of that country. Antonio Beuter, a traveller, about 1550, praises the fayence of Pisa with those of Pesaro and Castelli, but we have one only specimen bearing the name "PISA:" a large vase of fine form, covered with arabesques on white ground; in the collection of the Baron Alphonse de Rothschild.

PESARO.

We are indebted for all we know of the history of this *fabrique* to Giambattista Passeri, who has striven to do all honour to his native country, but as his account was not written until nearly two centuries after its establishment, we must make allowances for his *amour propre.* He has consequently been too liberal in assigning pieces to this locality. The manufacture of pottery has been traced by him to the year 1396, but it does not follow that this ware was the enamelled fayence which we call maiolica, probably the first allusion to it was in 1462, when a sum of money was lent for the enlargement of a manufactory; and other edicts are referred to, dated 1508 and 1552, to the "Vasari e Boccalari," vase and cup makers.

Passeri extols Guido Ubaldo II. della Rovere, who became Duke of Urbino, in 1538, for his patronage of the *fabrique* of Pesaro. At his death, in 1572, the pottery began to decline. The maiolica with yellow lustre, with blue outlines and imbricated borders, which are assigned to Pesaro, belong to the first part of the XVIth Century; many of these have portraits and scrolls inscribed with the name of the person to whom it was dedicated. Fig. 36 is a drug vase, painted with roses, inscribed "SIR DI CEDRO," of the XVIIth Century. When Passeri visited the town in 1718, there was only one potter, making ordinary vessels. Some years after, in 1757, he sent potters from Urbania and recommenced the manufacture. Many of these specimens are still preserved; one in the De Bruge Collection was inscribed Pesaro 1771; another in Mr. Fortnum's possession is dated 1763.

M. A. Jacquemart says, that two artists of Lodi—Filippo Antonio Callegari and Antonio Casali—were established here about the middle of the XVIIIth Century. A bowl and cover and a dish, painted and gilt with flowers, signed by them with their initials, in the collection of Mr. Reynolds, is given on plate xliii., fig. 37. There was another *fabrique*, established by Giuseppe Bertolucci of Urbania in 1757; Pietro Lei, a painter of Sassuolo, was engaged.

CASTEL DURANTE.

Castel Durante is a small town near Urbino, but a very extensive manufactory of maiolica; most of its early productions of the beginning of the XVth Century are confounded with those of Urbino, but we have evidence enough to show the beautiful character of the decorations employed there. The earliest dated piece is a splendid bowl, which belonged to the late Mr. H. T Hope; it is surrounded externally by blue scrolls on white, inside are painted the arms of Pope Julius II., supported by cupids, arabesques, &c., on deep blue ground. The inscription on the back informs us that it was made at Castel Durante, on the 12th September, 1508. Two other vases for druggists of the same character are in the British Museum and the South Kensington Museum, made at Castel Durante, in the botega or workshop of Sebastiano Marforio, the 11th October, 1519. A vase and a plate of about the middle of the XVIth Century, preserved in the South Kensington Museum, are here given, figs. 38 and 39. Other pieces are known with dates down to the year 1635, when the name was changed to Urbania in compliment to Pope Urban VIII. The Chevalier Piccolpasso, director of a botega for maiolica, at Castel Durante, circa 1550, wrote a treatise on the art of making and decorating it, whilst under the patronage of Guidobaldo II. The manuscript has been secured for the Art Library of the South Kensington Museum. This interesting work is illustrated with pen-and-ink sketches of all the details of manufacture and patterns of the ware, and the prices at which they were to be obtained; allusions are frequently made to other towns celebrated for the same industry; he also describes by name the principal forms of the vessels. He informs us that one potter, named Guido di Savino, worked at Castel Durante, and transported to Antwerp the knowledge of the manufacture of maiolica.

It was also from the same place that a family of the name

of Gatti, in 1530, introduced it into Corfu; and Francesco del Vasaro went to Venice and established himself there.

In 1722 Urbania was the only *fabrique* which remained in the Duchy of Urbino, where articles of utility only were made, but Cardinal Stoppani brought painters, and endeavoured to put fresh life into the potter's trade.

A great trade was carried on in pharmacy vases or Vasi da Spezieria, covered with grotesque heads, cornucopiæ, &c., designed and shaded with light blue, touched with yellow and orange, brown and green, the patterns being mostly in a bold style.

PADUA.

Vincenzo Lazari informs us, that in a street which still retains the name of *Bocaleri* (makers of vases) a few years since, were discovered, traces of ancient potter's kilns, and some maiolica triangular wall tiles, of blue and white alternately, of the end of the XVth or beginning of the XVIth Century, among which was a plaque, 20 in. in diameter, of the Virgin and Child between two saints, surrounded by angels. It is taken from a cartoon by Nicolo Pizzolo, a painter of Padua, pupil of Squarcione; on the summit of the throne is written NICOLETI, the name he usually adopted. It is now preserved in the Museum of that city. This city is is spoken of by Piccolpasso as possessing manufactories of maiolica in his time (1540).

There are some plates in the South Kensington Museum; one, of foliated scroll work and flowers on blue ground, with a camel in the centre, circa 1530; Bernal Collection. Another, with arabesques on blue ground, a coat of arms in the centre, reverse marked with a cross, circa 1550; also from the Bernal Collection.

Fig. 40 is a plate, painted on grey ground, with Myrrha flying from her Father, inscribed on the reverse with the name of the place and the date 1548; in the South Kensington Museum.

URBINO

Was the most celebrated of all the Italian *fabriques*, and must have had by far the most considerable trade, although no doubt many of those now attributed to this city were the works of other manufactories; however, we have a considerable number of signed and dated pieces, and the style and touch of the principal artists engaged here, may easily be detected. Pungileoni (*Notizia delle pitture in maiolico fatte in Urbino*) notices several early potters of Urbino, but we cannot identify any of them by their works until 1530. Federigo di Gianantonio, Nicolo di Gabriele, and Gian Maria Mariani in 1530; Simone di Antonio Mariani in 1542, and a few others, may be traced by their works. The botega of Guido Durantino was celebrated in the first half of the XVIth Century, for the Constable Montmorency, a great amateur, commanded a large service of maiolica in 1535, of which several pieces, bearing his arms, are still preserved. But the best known of all the keramic artists was Francesco Xanto Avelli da Rovigo, whose works are now so highly appreciated; he usually painted after the designs and engravings of Raphael, and other great masters, but seldom adhered strictly to the grouping of the originals; he also painted subjects from Virgil, Ovid, and other poets. The marks which he placed upon his works, consisted of one or more initial letters of his name, F. X. A. R., but usually the X. only, with the date. The works of Xanto are much sought after at the present day, and the prices they realize at sales by auction vary from £50. to £200., according to their importance. His pieces are dated from 1530 to 1542; on his best specimens we find touches of the ruby and gold lustre, which were evidently applied after the piece of maiolica had been painted and baked; it is therefore probable that as the knowledge of preparing the lustre colours was kept strictly secret at Gubbio, they were sent there to be lustred. On the backs of many of his works are long quotations from the poets, from whence his subjects were derived. A very fine plateau, signed by Xanto (fig. 41), represents the Marriage of Alexander and Roxana, after Raffaelle, dated 1533, now in the South Kensington Museum.

Another celebrated artist of Urbino, who flourished in the middle of the XVIth Century, was Orazio Fontana, whose family name was Pellipario, Fontana being a name taken in consequence of the profession of several members of the family. According to Mr. J. C. Robinson's account, the first whose name occurs is Nicola Pellipario, who was alive in 1540, and had a son, Guido, named in a document as early as 1520; the latter had three sons—Orazio, Camillo and Nicola. Guido, the father, who was also a potter, survived Orazio, and his name is found on a plateau in the Fountaine Collection, which states that it was made in Urbino, in the shop of Maestro Guido Fontana, vase maker. Orazio remained with his father till 1565, when he set up a botega on his own account in the Borgo San Polo; he died in 1571. His first work (if the monogram attributed to him be correct) is 1544.

The most exquisite specimen of painting on maiolica which is attributed to Orazio Fontana, is found upon a small vase in the possession of Mr. Mark Philips; around the body is a continuous frieze of nude figures fighting, executed *en grisaille*, on a black background, apparently after Giulio Romano. This unique gem formerly belonged to Mr. Gray, of Harringer House, at whose death it passed into the Stowe Collection for £35.; at the Stowe sale the present owner obtained it for 51 guineas, and it would, without doubt, at the present day realize considerably more. Fig. 42 is a charming plate, with Cupid riding on a dolphin. Figs. 43 and 50 two plateaus; fig. 44, a pilgrim's bottle; (pl. xxxi.) fig. 45, a salt cellar, and fig. 46, a cruet, are fine examples of the grotesque style of decoration of the middle of the XVIth Century. Fig. 47, an elegant vase, representing Apollo and Daphne; and fig. 48 (pl. xxxvi.), a plate, painted with Hercules and Omphale, and in the foreground a cartouche, inscribed "Omnia vincit Amor 1522." All these are in the S. K. Museum.

We pass over several artists of inferior note and close the series with the family of Patanazzi. Alfonso Patanazzi has signed his pieces in full, as well as Alf. P. and A. P., of the years 1606 and 1607. One of these, a plateau, subject—Romulus receiving the Sabine Women, now in the South Kensington Museum, is here represented (fig. 49).

In 1608 and 1617, we find the names of Francesco Patanazzi and Vincenzio Patanazzi, who, from the inscriptions, appear to have painted plates at the ages of 12 and 13.

At a more recent period, at the end of the XVIIIth Century, there still remained at Urbino a perhaps solitary potter, who appears to have been a Frenchman, making glazed fayence in the style of Moustiers, from which place or from Marseilles he probably came and established himself there. It is a pillar candlestick, in the South Kensington Museum, and underneath is inscribed "Fabrica di Maiolica fina di Monsieur Rolet in Urbino 28 Aprile 1773."

FAENZA,

If not the most ancient, was the most celebrated of all the manufactories of maiolica in Italy. It was this town that gave to France the name by which they have to the present day distinguished their enamelled pottery, as Spain had previously supplied the name to Italy. Thus in Italy it was called *maiolica* from Majorca, and in France, *faïence* from Faenza. In like manner the glazed pottery of Delft, so celebrated over Europe in the XVIIth and XVIIIth Centuries, gave the name of *delft* to the same descripton of ware made in England. The earliest dated piece we have seen is a plate in the Musée de Cluny, dated 1475, made by Nicolaus de Ragnolis. Another specimen, in the Sèvres Museum, is inscribed "Nicolaus Orsini, 1477;" and in the same collection is a plate, signed "Don Giorgio, 1485," probably that of Maestro Giorgio, before he went to Gubbio and was ennobled. Several early examples, preserved in the S. K. Museum, are here represented: fig. 51, a plate with the Virgin and Child, dated 1489; a plaque, fig. 52, dated 1491, with the sacred monogram in the centre; and fig. 54, a roundel, inscribed "Andrea di Bono 1491." Another specimen of about the same date is shown in fig. 55, a plate with an emblem of two hearts pierced with arrows, and the motto "En piu."

The products of this *fabrique* retained for a long time an especial character by which they are easily identified; at first the outlines of the figures were very simple and formal; they do not appear to have adopted the yellow lustre. Piccolpasso, who was in 1548 director of a rival manufactory at Castel Durante, and who wrote about the time when Urbino and Gubbio produced their finest works, gives the preference to the ware of Faenza.

In the XVIth Century a favorite decoration was grotesques and arabesques in blue *camaieu* on yellow ground, or alternately on the two colours. The reverses of the Faenza plates are frequently light blue, with concentric circles or spiral line in a darker colour; when white, with imbrications or zones alternately blue and yellow. Another peculiarity by which the Faenza ware is known, is the presence of red. Piccolpasso says it was only found in the manufactory of M° Vergilio, of Faenza. Towards the middle of the XVIth Century the painting cannot be distinguished from that of Urbino. Fig. 53 is a plate, blue ground, with arabesque border and a shield of arms in the centre; and fig. 56, a plaque, painted with Joseph sold by his Brethren. Both in the S. K. Museum.

The marks on the ware are very numerous; that of a circle intersected by cross bars, with a small pellet or annulet in one of the quarters, has been found in connection with the signature of a Faenza *fabrique*.

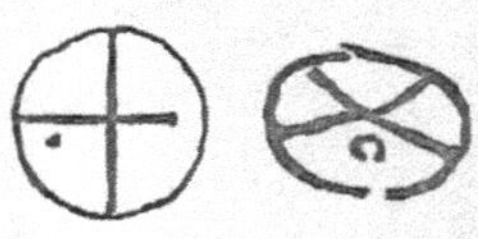

These initials are on the front of a large plaque, date about 1530, painted in rich deep blue, with green, yellow and brown; subject, Christ bearing the cross, and numerous figures, called "Lo Spasimo di Sicilia," after Raffaelle. Museum of Art, South Kensington.

GUBBIO,

In the Duchy of Urbino, is known to us principally by the works of Maestro Georgio Andreoli, who seems to have monopolized the secret of the ruby and yellow metallic lustre, with which he enriched not only his own productions but put the finishing touches in lustre on the plates of Xanto and other artists from Urbino as well as from Castel Durante. There is no doubt that the painting of the piece and the application of the metallic lustre colours were two distinct operations, and that it was painted and the colours fixed in the muffle kiln some months before it was touched with the lustre pigments, and again subjected to another baking. We may thus explain the anomaly of pieces having two distinct dates upon them: thus a plate in Mr. R. Napier's collection by M° Giorgio, has in front the date 1517 marked in blue, and on the reverse in metallic lustre 1518. Other instances are not unfrequently met with. Giorgio was the son of Pietro Andreoli, a gentleman of Pavia, and was established at Gubbio, when young, as a potter, according to Passeri, with his brothers, Salimbene and Giovanni. In 1498 he obtained the rights of citizenship, and filled some municipal offices. He was a statuary as well as a painter of maiolica, several of his sculptures in marble being yet extant. Many of his early pieces are without the lustre which subsequently rendered him so famous. The first piece on which his metallic lustre is revealed to us by his signature is dated 1517, the last 1537. Although M° Giorgio was probably not so good an artist as many of his contemporaries, he was unmistakeably a clever colourist, and his knowledge of the harmonious disposition of the rich lustres he had at his command is beyond dispute. Such brilliant and luminous displays as he sometimes exhibits on his ware would be admirable in any material.

An exquisite plate, showing the perfection of enamel glaze and richness of lustre, as well as correctness of drawing, representing the Three Graces, lately in the possession of

M. Roussel, was sold for 400 guineas a few years since; this, with several other splendid specimens of Maestro Giorgio's work, are in the rich collection of Mr. Fountaine at Narford. Another plate, painted with the "Stream of Life," from a print by Robetta, similar to that described below, was secured by the same gentleman at the Bernal sale for £142. There are also many fine *Giorgio* plates, as well as the ordinary Gubbio lustred pieces, in the Soulages Collection, S. K. Museum, of which we have selected two:—

Fig. 57 is a bowl plate, lustred and painted with nude figures of a man and woman standing beside a stream, landscape background, taken from a composition known as the "Stream of Life," engraved by Robetta, of brilliant ruby lustre; signed by M° Giorgio, diam. $7\frac{3}{4}$ inches, cost £100.

Fig. 58 is a vase with two handles and cover, lustred and painted with a shield of arms, by M° Giorgio, about 1520; height $10\frac{1}{2}$ inches.

Another painter in lustre, of the school of M° Giorgio, has signed his pieces with the letter N., which is supposed by some to be a monogram of Vincencio, the son of M° Giorgio.

A painter named Perestino, of Gubbio, has produced some very beautiful pieces, dated 1533 and 1536, sometimes with his name in full, as a bas relief of the Virgin and Child, in the Louvre; and others with the initial P. only, on a vase in the Campana Collection, and on a fine plate with the subject of the Redemption of Solomon, and the establishment of the Throne of David, taken from a lost work of Raffaele; in the Bracon Hall Collection.

The marks of all the artists of Gubbio are in lustre on the reverses of the pieces. Maestro Giorgio's signature consists of the letters *M° G°* usually accompanied by a date, sometimes more at length, "da Ugubio" being added.

As I have before observed, the secret of the metallic lustres employed at Gubbio seems to have died out altogether towards the end of the XVIth Century.

DERUTA.

Many of the lustred pieces of maiolica, with light yellow lustre edged with blue, which were attributed formerly to Pesaro, have been recently classed among the wares made at Deruta, from the circumstance of a plate in the Pourtalès Collection—subject, one of Ovid's Metamorphoses, being similarly decorated with the yellow lustre, and signed by El Frate of Deruta, 1541. For this reason, a plate in the South Kensington Museum, with St. Sebastian in relief, with the saint in blue and the arcade of this peculiar yellow lustre, dated 1501, may also be referred to Deruta. The earliest signed and dated piece, however, is not earlier than 1525. This and several other specimens have "*In Deruta*," inscribed at length; others have simply the letter D with a bar through it. Some very fine and early pieces have the signature of the painter, El Frate, before spoken of, but without the yellow lustre; as on a plate with the Marriage of Alexander and Roxana, in Mr. Barker's collection. The plate in the Hotel de Cluny, with Diana and Actæon, after Mantegna, designed in blue and yellow lustre, marked with a C and a bar through it, belongs to this *fabrique*.

As illustrations we reproduce fig. 59, a plate, blue and white, arabesque dolphin border, with laureated bust; in the centre, cupid on a horse; date about 1520. And fig. 60 (pl. xix.), a plate of lustred ware, in the centre a profile female bust, inscribed "SURA FIORE," and a border of arabesques; date about 1520. Both in the S. K. Museum.

FERRARA.

The maiolica of Ferrara is alluded to by Piccolpasso. Alphonso I., Duke of Ferrara, occasionally worked himself in a room attached to his palace, and is said to have discovered a fine white colour, which was adopted by the *fabriques* of Urbino. He died in 1534. His successor, Duke Alphonso II., summoned Camillo Fontana (son of the celebrated Orazio Fontana of Urbino) in 1567 to re-establish and give new life to the manufactory. In conjunction with a certain Giulio d'Urbino they produced some services for the Duke on the occasion of his marriage with Marguérite di Gonzaga. All the pieces (which are well known) bearing the *impresa* of the Duke, a flame of fire and the motto "ARDET ETERNUM," belong to this *fabrique*, about 1579. At a much later period, probably late in the XVIIth Century, there was still a manufactory here. There is a plateau in the South Kensington Museum painted with the Triumph of Bacchus, thus inscribed—

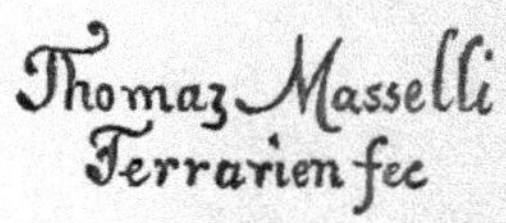

a representation of which is given, fig. 61.

BASSANO, NEAR VENICE.

A *fabrique* (according to M. V. Lazari) was founded about 1540, by Simone Marinoni, but it is not known how long it lasted. Later pieces of the XVIIth Century bear a certain resemblance to the Castelli ware. The only signatures found are those of Antonio and Bartolomeo Terchi, two brothers, of Rome, who appear to have travelled about from one place to another, working for various establishments. In 1728, a manufactory of maiolica was set on foot by the sisters Manardi, which was continued in 1735 by Giovanni Antonio Caffo; and sometime after, but previous to 1753, another was carried on by John Maria Salmazzo.

NOVE.

In 1728, Giovanni Battista Antonibon, established in the village of Nove, near Bassano, a manufactory of earthenware, and in April, 1732, he opened a shop in Venice for the sale of his wares. In 1741 it was still in a prosperous state and carried on by his son Pasqual Antonibon. In 1766 it consisted of three large furnaces: a smaller one and two muffle kilns. Pasqual took his son, Giovanni Battista Antonibon, into partnership, and in 1781 Sig. Parolini joined the concern, continuing the fabrication with great success until February, 1802, when they leased the premises to Giovanni Baroni, and the style was *Fabrica Baroni Nove.* It was at that time prosperous, and some beautiful examples were produced, as shown in the accompanying illustration.

Fig. 62 represents a splendid fayence presentation vase, oviform, of bleu de Roi ground, painted in colours, with Alexander and Darius, and another classical subject after Le Brun, richly gilt, evidently a chef d'œuvre of the manufactory, 2 ft. 6 in. high; it is in the possession of Mr. C. W. Reynolds, and is said to have been intended as a present from the city of Venice to Louis XVI., but never presented. The name "Fabrica Baroni Nove" is written on each side of the square pedestal. Fig 63 (pl. xiii.) is a tureen and cover, painted with masks and scrolls in blue, (S. K. Museum). Eventually the works were allowed to go to decay, and on the 1st May, 1835, the Antonibons again took possession of them, and they still continue to make *maiolica fina* or fayence only, not having revived the manufacture of porcelain, for which at one time they were so famed.

VENICE.

Piccolpasso, in his manuscript to which we have so often referred, speaks of one or more large manufactories at Venice, and describes a mill used there for grinding the clay, the various patterns made, and the prices charged for the maiolica. In the South Kensington Museum is a plateau, circa 1540, light blue ground with arabesques, and an amorino in the centre, inscribed "In Venetia in contrada di S[a] Polo in botega di M° Lodovico," underneath is a shield enclosing a cross. Another in the Narford collection, The Destruction of Troy, has "Fatto in Venezia in Chastello, 1546." Another by Zener Domenigo da Venezia, was also made at St. Polo in 1568.

The Venetian maiolica of the end of the XVIth and throughout the XVIIth Century is still involved in obscurity, but a number of pieces have lately been appropriated with some show of reason. The name of *Io. Stefano Barcella Veneziano* is found on a specimen of the XVIIth Century, and some others with a mark of a fish hook have come to light, and from the long intervals between its use, it evidently belongs to a *fabrique* and not a painter. It is so intimately allied to the grapnel used by the Bertolini in the subsequent century, that we are warranted in placing it as a Venetian mark. The first is dated 1571; a second, 1622; and a third has the name Dionigi Marini, 1636, all accompanied by the fish hook. As an example of Venetian maiolica, circa 1700, we give an illustration, fig. 64 (pl. xiv.), a plate painted with an architectural subject. S. K. Museum.

In 1753, the Senate of Venice conceded to the brothers, Bertolini, the establishment at Murano, of a kiln for making fayence. The products of this period may be distinguished by their fine quality and extreme lightness; the patterns of the borders are stamped in relief like repoussé metal, and they are very sonorous when struck. Some of these are marked with a grapnel or creeper, others with the monogram AF surmounted by two branches crossed and a Maltese cross surmounted by a coronet. This Murano manufactory did not succeed so well as the promoters anticipated, and it was probably discontinued about 1760, as the concession was annulled by a decree of April, 1763. We here give a representation of a very fine plateau of this period (fig. 65), painted with a classical subject and scroll border in relief; mark the double anchor; in Mr. C. W. Reynolds' collection.

SAVONA.

The manufactory of Savona was founded, according to Mr. Marryat, in the beginning of the XVIIth Century by Gian Antonio Guidobono, of Castelnuovo in Lombardy, assisted by his sons, Bartolomeo and Domenico. The spot chosen was at the village of Albissola, situate on the sea, near

Savona. The *faïence de Savone* was well known throughout Italy and France in the XVIIth and XVIIIth Centuries. The ware is ornamented generally in blue on white ground, the designs are roughly executed, and the mark is often seen on the reverse of the piece, consisting of a shield of arms of the town—in chief *arg.* a demi eagle issuant *az.* in point *az.* paly *arg.* There are some other marks attributed to Savona: a double triangle with the letter S is called the "knot of Solomon" (Salomone); the sun with G.S.; the falcon mark; the tower mark; and the anchor mark, so called from these emblems being depicted on the ware. The illustrations here given are of the XVIIIth Century: fig. 66 is a basket, perforated, with two handles, painted rudely with scrolls in yellow, blue and green; in the centre, a cartouche with the letters S.A.G.S.; and a plateau, fig. 67, painted in blue and white with warriors on horseback; both in the South Kensington Museum.

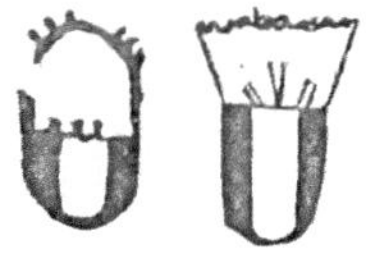

It was a native of Albissola, Domenique Conrade, who introduced the art into Nevers. It was in full activity during the first half of the XVIIIth Century. Among the decorators were Gian Tommasso Torteroli, Agostino Ratti, and Jacques Borrelly, whose name is signed on a large vase—"Jacques Borrelly Savonne, 1779, 24 Sept." The name is also on a vase in the M. D'Azeglio's Collection; perhaps the father; "Primum opus M. A. Borrelli Mense Julii 1735," and his name occurs on the pottery of Marseilles, sometimes *Giacomo* Borrelly, at others *Jacques* Borelly, on pottery about 1780.

MONTE LUPO.

The plates and dishes of coarse heavy earthenware, rudely painted with large caricature figures of soldiers and men in curious Italian costumes of the XVIIth and XVIIIth Centuries, in menacing and warlike attitudes, striding across the plates, holding swords, spears and other weapons, are usually attributed to Montelupo, near Florence, but they also produced chocolate brown vases of a more artistic character in the style of Avignon. The manufactory is still in existence.

A plate in the S. K. Museum, fig. 68, represents three cavaliers, signed on the back "Raffaele Girolamo fecit Monte Lupo 1639;" and another plate in the same collection, rudely painted with a musqueteer, is here given (fig. 69), date about 1630.

GENOA

Is spoken of by Piccolpasso as a great mart for maiolica about the year 1540. He tells us the patterns painted and the prices charged, arabesques, leaves, landscapes, &c., but no specimens of this early date have hitherto been identified. The fayence of the XVIIIth Century, however, is of frequent occurrence; its character is much the same as that of Savona, viz. rude and hasty sketches in blue *camaieu*, sometimes with small caricature figures in the style of Callot. In consequence of its maritime position, the mark selected for this ware was a beacon, by some erroneously called a light-house, from which some object is suspended on a pole. Swinburne, describing the tower of signals at Barcelona, observes: "If one ship appears a basket is hung out, if two or more it is raised higher, and if a Spanish man-of-war they hoist a flag."

Fig. 70 is a Bottle, painted in blue with birds and scroll ornaments, of the XVIIIth Century, with the usual mark; in Mr. C. W. Reynolds' Collection.

LORETO.

In the Santa Casa, at Loreto, are still preserved upwards of 350 maiolica vases, mostly with covers, painted with designs from the great masters. All these, which are arranged in two large rooms, came from the Spezieria or Medical Dispensary, attached to the Palace at Urbino. The last Duke of Urbino, Francesco Maria II., in his dotage, had abdicated his duchy in favour of the Holy See, and at his death, in 1631, his heir, Ferdinand de Medicis, removed the more ornamental pieces to Florence. The vases from the Spezieria he presented to the shrine of our Lady of Loreto, called Santa Casa. This splendid collection did not consist alone of vases for containing drugs, but many other choice specimens were included; and it consequently became the envy of more than one crowned head: the Grand Duke of Florence proposed to give in exchange for them silver vases of equal weight; Queen Christina was heard to say that of all the treasures of Santa Casa she esteemed them the most; and Louis XIV. is said to have offered for the Four Evangelists and the Apostle Paul the same number of statuettes in solid gold.

Although Loreto is not strictly speaking a *fabrique* of maiolica, yet an account of its keramic treasures will interest the reader, and it enables us to introduce some pieces of maiolica actually made within the precincts of the sanctuary, inscribed "Con Pol di S. Casa," *Con polvere di Santa Casa* (with the dust of Santa Casa), with a representation of our Lady of Loreto and the Infant Saviour, and in the distance a view of the Sanctuary. These cups are made of clay, mixed with the dust shaken from the dress of the Virgin and walls of the sanctuary, and in this form are preserved by the faithful as tokens of their visit to the shrine.

Figs. 71 and 72 (pl. xli.) are two varieties of these bowls, in the possession of Mr. C. W. Reynolds.

CASTELLI.

Castelli is a town or hamlet in the Abruzzi, north of the city of Naples. No time can be assigned for the commencement of the making of maiolica; but previous to 1540 it was celebrated fór the excellence and beauty of its pottery. Passeri quotes the testimony of Antonio Beuter in his "Cronica generale di Spagna," who wrote at that date; he says—"Corebœus, according to Pliny, was the inventor of pottery in Athens. He did not make them better, nor were the vases of Corinth of more value than the works of Pesaro, Pisa, or of Castelli, in the Sicilian valley of the Abruzzi, nor of other places, for fineness and beauty of work." However, we have no opportunity of judging of the correctness of this flattering encomium, for no specimens are known of the Castelli maiolica of the XVIth Century. Few of the early manufactories of Italy, which were so famous for their maiolica, survived much beyond the beginning of the XVIIth Century. Castelli alone appears to have stood its ground, and towards the end of the XVIIth Century was as flourishing as ever in this particular branch of industry. Francesco Saverio Grue, a man of letters and science, became about this time director of the Neapolitan maiolica *fabrique*, at Castelli. The ware was ornamented with subjects of an important nature, correctly designed and well painted; sometimes the landscapes were delicately heightened with gold. His sons and brothers continued to add lustre to his name for nearly a century. Francesco Antonio Grue's works, which have dates, range from 1677 to 1722, principally scriptural subjects as well as mythological. Luigi Grue, about 1720-1740, painted landscapes and figures. Ioanes Grue or Grua, painted scriptural subjects from about 1730 to 1750. Saverio Grue was the re-inventor of gilding on fayence, some of his pieces are dated 1749 and 1753; his earliest paintings are without gold, consisting of classical subjects and mottoes on plaques. C. A. Grue was a painter about the same time.

Many distinguished artists proceeded from this school, among which may be noticed Bernardino Gentili, Fuina, G. Rocco, Math Roselli, and Giustiniani. The manufacture was patronized by Carlo Borbone and his son Augusto, who emulating the Medici of Tuscany, raised the keramic art of the kingdom of Naples to great celebrity.

We give the following examples of this interesting and artistic ware:—Fig. 73 is a bowl and cover, painted with nude figures after Annibale Caracci, filled in with fruit, foliage and cartouches, signed "Liborius Grue P." XVIIIth Century; in the S. K. Museum. Fig. 74 is an ewer and basin, decorated with a cardinal's arms, cupids and flowers; in Mr. C. W. Reynolds' possession. Fig. 75 is a fine plateau, painted with a landscape and figures, and a border of cupids, masks and flowers; in the same collection.

NAPLES.

We know nothing of the maiolica of the XVIth Century made in the city of Naples. Three vases have been recently put forward as examples of this period, and it is a curious fact that although two of the greatest Parisian authorities have had the opportunity of examining them minutely, and have copied the inscriptions in their published works, they cannot agree as to the date: M. A. Jacquemart assigns them to 1532, and M. Demmin to 1682. One of these vases is inscribed "Franc° Brand Napoli Casa Nova;" another "Paulus Franciscus Brandi Pinx;" and the third, "P. il. Sig. Francho Nepita." With this conflicting testimony before us, we must judge for ourselves, and looking at the character of the decoration, which evidently shows the decadence of the art, as well as the style of the monograms, which assimilate with those of Savona, Venice, and other Italian manufacturers of the latter half of the XVIIth Century, they belong doubtless to the later period (see Chaffers' *Marks and Monograms*, page 128). Examples of the fayence of the XVIIIth Century are frequently met with, signed FDV—F. del Vecchio; Giustiniani; the letter N crowned, and sometimes the letters H.F.

TURIN.

The maiolica manufactories of Turin have hitherto escaped observation, probably from the scarcity of the ware or the difficulty of identifying unsigned pieces, and the silence of early writers. The Marquis D'Azeglio, in his endeavour to illustrate the early pottery and porcelain of Italy, has become possessed of a few interesting specimens of Turin fayence, which throw a ray of light upon the subject, and will probably lead to further investigation. That there was a manufactory of maiolica at Turin in the XVIth Century, is proved by the recent acquisition by Mr. Reynolds of a *fruttiera* with pierced border, painted on the inside with a boy carrying two birds on a long pole; it is marked underneath—Fatta in Torino adi 12 di Setēbre 1577, as shown in the cut and represented in fig. 76. Towards the end of the XVIIth Century we find that the manufactory was in existence, by a plateau, painted in blue with animals, bearing the mark of a cross on a shield (the arms of Turin), and being crowned, we may infer it was under Royal patronage. Another large dish confirms this, being inscribed on the back of the rim:—"Fabrica Reale di Torino GR 1737." In the centre of the reverse is a monogram composed of F. R. T. (Fabrica Reale Torino). There is another plateau of about the same date, painted with Susanna and the Elders, having the potter's name, *Gratapaglia. Fe. Taur.*, perhaps the same whose monogram appears on the preceding piece. All these are in the collection of the Marquis D'Azeglio.

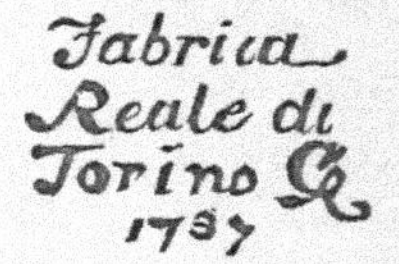

MILAN.

We have no specimens that can be identified of an earlier date than the XVIIIth Century. The fayence is usually painted with grotesque figures, but sometimes with flowers and scrolls in relief, also with Watteau subjects. An ecuelle and dish, figs. 77 and 78, in the possession of Lady Charlotte Schreiber, are painted with carnival figures; and two other specimens in Mr. Reynolds' Collection, figs. 79 and 80, are here represented. Sometimes the abbreviation *Mil.* is used, as on a service painted with Japanese patterns in the Museum of Sigmaringen.

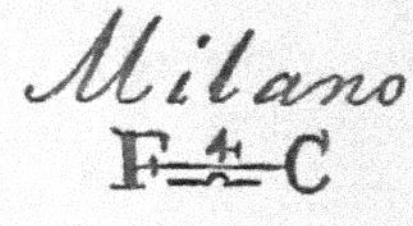

Some pieces, apparently of a later date, are from the manufactory of Pasquale Rubati, usually signed with his initials thus: reading *Fabrica Pasquale Rubati Milano.*

FLORENCE.

Of the early maiolica made here little is known, but fayence of the XVIIIth Century is occasionally met with, marked with the letter F or FI. Fig. 81 represents a cup and saucer, painted with birds and flowers; in Mr. C. W. Reynolds' Collection.

LUCA DELLA ROBBIA.

Although the works of this great artist come more properly under the denomination of Italian sculpture, yet our work would be incomplete if we omitted to notice his enamelled terra cottas. Luca della Robbia was born at Florence, A.D. 1400, and commenced his career as a goldsmith, but afterwards became a sculptor, and attained considerable eminence in that profession. He discovered the art of covering his bas-reliefs with a stanniferous enamel, which rendered them impervious to the action of the elements and extremely durable. His early relievos consisted of scrolls, masks, birds and Renaissance ornaments, with fruit and flowers in natural colours; these usually formed the borders of his subjects, which were principally of a religious character. He was succeeded by his nephew, Andrea della Robbia, born in 1437, died 1528. After his death, his four sons, Giovanni, Luca, Ambrosio, and Girolamo, continued making the same description of coloured reliefs, but greatly inferior; the last named went to France, and was employed by Francis I. in decorating the Chateau de Madrid, in the Bois de Boulogne, and died there about 1567.

As an illustration of the work of Luca della Robbia, we give fig. 82, a beautiful altar piece of coloured enamelled earthenware of the latter half of the XVth Century. The subject is the Adoration of the Magi, a composition of more than twenty figures; on the right is the Virgin seated, holding the Saviour on her knee, at her back St. Joseph standing, and in front one of the Magi kneeling in adoration, behind whom are two other kings holding cups, with attendants; in the distance are soldiers on horseback and buildings, at the back of the holy family is seen the stable in which are two oxen, and at the summit two angels holding up the guiding star. Several of the figures in the background are portraits of the artist's contemporaries; the head between the two kings is that of Pietro Perugino. The subject is here given without its frame, which consists of a predella, on which are festoons of fruit, two pilasters at the sides with arabesques, and a frieze of cherubs' heads at the top, on the lower corners are two shields of arms of the Albizzi of Florence. Its original locality is unknown, but it was purchased in Paris in 1857 for £100. Total height 7 ft. 8 in., width 6 ft. S. K. Museum.

Spain.

The maiolica of Spain was for a long time confounded with that of Italy, and it was not until 1844 that M. Riocreux, the Curator of the Sèvres Museum, distinguished its peculiar characteristics and established its Spanish origin. Lustred maiolica was made by the Moors and Saracens at a very early period, and manufactured by them wherever they had dominion. The Hispano-Arabic period dates from the VIIIth Century, when the mosque of Cordova was built, until the XIIIth Century.

We give illustrations of two vases of ancient maiolica of the XIIIth Century, now in the S. K. Museum. They are described in the catalogue "Siculo Arabic," from their similarity to others found in Sicily; they are evidently of Arabic origin, but whether made in Sicily or Spain is uncertain. There is a certain resemblance in the ornamentation to the vase of the Alhambra, which is supposed to have emanated from the *fabrique* of Malaga: the winged horse on the one and the Arabic inscription on the other, interspersed with arabesques and foliage, point to the same origin. Fig. 83 is an oviform vase, white ground, with winged horses and birds in black tinted with blue; height 15 in. Fig. 83*a* is a vase of similar form, white ground, with Arabic inscriptions and a frieze of blue birds round the neck.

The Hispano-Moresque period, which is best known to us from the numerous specimens preserved to our time, commences from the XIIIth Century, when the Alhambra of Grenada was erected by the Moors.

Fig. 84 is a vase with flat expanded handles, spherical body, the whole surface diapered with leaves and conventional flowers, in reddish yellow lustre and blue, of the XVth Century; height 20¾ inches. South Kensington Museum.

The earlier pieces of the XIVth and XVth Century may be distinguished by a golden yellow metallic lustre, and blue enamelled on white ground. The designs are Moorish, consisting of diaper patterns, foliage, fantastic and other animals, shields of arms of Spanish Princes, &c., and sometimes Arabic inscriptions, transformed into ornamental designs. The forms are vases with two winged handles, these are rare; large and small basins, spherical vases on conical feet, dishes, &c.

The *azulejos* or enamelled tiles of the Alhambra are well known, bearing passages from the Koran, shields and other devices, they are of the beginning of the XIVth Century. Three specimens of these are represented, figs. 85, 86 and 87, in the Geological Museum.

MALAGA. The principal centre as well as the earliest of the manufactures of fayence was, according to M. Charles Davillier (who has written a history of the Hispano-Moresque pottery) at Malaga. A traveller, who visited this city about 1550, Ibn Batoutah, tells us: "They make at Malaga the fine pottery or gilt porcelain, which is exported to the most distant countries." The finest specimen of Moorish fayence known is the celebrated vase of the Alhambra, which is supposed to be as early as the palace itself, viz. the XIVth Century, and was probably made at Malaga. The history of this vase is worthy of note; we learn from the "*Promenades dans Grenada,*" by Dr. Echeverria, that three vases full of treasure were discovered in a garden at Adarves, which was put in order and tastefully laid out by the Marquis de Mondejar in the XVIth Century, with the gold contained in the vases, and to perpetuate the remembrance of this treasure trove, they were arranged in the garden; but the vases, being exposed to public view, unprotected, sustained considerable injury by being rubbed and handled, and eventually one got broken, and every traveller who visited the garden took a piece as a souvenir until all of it was gone. In 1785 two were yet preserved intact, but about the year 1820 another disappeared altogether, and of the three only one is now extant; it measures 4 ft. 7 in. in height. The colours of the decoration are a pure blue enamel, surrounded or heightened with a yellow lustre on white ground.

Figs. 88 to 91, are four other specimens of the Spanish lustre ware, with shields of arms; of the XVth or XVIth Century; in the S. K. Museum.

MAJORCA was the second in rank and next in importance as regards its ancient manufacture, but it must have had a very extensive trade in fayence, for it was exported to almost every part of the globe, and as we have seen gave its name to all fayence. The first mention we find of it, is a treatise on Commerce and Navigation by an Italian—Giovanni de Bernardi da Uzzano. This author, writing in 1442 about the productions of the Balearic Isles, says, *the fayence of Majorca has a very extensive sale in Italy.*

As the keramic art in Spain declined, we find later pieces change the style of decoration. The Arabic inscriptions, which were perfect on the early vases like that of the Alhambra, were copied, but the painter not knowing their signification, employed them as ornaments, until at last they became altogether confused and illegible. The arabesques were not in such elegant taste, and large coats of arms entirely filled the centres of vases and plates. J. C. Scaliger, who wrote in the first half of the XVIth Century, extols the vases of Majorca and compares them to the Chinese porcelain, and says that although imitations they were not inferior in form or brilliancy, but actually surpassed them for elegance.

VALENCIA was also celebrated for its fayence, and may be traced back to the Roman time, for Saguntum, now Murviedro, is mentioned by Pliny and others, as noted for its jasper red pottery. It is impossible to trace the origin of the *lustred* pottery of Valencia, but it was probably about the beginning of the XVth Century, when it became the most important in Spain. Lucio Marinao Siculo, in 1517, says it was much esteemed, being so finely made and so well gilt. The pieces attributed to this place are of the XVth Century, and have christian devices; many of them have the inscription "In principio erat Verbum et Verbum erat apud Deum" from the 1st chap. of St. John, and the eagle displayed (not in an escutcheon as the arms of Aragon); St. John was particularly venerated at Valencia. Of its earlier productions of the Moorish period we know nothing.

Valencia has from time immemorial been celebrated for its *azulejos* or enamelled tiles. There are many houses of the XVth and XVIth Centuries still existing in the ancient cities of Spain, the walls of the rooms being covered with tiles ornamented with borders, scrolls and geometrical designs. The celebrity of this manufacture is maintained to the present day. In the chapter-house of the cathedral at Zaragoza is an elegant example of flooring, the tiles averaging about 8 inches square, decorated with scrolls, medallions of landscapes, flowers, &c.; it is inscribed "Real[s]. Fabricas de D[a] Maria Salvadora Disdier. Brit. ft Anno 1808." In 1788 Gournay, in his almanack, mentions three *fabriques* of tiles at Valencia: those of Disdier, Cola and Casanova. In the Sèvres museum is a later example with landscape and figures, inscribed "De la Real Fabrica de Azulejos de Valencia Anno 1836." Fayence of all descriptions was extensively made here through the XVIIth and XVIIIth Centuries.

Fig. 92 represents a barrel mug of this *fabrique*, height 10 inches, painted in blue and white, inscribed "S[n] Geronimo de Buena Vista," having belonged to the monastery of that name at Seville; and fig. 93 is a blue and white dish with a lion in the centre. Both in the possession of Lady C. Schreiber.

Manises, near Valencia, was also celebrated from the XVIth to the XVIIIth Century. The decorations appear to be of Oriental patterns, executed for the most part in a rich copper coloured lustre. Mr. Talbot Dillon in 1780

(Travels through Spain), says "About two leagues from Valencia, is a pretty village called Manisès, composed of four streets. The inhabitants are mostly potters, making a fine fayence of copper colour, ornamented with gilding. The people of the country employ it both for ornament and domestic use." Some of these dishes with copper colour lustre have upon them a mark of an open hand, which may be the emblem of the place, and are dated 1610 and 1611.

TRIANA, near Seville. There were several *fabriques* here, one for the manufacture of spires or ornaments of earthenware, with which the gables of the buildings were crowned; others for *azulejos* or tiles so much used in Spain, and for fayence vessels of all descriptions. We give a representation, fig. 94, of a curious bottle, 14 in. high, in form of a lady in the costume of Louis XIV., *en grande tenue*; inside the *fontange* or top knot of the head dress, which forms the spout, is written "Victor. I. Viva. Mi. Amo. Don. Damian. Sant. ✠" In the possession of Lady C. Schreiber. Fig. 95 is a dish of this *fabrique*, painted with a landscape and figures, dated 1774; from the same collection.

ALCORA. There was a very important *fabrique* of fayence at this place, carried on by the Count D'Aranda, in the XVIIIth Century. Mr. C. W. Reynolds has recently obtained from a palace in Spain a series of twenty-four plaques, with frames of rococo scrolls and masks in relief, the medallions and frames being in one piece, some of large size. The paintings are very much in the style of Castelli, of mythological and classical subjects, the seasons and Spanish costumes; fig. 96 represents one of these plaques. A very fine fayence cup, in the possession of Baron C. Davilliers, is painted with the Family of Darius, after Le Brun, marked underneath "ALCORA ESPANA. SOLIVA." This painter's name, *Soliva*, is also found on the Moustiers ware. Fig. 97 is a plate, painted with sea view and sunset, in Lady C. Schreiber's Collection.

The usual mark upon this fayence is the letter A in gold or colour.

Persia.

THE ware which has been assigned to Persia is undoubtedly of Oriental origin, from the peculiar patterns with which it is decorated. The designs remind us of the embroideries and rich stuffs produced there, and the manuscripts and illustrated books of that country confirm the opinion in preference to a recent theory referring this fayence to a Rhodian origin. Some of the Persian fayence is of early date. M. Piot *(Cabinet de l'Amateur)* discovered some plaques and a number of fragments of bottles, inlaid in white marble, round a portion of the church of St. Giovanni del Torro de Ravello, in the kingdom of Naples, built in the XIIth and XIIIth Centuries; and Mr. C. D. E. Fortnum found others decorating the church of St. Andrea, at Pisa.

The Persian ware is distinguished by the great brilliancy of its enamel colours, the principal of which are a deep lapis lazuli blue, turquoise, a vivid emerald green, a red of a dark orange tone, orange or buff, olive green and black. The lustres are a rich orange gold, a dark copper colour, and a brass lustre. The patterns upon the tiles and vases are similar, and consist of elegant arabesques, foliage and ornamented flowers, more or less in imitation of nature. Among these we notice the tulip, the Indian pink, the rose, and other flowers. The tulip in Persia is the emblem of Affection, and is thus symbolized at the present day; in the barracks in the

Bird-cage-walk is a monument erected by a Persian lady to a Crimean officer, ornamented with a wreath of yellow tulips. The bowls and vases are sometimes ornamented with fabulous birds, gazelles, antelopes, hares, &c., mixed with scrolls and foliage. The forms are various, hemispherical and cylindrical cups, vases and bowls on conical feet; a common form is a bottle with a very long neck, divided in the centre by a boss, probably used to hold wine; ewers and basins, the former like a bottle with handle and long spout, used especially for ablutions, the latter with a pierced cover. The tiles being mostly made to cover walls have continuous arabesques, which joined when placed side by side. Chardin says of them, "In truth, nothing can be seen more lively or more brilliant than this sort of work, nor of equally fine design."

The Persian fayence was probably the same as the Gombroon ware, which was shipped by the English East India Company from a port of that name in the Persian Gulf, where they formed their first establishment, about the year 1600, and whence the great bulk of Chinese porcelain was exported. A Persian jug in the possession of Mr. T. G. Sambrook, is mounted in silver, bearing the English hall mark for the year 1596, and was perhaps one of the first brought to this country; another, mounted in silver, of the same date, belongs to Mr. C. Winn—proving how much the ware was prized in England at that time.

Figs. 98 and 99 are two tiles, ornamented in relief and coloured with flowers, and a man on horseback; and fig. 100 a plate, painted with green, white and blue scrolls. These are in the S. K. Museum.

It has long been a *vexata questio* whether porcelain was ever made in Persia, some say the idea is altogether chimerical, but M. Jacquemart endeavours to prove that both hard and soft porcelain were made at Iran, and has devoted three or four long chapters recently in support of his theory; *(Les Merveilles de la Ceramique)*. If there be any truth in this, he certainly has the credit of being the first positively to assert it as a fact beyond dispute. He adduces several instances of hard porcelain vases with Persian inscriptions, and others with arabesques in the Persian style, but judging from the engravings he gives, they resemble so much in many points the Chinese, that it seems to admit of doubt.

The nearest approach to porcelain I have seen in Persian ware is a sort of siliceous frit or fine stone ware, which possesses a very slight degree of translucency, but is not the true porcelain, composed of kaolin and petuntse like the Chinese.

France.

FAYENCE.

HENRI II. WARE.

THIS elegant ware is of a distinct character and ornamentation to every other class of pottery. It is only by a recent discovery that we have been able to assign this manufacture to its original source. It seems to have been the opinion of all the most able writers on the subject, that it was made in Touraine. The first who promulgated it was M. André Pottier of Rouen; he says that of the *twenty-four* pieces then known (in 1839) about one half came from the neighbourhood of Thouars. M. Brongniart states that the majority of the *thirty-seven* pieces, known at the time he wrote in 1844, came from the south-west of France: Saumur, Tours and Thouars. M. Labarte, in his introduction to the De Bruge catalogue (in 1847), also refers the greater number to Touraine and La Vendée. Le Comte Clement de Ris in the *Gazette des Beaux-Arts* (1860), confirms these statements, and says that ten or twelve pieces came direct from Thouars, which he considered the original place of their production. He also noticed the great resemblance that existed between the interlaced ornaments on the Henri II. ware and the book bindings of Grolier and the Maioli, and even suggested the use of bookbinders' tools in stamping the patterns on the clay.

These shrewd conjectures have been in a great measure verified by the researches of M. Benjamin Fillon, of Poictiers, who in a letter to M. Riocreux, Curator of the Sèvres Museum, solves the problem, and clears up the mystery which had hitherto enveloped the origin of this pottery: it is headed, "*Les Faïences d'Oiron*," and the writer says that these wonders of curiosity, which have turned the heads of so many amateurs, were actually fabricated at Oiron, near Thouars, with clay from the immediate neighbourhood. Two artists assisted in the work: a potter named François Charpentier, and Jean Bernard, Librarian and Secretary of Hélène de Hangest-Genlis, widow of Artus Gouffier, a superior woman and cultivator of the arts. After the decease of this lady in 1537, they both entered the service of Claude Gouffier, her son, who had inherited the tastes of his mother. The librarian had, while in the service of Hélène de Hangest-Genlis, furnished designs for the ornamental bindings of books and frontispieces.

The arming of the Protestants put an end to a fabrication, which could no longer maintain itself; for this reason, that its only object being to supply the *dressoirs* and furnish the chapels of one family, their relations and personal friends, and not for commercial purposes; it followed the fortune of its patrons, in a country menaced like Poitou, with the horrors of a religious war.

We will now briefly notice the monograms and initials placed upon the pottery of Oiron, viz. the sacred monogram; that of the Dauphin Henri (afterwards Henri II.); Anne of Montmorency; and of Claude Gouffier, composed of an H., in memory of his mother, and a double C. Mr. Magniac's ewer has the letter G repeated several times round the body, the initial of Gouffier; and the candlestick belonging to Mr. Fountaine has the letter H, the initial of his mother's name—Hangest. The arms upon this pottery are those of the King, Francis I.; of the Dauphin Henri; of Gilles de

Laval, Seigneur de Bressiure; Anne of Montmorency; François de la Tremouille, Vicomte de Thouars; and of William Gouffier. This last occurs on a plate in the Kensington Museum, which has in the centre an oval escutcheon, surrounded by fruit, cherubs' heads and flaming rays, all in relief; in the centre are the arms of William Gouffier, third son of Admiral de Bonnivet, when he was a knight of Malta, that is to say, before he was raised to the episcopal chair of Beziers, in 1547. The emblems are the salamander of Francis I., and the crescents of Henri II., which were never used by Diana of Poictiers, as is generally supposed.

The distinguishing characteristics of this curious ware are, in the first place, the body, which is a creamy white pipe clay, very compact and of fine texture, so that it does not, like the ordinary fayence, require an opaque white enamel, but merely a transparent glaze; and secondly, that instead of being painted with enamel colours over the surface, it is inlaid with coloured pastes, in the same manner as the *champ levé* enamels or niello work in metal. Its fabrication must have required great care and diligence.

The number of pieces of this ware known to be in existence is 53. They are at the present day equally divided between England and France, each having 26; the odd one belongs to Russia. For a more detailed account of this ware, consult Chaffers' *Marks and Monograms on Pottery and Porcelain*, pp. 157-163.

Examples.

Fig. 100*a* is a candlestick of cream-coloured ware, inlaid with arabesques and other patterns, in dark brown and reddish brown, with reliefs of three boys, tragic masks and shields of arms of France, and the cipher of Henri II., and above, three terminal figures of satyrs; date about 1540. In the S. K. Museum.

Fig. 101 is a *biberon* of elegant form, gourd shaped, resting on a foot, with a short tubular spout richly moulded, and a bucket-shaped handle over the mouth; the whole surface of the vase is inlaid with interlaced bands and scrolls, rosettes, guilloches, masks, &c., in a reddish colour; a curved band on the neck has a row of ciphers, being the letters A.M., elegantly arranged as a decorative monogram, probably that of the Constable Anne de Montmorency; height 9¼ inches. This beautiful piece is the property of Andrew Fountaine, Esq.

FAYENCE.

Maiolica and Fayence are essentially the same, being composed of the same material and covered with a tin glaze or opaque white enamel, serving to hide the dingy colour of the clay, and forming a fine ground for the reception of colours.

Before describing the various manufactories of France, we will, as briefly as possible, give a description of the methods employed in fabricating this ware. The paste or body of fayence was composed of two parts clay and one part marl. These earths, mixed together, were placed in barrels half filled with water, and men with long poles beat and turned it about until it was reduced to a fine creamy pulp; this pulp was let out at the bottom of the barrel, and passing over a sieve fell into a reservoir; it was again stirred about with a pole, having a transverse piece of wood at the end, until thoroughly mixed; when the earth from mechanical suspension had gradually subsided, the water was drawn off, the clay, being about the consistence of dough, was cut into pieces and placed on shelves to dry, and subsequently thrown into a cave or cellar, where it remained a year before it was considered fit for use. When required, the earth was removed from the cellar and again trodden and thoroughly kneaded, until it became of suitable malleability. The potter, sitting at his wheel, which he set in motion with his feet, then took a ball of clay, proportioned to the size of the piece he wished to fabricate, and fixing it on the girelle or circular revolving table, with his left hand (the thumb being forced into the middle of the lump) he hollowed it out, his right hand first being dipped in *barbotine* (or the same earth mixed with water) was passed round the exterior, his left hand pressing outwards the inner surface; thus the turner could enlarge, reduce, or lengthen the piece as desired; when nearly finished he took a tool to form the contour of the vessel more correctly; the piece being thus perfectly formed, was placed in the air to dry, and then put into the kiln for the first baking, where it remained two or three days. The paste in this state was called *biscuit*, which although a misnomer, having been only once baked, is invariably called so, perhaps from its similarity to the baker's biscuit. After the vessel was baked it was dipped into a stanniferous enamel; this enamel owes its opacity and whiteness to the oxide of tin, the basis is obtained by the calcination of one hundred parts of lead and twenty parts of tin, prepared in a special furnace. The result of this first operation is a yellow powder, insoluble in water; it is then mixed with proportions of sand and salt and fused, when cold, this substance becomes a solid mass of opaque white glass; it is then broken and ground in water, and placed in a large bucket; into this liquid enamel the vase to be decorated was plunged, taking up a sufficient quantity of the enamel to entirely cover the surface; it was then ready for the decorator or painter. The biscuit, thus dipped into the liquid enamel, readily absorbed all the water, leaving on its surface a pulverized and fugitive coating, easily removed by the least shock, and it was on this fragile surface that the painter displayed his ability; which required great care in handling the brushes, with little or no opportunity of retouching or correcting mistakes. When decorated it was placed in an earthen case, called a *seggar*, to protect it from contact with the flame and the dust of the ashes or cinders, and again put for the second time into the kiln, which was heated to a much higher degree than the first, and occupied about twenty hours.

The blue was one of the most important colours in the decoration of fayence, and much employed for painting *en camaieu;* obtained from *cobalt*, prepared by calcination and extracting the arsenic and other volatile bodies, mixed with four times its weight of sand and three of salt, being of a gray colour before it was fired; this blue when prepared was called *zaphir* or sapphire. Two sorts of yellow were used, one transparent, the other opaque or thick, composed of sulphate of antimony, litharge and sand; the flesh tints were usually in this colour. The red was seldom or never used on fayence; cobalt blue, antimony, yellow and chrome green, will not change by the excessive heat of the kiln, but red, from the protoxide of iron of which it is made, is converted into brown or black; thus in the time of the French Revolution, when the figure of La République had to be represented, the Phrygian bonnet was painted yellow as a substitute for the redoubtable "bonnet rouge."

BEAUVAIS was celebrated for the manufacture of decorative pottery in the XIVth Century, and the descriptions of cups of the *terre de Beauvais* in early inventories frequently occur. Rabelais speaks of the "Poteries Azurées," of Beauvais, and several specimens of it are still in existence; they are of red, green or blue glaze, with gothic inscriptions and arms in relief of various provinces of France.

APT. The fabrication of fayence is said to have commenced here about the middle of the XVIIIth Century, principally in imitation of jasper and brocatelle marbles. A vase made by M. Moulin in 1780, is in the Sèvres Museum, with ornaments in relief and festoons of coloured pastes. In the same museum are some specimens made by Veuve Arnoux in 1802. The manufacture of M. Bonnet, established about 1780, and still carried on by his successor, produces marbled ware and vases of a yellow colour.

Fig. 102 is a yellow vase with masks and vine leaves, in the possession of Lady C. Schreiber.

BLOIS. A manufactory of fayence was in existence here through the XVIIth and XVIIIth Centuries. M. Ulysse Besnard, Curator of the Blois Museum, informs us that it was of a superior quality, similar to that of Nevers and Rouen. Some specimens are signed Lebarquet.

Fig. 103 represents a pair of candlesticks, painted with mermen, masks, &c., in the S. K. Museum, which are marked "Blois."

Avignon flourished as a manufactory of pottery from about 1650 to 1780, but there were also potteries here early in the XVIth Century. The pottery known to us is of a chocolate brown, with a fine metalloid glaze like bronze or tortoiseshell. The ewers and bottles are of elegant forms, resembling those of Italy, sometimes perforated and ornamented with masks and flowers in relief, or painted yellow.

Paris. François Briot was a celebrated artist, modeller, goldsmith, and likewise a manufacturer of fayence. His works in gold and silver have disappeared with the other superb jewels, described in the inventory of Henri II. in 1560, but some of his extraordinary works are preserved to us both in pewter and in enamelled pottery; in fact all the goldsmiths of the XVIth Century were acquainted with the potters' art of moulding in clay, for the purpose of reproducing their works in the richer metals. Benvenuto Cellini praises the extremely fine quality of the sand on the banks of the river of the Isle S[te] Chapelle, at Paris, and it was probably of this material Briot composed his pottery. His enamelled ware has erroneously been attributed to Bernard Palissy, but it is a distinct manufacture, and executed by Briot in a rival establishment. The enamel is more vitreous and transparent, the colours more brilliant, and of a higher finish than any produced by Palissy, and more nearly resemble enamel on metal. Sir Edward Marwood Elton possesses a circular salver, which is supposed to be the finest of its kind extant, enriched with very elaborate ornamentation in relief, enamelled with the most brilliant colours; in the centre, a figure of Temperantia surrounded by medallions of the elements and the arts and sciences, terminal figures between; in the Fountaine Collection at Narford, is an ewer to match. M. Calixte de Tussau has a fine example, stamped with Briot's monogram F.B. Another in the Soltykoff Collection, was sold for £400. to the Baron Sellière. There were also some smaller enamelled plates, representing the earth and the air personified, and the Judgment of Paris, sold for £70.

BERNARD PALISSY was born at La Chapelle Biron, in Perigord, A.D. 1510. He was originally a painter on glass; in 1539 he married, and established himself at Saintes, near Rochelle. After many years of diligent research and great patience, under trying circumstances, including the reproaches of his wife, which were to be expected (for it is related he actually burned his tables and chairs to heat the furnace for his experiments), he at length succeeded in discovering the enamel which decorates his ware. His rustic pottery *(figuline rustique)* and other beautiful productions, once perfected, were soon appreciated, and he rose to opulence. He made large pieces, such as vases and statues, for Henri II. and his Court, to ornament their gardens, and decorate their palaces and mansions. Being a Protestant, he was, after the Edict of 1559, taken under the protection of Catherine de Medicis and settled in Paris, thus escaping the Massacre of St. Bartholomew. In 1588 he was confined in the Bastille for his religious opinions, and lingered in those dungeons until his death in 1589. His brothers, Nicolas and Mathurin, who were associated with him in his keramic productions, and his successors, executed very inferior specimens. Clerissy, of Fontainebleau, was also a continuator of his style in the XVIIth Century. Palissy's first experiments were made with a view to discover a white enamel glaze, suitable for covering his ware, which would display brilliant colouring; but in this he was not successful, and it is remarkable that although the stanniferous enamel had been long known in Italy, and was at that time in general use, and the maiolica must frequently have come under his notice, yet he never succeeded in discovering its properties. However his earthenware, as well as his style of decoration and beautiful modelling, were quite original. The natural objects found upon his ware are true in form and colour, being mostly modelled from nature; the shells are copied from tertiary fossils found in the Paris basin; the fish are those of the Seine, and the reptiles and plants such as he found in the environs of Paris. To give some idea of the appreciation of true pieces of Palissy at the present day, we may mention the prices some have recently produced: a round basin with Diana of Poictiers, *en chasseresse*, leaning on a stag, brought in the Soltokoff sale £292.; a basin with masks and flowers, £160.; a pair of salt cellars, £80.; two statuettes of Mercury, and a player on the bagpipes, £103.

Examples of Palissy in the S. K. Museum.

Fig. 104. Ewer, dark blue ground with masks, cartouches and scroll foliage in various colours. The handle of scroll form, decorated with a nude female figure in high relief holding a cornucopia. XVIth Century. (Soulages Collection).

Fig. 105. Plateau. "La belle Jardinière." In the centre a figure of Flora, at her feet gardening implements, the border decorated with an embossed arabesque design. XVIth Century. (Soulages Collection).

Fig. 106. Dish with reptiles, fish, shells plants, &c., in proper colours in relief, on deep blue ground. XVIth Century. (Soulages Collection).

Fig. 107. Plate, round the edge daisies in relief, floral medallions in the centre upon a perforated ground. XVIth Century. (Pourtalès Collection.)

NEVERS was celebrated for its pottery in the year 1590. The alchemist, Gaston de Cleves, dedicated a book to Louis of Gonzaga, Duke of Nevers; in the dedicatory epistle he extols this prince for having brought into his States expert artists and workmen in the arts of glass making, pottery and enamel. The quotation is given by Marryat at some length. The earliest evidence of the making of fayence at Nevers, is the foundation of a *fabrique* by Domenique Conrade, a gentleman of Savona, a native of Albissola, where the Savona maiolica was made, and which was well known in Italy in the latter half of the XVIth Century. In 1578 he obtained letters of naturalization from Henri III., and commenced making his ware. His brothers, Baptiste and Augustin, were probably associated with him. His son Antoine, and his grandson Domenique, continued this establishment till towards the end of the XVIIth Century. In 1652, Pierre Custode established another *fabrique*, which was equally successful, and seven generations of this family successively were employed in it. At the beginning of the XVIIIth Century, in consequence of the success of the Conrades and the Custodes, several other manufactories were started, and in 1743 a decree restricted the number to eleven, to which another was added in 1760. In 1790 these were all in active operation, but shortly after, in consequence of the French Revolution, and especially the treaty of commerce between France and England, by which the English potters were enabled to pour in their earthenware at so cheap a rate that the French could not compete with them, added to this, the price of lead and tin, which came principally from England, was raised; all these disadvantages came so quickly upon them, and all the *fabriques* of the south of France, that a panic ensued; and in 1797 six had absolutely suspended their works, and the other six were reduced to half their number of workmen.

The fayences of the 1st epoch, 1600 to 1660, have frequently been confounded with Italian maiolica, but a little attention will show the points of difference. In the Nevers ware the figures are always yellow on blue ground; the Italian figures are usually blue on yellow. At Nevers they never employed red or metallic lustre, and the outlines are always traced in manganese violet, never in purple or black. During the 2nd epoch, the ground was a peculiar lapis lazuli blue, like the Persian called *bleu de Perse*, entirely covering the piece, spotted or painted with white, sometimes in yellow and orange, and painted with flowers and birds. The Chinese patterns are in light blue *en camaieu*, sometimes intermixed with a sort of brown lilac. Those of the other periods, in the style of Rouen and Moustiers, and the Saxon style, are well known; some also of the later time have verses and inscriptions of a popular character, and revolutionary sentences and republican emblems, having fallen to the last degree of decadence at the end of the XVIIth Century. (Consult Chaffers' *Marks and Monograms on Pottery and Porcelain*, pp. 182-189.)

Examples in the S. K. Museum.

Fig. 108. Pilgrim's bottle; *bleu de Perse* ground, painted with birds and flowers, in white and yellow; 1650 to 1680; height 11½ inches.

Fig. 109. Vase, one of a pair, painted with Japanese figures and landscapes in blue and manganese on white ground; 1650 to 1750; height 15⅜ inches.

Fig. 110. Vase, painted in blue and yellow, with boys reposing on dolphins, and marine animals; 1602 to 1660; height 9¼ inches.

Fig. 111. Cup, lobed, with double spout and small handles, chocolate ground mottled white; 1640 to 1700; height 3 in.

Fig. 112. Pilgrim's bottle, Apollo and Daphne; *rev.* a Bacchanalian scene.

ROUEN. There was a manufacture of pottery at Rouen early in the XVIth Century, which was evidently in great prosperity in 1542. There are two large pictures in the conservatory of the mansion of the Duc d'Aumale, Orleans House, Twickenham, they were brought from the Chateau d'Ecouen, and bear the arms of Montmorency. These pictures are formed of square tiles, representing the stories of Marcus Curtius and Mutius Scævola, and on them is written "Rouen, 1542." From this period until the middle of the XVIIth Century the records are wanting and no specimens are known, but towards the end of the century there were many establishments; among these, we find one belonging to Nicholas Poirel, Sieur de Grandval, privileged in 1646 for fifty years; another grant of privilege was accorded to Edmé Poterat, of St. Sever, Sieur de St. Etienne, in 1673, who was succeeded by his son Louis Poterat. At the commencement of the XVIIIth Century, the Chinese style pervaded all the Rouen fayence, but it was transformed or travestied and possessed a special physiognomy, the subjects were landscapes and buildings with figures, fantastic birds, dragons, &c., in blue, green, yellow and red, bordered with the square Chinese ornaments. When Louis XIV. sent his silver plate to the Mint to assist in defraying the war expenses, he had a service made at Rouen, which bears the mark of the *fleur de lis;* these pieces were made in the forms of birds and animals, such as were served at table. At a later date, the decoration consists principally of flowers issuing from cornucopiæ and rococo ornaments; this sort of style is called in France "*à la corne*." The paste of the Rouen fayence is heavier and thicker than that of Delft, but the designs and ornaments are full of taste, decorated in blue *camaieu* and in polychrome, some in the style of Nevers, of white on *bleu de Perse*, but of paler colour. It is the most artistic of all French fayences, by reason of the national character of its decorations. The pieces were frequently of large size, as fountains, consoles, vases, &c. There are four terminal busts of the Seasons at Hamilton Palace; and a large bust of Flora, on a high pedestal, in the S. K. Museum, presented by the late Duke of Hamilton.

We are inclined to think there was really no special mark of this *fabrique*, for having no rival or competitor, it was not necessary to have a distinctive sign. It is true, the *fleur de lis* was occasionally used, but the pieces so marked form the exceptions, and the innumerable monograms found upon the Rouen ware are probably those of the painters. For the marks used by them, the reader is referred to Chaffers' *Marks and Monograms*, pp. 189-192.

Examples in the S. K. Museum.

Fig. 113. Aiguière, one of a pair; the neck and mouth fluted, the body swelling from below, with raised ornament on the body and the handle; painted with polychrome decoration of landscapes within medallions, flowers, scrolls, and arabesques; period of Louis XIV.; height 26⅜ inches.

Fig. 114. Plate, painted in centre with a group in blue of two figures after Klingstedt, surrounded by polychrome decoration, scroll border round the rim, and a shield of arms; period of Louis XIV.; diam. 9½ inches.

Fig. 115. Plate, octagonal, painted in the centre with a rose ornament, with medallions and scrolls round the rim, in blue and orange; period of Louis XIV.; diam. 10 inches.

Fig. 116. Ewer, helmet-shaped, with scroll handle, painted in blue with medallions, arabesques and flowers; period of Louis XIV.; height 9¾ inches.

Fig. 117. Compotier, gadrooned, painted in blue with a centre rose ornament, surrounded by garlands, and border of arched pattern; period of Louis XIV.; diam. 9¼ inches.

Fig. 118. Sugar sifter, baluster form, with dome-shaped and pierced cover, painted in blue with scrolls and flowers; period of Louis XIV.; height 9⅛ inches.

Fig. 119. Dish, octagonal, painted in blue with a central figure subject after Klingstedt, and polychrome border of medallions, scrolls, and flowers; period of Louis XIV.; length 15⅛ inches.

Fig. 120. Compotier, octagonal, with indented edge, painted in polychrome with a cornucopia, flowers and insects; period of Louis XV.; diam. 9⅝ inches.

Fig. 121. Compotier, painted with Chinese figures, landscape, and flowers, in polychrome; period of Louis XV.; diam. 10 inches.

Fig. 122. Dish, oblong, with curved outline, painted in the centre with a shield of arms, and surrounded by a bold border of flowers, in polychrome; period of Louis XV.; length 19¼ in.

Fig. 123. Jug for cider, pear-shaped, painted with S. James standing in a landscape, under which is inscribed "I. 1737 D." cornucopiæ, flowers, and arabesques, in polychrome; height 13¼ inches.

STRASBOURG and HAGUENAU were noted for the manufacture of fayence, established by Hanung about 1750. It was called in France "poterie du Rhin," and is of a peculiar character, and easily known, being generally decorated with flowers and scrolls in red, rose colour and green. The fayence of Strasbourg has been imitated in the south of France, especially at Marseilles. The manufacture of hard porcelain was commenced here, but in consequence of the monopoly of Sèvres, he removed this to Frankenthal, leaving his sons Paul and Joseph Hanung to carry on the making of fayence at Strasbourg. The marks I.H. and P.H. in monogram are frequently found upon this ware, accompanied by numbers and letters indicating the patterns, to enable the merchants to give orders to the manufacturers: a plan also adopted in many *fabriques* at Delft.

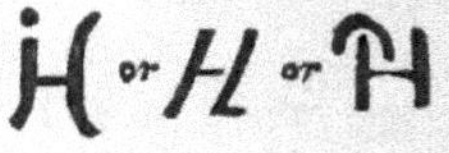

Examples in the S. K. Museum.

Fig. 124. Fountain, in three pieces, the cistern of scroll outline with raised ornament of a dolphin, a tree, on the stem of which is a crocodile, and a mask; in the mouth the tap is fixed; on the top is a swan; the basin has a scroll bordering, and is ornamented with raised medallions and flowers; polychrome decoration; it bears the initials of Paul Hannong; 1750 to 1760; total height 22¼ inches.

Fig. 125. Clock case, in three pieces, of scroll outline, with projecting busts on the sides, a figure of Time on the top, and bold scroll bracket beneath, enriched with marbled mouldings, and coloured in morone, yellow, blue, and green; it bears the mark of Paul Hannong: 1750 to 1760; total height 3 ft. 9 in.

MOUSTIERS. Fine fayence; 1686 to 1800. We have no record of the origin of this important *fabrique*, but a manuscript in the library at Marseilles informs us that the fabrication of fayence in Provence commenced at Moustiers, and that the Spanish Government wishing to improve their own manufacture, the Count d'Arenda then minister (1775-1784) engaged workmen from Moustiers and Marseilles to go to Denia, where, having expended a great deal of money in experiments, especially in improving the colours and the fine blue (hitherto only known in France), it was at length abandoned. One of the artists, named Olery, returned to Moustiers and established himself there, where Clerissy also had already made beautiful fayence, and was making a rapid fortune; with the knowledge he had acquired in the employment of colours, and the introduction of new forms, he soon surpassed Clerissy, but not being prudent, economical or rich, his secrets became known and he sank into mediocrity. It is only within a few years that the fayence of Moustiers has become known to amateurs. M. Brongniart makes no mentions of it in his treatise on pottery in 1844. It has been indiscriminately attributed to Rouen, Marseilles, and even to St. Cloud, but the researches of M. Riocreux of Sèvres, M. Jacquemart, M. Davillier, and others, have thrown considerable light on its early history.

Pierre Clerissy was a manufacturer here in 1686, and this is the earliest record we have; he directed his *fabrique* for forty years. A second Pierre Clerissy succeeded him, associated with Joseph Fouque, to whom it was eventually ceded about 1750, and remained uninterruptedly in the same family until 1850. We have, therefore, evidence of three potters at Moustiers in 1745, viz.: Clerissy, Olery, and a certain Pol Roux. In 1756 there were seven or eight, and in 1789 they were increased to eleven, whose names are all known, and need not be enumerated here.

The products of the Moustiers *fabriques* may be divided into three periods :—

1st Epoch. Towards the end of the XVIIth Century. The subjects are hunting scenes, &c., painted in blue; champêtre scenes and figures in costume of Louis IV.; mythological and biblical subjects with arabesque borders; the outlines are sometimes lightly indicated in violet of manganese.

2nd Epoch. From the commencement of the XVIIIth Century to about 1745. The specimens of this period are the best known and are not so rare; they are also in blue *camaieu*, in the style of Jean Bérain and André Charles Boulle, with highly finished and graceful interlaced patterns, among which are cupids, satyrs, nymphs and terminal figures, flowers, masks, &c.; canopies with draperies resting upon consoles, vases, fountains, &c.

3rd Epoch. From 1745 to 1789. The fayence is mostly painted in polychrome; the colours are blue, brown, yellow, green, and violet. The decorations are flowers, fruit, and foliage, sometimes mythological subjects. Other patterns of this period consist of grotesque figures, and caricatures in the style of Callot. These are by Joseph Olery, and may be easily recognized by his trade mark, an O traversed by an L, and sometimes the initials of the painter. The outlines of the designs were transferred to the surface of the ware by means of paper patterns, pricked with a fine needle and powdered over with charcoal, so that the subject could be reproduced as often as wanted. M. Davillier has a great number of these patterns, dated 1752 to 1756, their authenticity being proved by the paper marks.

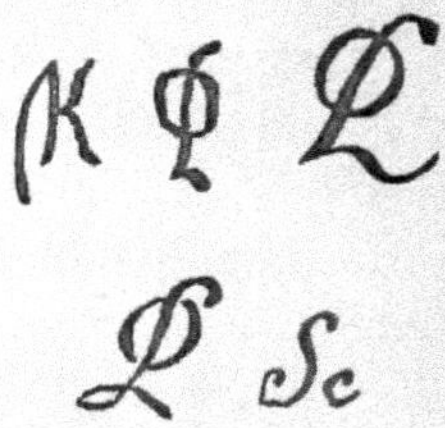

Examples in the S. K. Museum.

Fig. 126. Dish or plateau, oblong, with curved outline, painted in blue with amorini seated on scroll ornaments, surrounded by arabesques, in the style of Bérain; 1680 to 1720; length 17¼ inches.

Fig. 127. Plateau, round, with curved outline, painted in green *camaieu* with a rustic subject in the style of Boucher, with polychrome floral border; 1720 to 1760; diam. 11⅛ in.

Fig. 128. Compotier, painted with a central hunting subject, after Tempesta, surrounded by a floral border, and outer border of garlands, in polychrome; 1680 to 1720; diam. 10⅜ inches.

Fig. 129. Plate, octagonal, with curved outline, painted with central medallion of Juno standing in a landscape, surrounded by a garland, and round the border the busts of divinities within medallions, and garlands, in polychrome; 1680 to 1720; diam. 10 inches.

Fig. 130. Barber's basin, oblong, with curved outline, painted with central subject of Diana and Actæon within a scroll surrounded by satyrs and monkeys, with border of garlands and insects, and shield of arms, in polychrome. It bears the mark of Olery; 1680 to 1720; length 15 inches.

VARAGES, about six leagues from Moustiers, was also a manufactory for fayence in the style of Moustiers, established about 1730. There were five *fabriques*. Some of this ware bear the mark of a cross, and was called "Fayence à la Croix."

MARSEILLES. The manufacture of fayence at Marseilles, and the South of France, must have been in activity early in the XVIIth century; for several of the laboratories, especially the hospital at Narbonne, are completely furnished with drug vases, made at that time. M. Davillier has a very interesting plate which proves the existence of a pottery at Marseilles in the year 1697. It is inscribed "A. Clerissy à St Jean du Dezert à Marseille 1697" and this is the earliest authenticated piece known having a name and date. Another potter is known to have been at Marseilles in 1709, named Jean Delaresse. A little after 1750, twelve *fabriques* of pottery were in existence. In 1790 there were eleven manufactories existing, but most of them ceased about 1793, for the reason above stated—the Treaty of Commerce with England. The Revolution of 1793 gave an additional blow to the keramic industry of Marseilles. In 1805 there were only three, employing 20 hands. In 1809 only one.

From 1709 to 1749, nothing is known of the state of the manufactories here, but in the last-named year we hear of Honoré Savy being established at Marseilles; he discovered a green colour superior to any other, called "Le Vert de Savy." His establishment was by far the most important, and was under the protection of the Comte de Provence, the king's brother. Joseph Gaspard Robert was another celebrated potter, he signed his works J. R., sometimes at length. The widow Perrin and Abelard fabricated a great quantity of fayence, and pieces are more frequently met with than any other, they are signed VP (veuve Perrin).

The fayence is much the same character as that of Moustiers, sometimes like Strasbourg. The decorations are frequently in red or green, sometimes with Chinese designs. There is one peculiarity about the Marseillaise fayence which at once fixes its identity, and this is, three green leaves or marks painted on the backs of plates and dishes, to hide the imperfections in the enamel caused by the pernettes or points of support on which they rested in the kiln. There is also a great resemblance between the early ware made here and at Genoa, in consequence of the emigration of many workmen, as we learn from a complaint made on the subject by the potters of Marseilles to the Intendant of Provence in 1762, by which it seems they took a great number of apprentices at very low wages, and the wages were paid in fayence, which mode of payment they said deteriorated the quality, and caused the workmen to emigrate to Genoa. Also they complained that great quantities of Genoese fayence were imported into Languedoc and Provence, and spread over France, which was absolutely ruinous to the trade of the two provinces, especially to Marseilles. Among the artists who emigrated to Italy may be mentioned Jacques Borrelly and M. Rolet, whose names we find on fayence, the former at Savona in 1779, the latter at Urbino in 1772. The mark used by Savy after the visit of the Comte de Provence, in 1777, when under the protection of Monsieur the king's brother, was the fleur-de-lis.

Examples.

Fig. 131. Soup tureen, cover and stand, with scroll handles and feet, the handle of the cover formed of a cluster of fruit, with polychrome flower decoration and gilding; made by Savy, about 1750; length of tureen $15\frac{1}{2}$ in. S. K. Museum.

Fig. 132. Plate, painted with a landscape by Veuve Perrin. Mr. C. W. Reynolds.

Sinceny in Picardy, formerly written St. Cenis. A pottery was established here in 1733, by Jean Baptiste de Fayard,

Gouverneur de Chaunay et Seigneur de Sinceny. Dr. Warmont (*Recherches Historiques sur les faïençes de Sinceny, &c.*, Paris, 1864,) divides the products of this manufactory into three periods:—

1. Rouennaise, 1734 to 1775.
2. Faïence au feu de réverbère, 1775 to 1789.
3. Décadence de l'Art, 1789—1864.

The first director was Pierre Pellevé, and a numerous staff of painters, some of whom, Pierre Jeannot, Le Cerf, and Bertrand, placed their initials upon the ware. The earliest pieces were painted in blue; the next in blue touched with red or green and yellow, decorated with *lambrequins* (mantlings), *à la corne* (cornucopiæ), birds and butterflies. Chinese figures, which, from the frequent repetition in the same outlines, were doubtless stencilled by pricked papers and charcoal powder. Drinking cups, and small statuettes and figures were also produced about 1760, by a modeller named Richard; toy figures for children, &c. &c.

About 1775 a great improvement was perceptible in the fayence of Sinceny; the paste was finer in quality, the colours brighter and more varied, in more exact imitation of the porcelain of Japan,—this was accomplished by what is called *au feu de réverbère* in contradistinction to the old process *au grand feu;* the latter being only one baking, while in the other the ware was placed a second time in the kiln, and the pigments not exposed to so great a heat, allowing the employment of brighter colours. This new process was very costly, and required, as it were, a fresh apprenticeship; and the proprietors were compelled to procure hands from Lorraine, where it seems to have originated. They produced table services decorated in polychrome, with branches of roses, sometimes in green *camaieu;* delicate wicker baskets, watch stands, &c., painted with Chinese figures, rococo scrolls and other ornaments. The mark S. c. y was used at this period, and some-

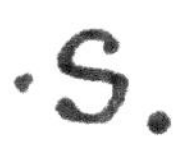

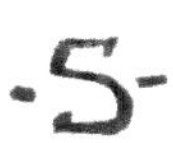

times the name at length. From 1790 the fayence *au feu de réverbère* was discontinued on account of its expensive character and the introduction of English ware at a lower price; but still, both descriptions were occasionally made. The original manufactory is still carried on.

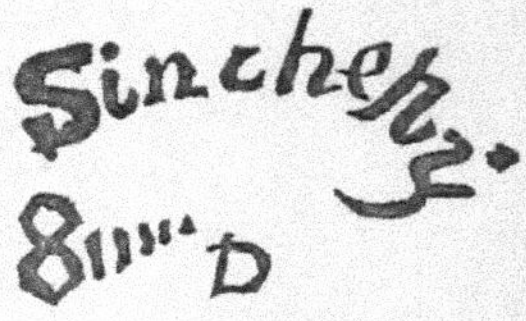

LUNEVILLE. An establishment of fayence was founded in 1731, by Jacques Chambrette; it was called *La Manufacture Stanislas*; he was succeeded by his son Gabriel and his son-in-law Charles Loyal. They made fayence of blue decoration like Nevers, and sometimes rose and green colours like the old Strasburg ware. Large figures of lions, dogs, and other animals of natural size are frequently met with.

Examples in the S. K. Museum.

Fig. 133. A pair of statuettes; rustic male and female figures, with polychrome decoration; about 1775; height 8¾ in.

Fig. 134. Dish, oblong, with waved edge, painted with centre group of an eagle attacking birds of rich plumage, and border of insects, in polychrome; about 1760; length 13¼ in.

Fig. 135. Dish, oblong, with waved outline, painted with centre group of birds with rich plumage, and smaller birds, insects, and diaper pattern round the border, in polychrome; about 1760; length 15½ inches.

APREY, near Langres. A manufactory was established, about 1750, by Lallemand, Baron d'Aprey. About 1780 it was conducted by M. Vilhault, who made a superior kind of fayence. The process adopted by him was considered the best then existing, and formed the subject of a lecture by M. Bosc d'Antic, before the Academy of Dijon, on "an improved method of making fayence." The early style is that of Strasbourg with rose colour, green and yellow predominating. The marks used were the letters A. P. in monogram.

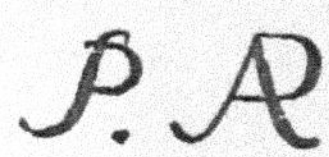

Fig. 136. Plate, with waved eged, painted in polychrome

with groups of flowers; about 1780; diameter 9⅜ inches. S. K. Museum.

MANERBE, near Lisieux in Normandy, and at MALICORNE IMFREVILLE, CHATEAU-LA-LUNE and ARMENTIÈRES, were constructed those elegant glazed earthenware pinnacles which adorn the gables of the old mansions in various parts of Normandy. They are 5 or 6 feet long, being a series of small ornaments placed one above another on an iron rod, and partake of the character of the *figulines rustiques* of Palissy, and have frequently been sold as such.

ST. CLEMENT. Established about 1750, Little is known of this *fabrique.* There are some specimens in the Sèvres Museum; also some others of later date, 1819 and 1823.

Fig. 137, is an écuelle, with gilt scrolls on white ground; in the possession of Lady C. Schreiber.

TOULOUSE. A manufactory was established here in the XVIIIth Century. The ware is very similar to the style of early Rouen.

Fig. 138, is a large hunting bottle, with loops for suspension, painted with blue flowers, and round the neck "Laurens Basso a Toulousa Le 14 Maÿ 1756." In the possession of Mr. C. W. Reynolds.

NIDERVILLERS. This important manufactory of fayence was established in 1760, by Jean Louis, Baron Beyerlé. It was in the German style, potters from Germany having been employed, and is remarkable for the richness and delicacy of its decoration, most frequently painted with flowers in bouquets and garlands. The buildings were constructed after his own plans; and being a good chemist, he brought his ware to great perfection. His fayence figures and groups are well modelled; about 1780, four years before his death, the estate was purchased by Genl Count Custine, and carried on by him under M. Lanfray, principally in the manufacture of porcelain, which will be subsequently referred to. Count Custine's mark is here given.

Examples in the S. K. Museum.

Fig. 139. Compotier, one of a pair; shell-shaped, painted with flowers in polychrome; it bears the initials B. N., the mark of Baron Beyerlé; about 1770; length 9⅛ inches.

Fig. 140. Tray, oblong, painted to resemble deal, with representation in the centre of an unrolled piece of paper, on which is a landscape with ruins in rose *camaïeu*, inscribed "J. Deutsch del. sculpt. à Niderwiller, 1774;" length 13⅛ in.

Fig. 141. Vase with cover, one of a pair; urn shape, painted to resemble deal, with medallions containing landscapes in rose *camaïeu*, and borders of bay leaves. It bears the mark of Count Custine; about 1774; height 17⅜ inches.

DOUAI. Two brothers of the name of Leech, from England, were engaged, in 1782, by M. George Bris, of Douai, to superintend the manufacture of English pottery on a large scale, in the Rue des Carmes (now a Normal School). The products of this manufactory are much sought after by amateurs, on account of their elegant forms. It was one of the first of the kind established in France. The chief workmen, who came originally from England, instructed pupils, who carried the new process to Chantilly, Forges, and other places in France.

VINCENNES. The existence of this manufactory is made known to us by a patent of 31 December 1767, from which we learn that M. Maurin des Abiez desired to undertake a manufacture of fayence in the manner of Strasbourg; it being notorious that there did not exist in France any fayence comparable to it in beauty and solidity; he had purchased the secret, and brought to Paris a staff of workmen who had been engaged there, and he had already expended 100,000 francs to arrive at the desired perfection. He also included in his request the manufacture of porcelain, and stated that he required a large and commodious building for the purpose, which he could not obtain without a great outlay of capital. It was accordingly decreed that he should have possession, for twenty years, of the Chateau de Vincennes, in a square enclosure, which had formerly been employed for the ancient manufacture of porcelain. Pierre Antoine Hanung was engaged as director, and it was carried on for four years, until 1771, when Hanung petitioned for assistance, having got into difficulties, in consequence of the undertakers having ceased to furnish funds necessary to carry on the works, but as he could not obtain it, they altogether ceased.

SARREGUEMINES was a manufactory of great importance, established about 1770 by Paul Utzschneider. This beautiful fayence is in imitation of porphyry, jasper, granite and other variegated hard marbles, sometimes cut and polished by the lathe; frequently also with white raised figures on blue in the style of Wedgwood, and red ware like the Japanese. There are many specimens in the Sèvres Museum. The name is impressed on the ware.

ST. AMAND, near Valenciennes. A manufactory was founded about 1750, or a little earlier, by M. Fauquet, and continued by his son. In *Le Calendrier du Gouvernement de Flandre & Hainault*, for 1775, it is stated, that, there were two important manufactories of fayence, which equalled that of Rouen, and in 1778 the inspector of manufactures reports the satisfactory state of the *fabrique* of St. Amand, conducted by M. Fauquet fils. In 1775 he married a sister of Lamoninary of Valenciennes, and occupied himself especially with the gilding of his ware, which gave his neighbours the opportunity of saying, he melted all his Louis d'ors in making his experiments and ruined himself. In 1785, M. Fauquet established a porcelain manufactory at Valenciennes, but carried on that of fayence at St. Amand simultaneously. In the revolution of 1789 he emigrated, and all his goods were confiscated. In 1807 he attempted to revive the *fabrique*, and advertized that the St. Amand works were in full activity, making white fayence in the style of Rouen. Three painters were attached to this *fabrique*: Bastenaire Daudenart, Desmuralle, a flower painter, and Louis Alexandre Gaudry, a landscape painter.

M. le Dr. Lejeal *(Note sur une marque de Faïençe Contestée)* has thought it of sufficient importance to publish a pamphlet respecting a curious mark, sometimes found upon fayence, which had been long wandering about from one locality to another, but which he at length has found a resting place for at St. Amand. His authority is a plate of fayence, beautifully painted with flowers, which belonged to a family for eighty years, and was presented by Fauquet himself. Bastenaire Daudenart, the painter, acknowledged it to be the finest piece ever produced there; this piece bears the mysterious mark which has given rise to so much discussion. This mark is an imitation of that of Sevres. The two F's interlaced and the two L's are the initials of Fauquet and Lamoninary. Another mark is given by Dr. Lejeal, in which the two F's are more distinctly traced, and the letters S.A. at the side being the initials of St. Amand, corroborate the doctor's hypothesis.

SCEAUX PENTHIÈVRE. In a decree, dated 1753, we read that Sieur Jacques de Chapelle had established a manufactory of a particular sort of fayence at the village of Sceaux, of which he alone possessed the secret, and being much appreciated by the public on account of its good qualities and the sale increasing, he was permitted to carry on his trade. The ware is in the style of Strasbourg, the rose colour and green prevailing and painted with flowers, but more carefully finished, landscapes, &c. Until 1760 the ware was marked with the letters S. X., and it was continued by his successor, Jullien, to 1772, at which date Glot, a sculptor, became proprietor, who marked *Sceaux* at full length. When the Duc de Penthièvre became patron, the anchor was used, he being Lord High Admiral.

Fig. 142 is a plate painted with birds; in Mr. Reynolds' Collection.

BOURG-LA-REINE. Established in 1773 by Messrs. Jacques and Jullien, who removed hither from Menecy. The early ware is very similar to that of Sceaux. A *fabrique* of fayence is still carried on by M. Laurin, who uses the old mark placed upon the porcelain. Besides the white fayence for domestic use, more artistic pieces are produced, painted on the enamel after it has received a slight baking; it is principally in imitation of the Italian. The painter attached to the manufactory of Bourg-la-Reine is a pupil of Sèvres, named Chapelet, who marks his decorations with a chaplet.

Creil had a manufactory of fine fayence, established by M. St Crique; they made opaque porcelain and stoneware in the English style, and transferred prints on to the ware.

Fig. 143 is a plate of this *fabrique*, yellow border with transfer printed landscape. Lady C. Schreiber.

Montereau. On the 15th of March, 1775, Messrs. Clark, Shaw & Co., natives of England, obtained letters patent to carry on a manufactory of English fayence, called Queen's ware, from clay found in the vicinity; they were empowered to bring over from England two other workmen, making with their wives and families seventeen persons, and in consideration of their expenses, a concession was made of 1200 francs a year for ten years. This English ware had a very extensive sale, and was a great blow to the manufacture of French fayence. It soon spread over France, and was extensively made at Toulouse, Creil, Sarreguemines, and other places.

Russia, Denmark and Sweden.

FAYENCE.

St. Petersburg. About the year 1700, Peter the Great, during his stay at Saardam, induced some potters of Delft to emigrate to St. Petersburg, where he established a manufactory. We have no information on the subject, except a notice of it in the "*Connaissances Politiques*," of Beausobre, published at Riga in 1773: "There is also among the porcelain manufactories at St. Petersburg a *fabrique* of fayence, on the other side of the Neva, where they make every description of vessels of correct design and in good taste. A private gentleman of Revel, has also established at his own cost, near this city, a *fabrique* of fayence, and has obtained painters and potters from Germany."

Rorstrand is the name of a suburb of Stockholm, where earthenware was made. Established in 1727. The king granted the proprietors a monopoly in Sweden, which was renewed in 1735, and ceased in 1749. The manufactory was continued down to the present day. In 1772 it was under the direction of Nordenstople, and later under Geyer.

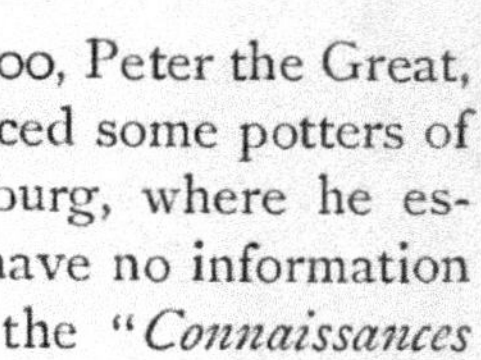

Examples.

Fig. 144. Tureen and cover, white, with coloured flowers and scroll margin, the cover surmounted by the half figure of a deer; dated 1770. S. K. Museum.

Fig. 145. Butterboat, leaf shaped, painted with flowers; dated 1771; in Mr. C. W. Reynolds' Collection.

STOCKHOLM is the same manufactory as Rorstrand, but the mark was altered when it was united to the capital. The mark is the name at full length, with the initials of the painters and sometimes dates.

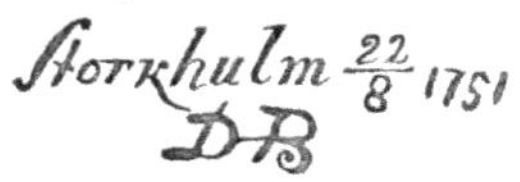

MARIEBERG near Stockholm. The second Swedish pottery was established in 1750, on the expiration of the monopoly of Rorstrand, by M. Ehreinrich, under the patronage of Count Scheffer, Councillor of State. The fayence was something like Delft ware, and they also ornamented it with transfer printing. The mark is three crowns, for Denmark, Norway and Sweden, accompanied by dates and initials of the directors. In this instance the date is the 14th of October, 1768.

Examples.

Fig. 146. Vase and cover, with branches and flowers; coloured in relief; on the cover a sitting bird; date about 1770. S. K. Museum.

Fig. 147. Vase and cover, with printed transfer landscape and figures; on the pedestal a mouse; dated 1774. Lady C. Schreiber.

Fig. 148. Plate, pierced border, with a shield of arms and flowers; dated 1768. Mr. C. W. Reynolds.

Fig. 149. Bowl, painted with arms and flowers; satyr's head handles; dated 1769. Mr. C. W. Reynolds.

KIEL, on the shores of the Baltic, was also noted for its

fayence about 1770; it was under the direction of M. Buchwald. The paintings of landscapes and flowers in colours are well finished; sometimes marked *Kiel* at length, and sometimes *K* only, with other letters under, separated by short lines.

Fig. 150 is a very fine bowl, with a cover in form of a mitre; in Mr. Reynolds' Collection; it was used for a kind of punch, called bishop; it is painted with a party of ladies and gentlemen drinking this beverage from a similar bowl; and on the reverse soldiers skirmishing. Inscribed "Kiel. Buchwald Director. Abr. Leihamer fecit," as here given.

Germany, Holland and Belgium.

FAYENCE AND STONE-WARE.

THE pottery of Germany consists of two distinct classes. The fayence with the opaque white stanniferous glaze; and that which was made to a great extent in these countries (especially in Germany) called in England stone-ware; in Germany *steingut;* and in France *grès* or sandstone. These epithets exactly describe the quality of the last-named ware. It was very serviceable for domestic purposes, drinking bottles and vessels of every-day use, and was covered with a thin transparent glaze, effected by throwing common salt into the kiln when the ware was nearly baked—the salt vaporized by the heat, surrounded the vessels, and acting upon the silica of their surfaces, produced a thin gloss of silicate of soda over the ware, rendering it perfectly impervious.

NUREMBERG. The celebrated Viet Hirschvogel, of Schelestadt, was born 1441, and died in 1525; he was a great potter, contemporary with Luca della Robbia of Florence, who was born in 1400 and died in 1481. The invention of the stanniferous glaze, which has been attributed to the latter, we have shewn was nothing more than the appropriation of it to the purposes of sculpture, and well known long before his time. We may also safely conclude that it was used in Germany quite as early as in Italy. The early pieces of pottery are somewhat like maiolica, but the colours are brighter, the green predominating in many specimens; figures in relief in niches are frequently seen on vases. Several chimney pieces of the XVth Century are still in existence, one is in the Chateau de Saltzburg, and many pieces are treasured up in the Museums, supposed to have been made by Hirschvogel himself. In the Dresden Museum is a pitcher of green glaze, with a scripture subject in relief, dated 1473, and another in the Berlin Museum, dated 1470. The Nuremberg pottery of the XVIth and XVIIth Centuries is common. Hirschvogel was succeeded by his sons and a host of continuators. Fayence of the XVIIIth Century is also met with, painted with scriptural subjects, sometimes in blue *camaieu*, sometimes in other colours. On pieces of this character names are occasionally found, as Gluer, 1723; Strobel, 1724 and 1730; and Greber, 1729.

Examples.

Fig. 151. Group, in high relief, of enamelled earthenware, representing a sleeping knight, by whose side stands a man in civil costume, wearing a winged cap and holding a globe; XVIth Century; height 18 inches. S. K. Museum.

Fig. 152. Jug, of enamelled earthenware, in various colours, with figures in low relief; in front two armed figures in full relief, on each side of a tree; attributed to Viet Hirschvogel; XVth Century; height 13 inches. S. K. Museum.

Fig. 153. Dish, painted in the centre with Christ rising from the tomb; signed with the painter's name Glüer, 1723. Mr. C. W. Reynolds' Collection.

LEIPSIG. In the convent of St. Paul, which was built in 1207, there was a frieze of bricks, covered with tin enamel glaze, representing in relief the heads of Saints and Apostles, 20 in. by 15 in., $2\frac{1}{2}$ in. thick. On the demolition of the convent a selection of these were deposited in the Dresden Museum; they are of Byzantine character, in green enamel shaded with black, the hair, beard and eyes are coloured.

STREHLA. A manufactory for earthenware was in existence for many centuries. A pulpit of enamelled earthenware still exists at Strehla, supported by a life-size figure of Moses, ornamented with eight plaques of religious subjects and the four Evangelists, bearing the name of the potter and date 1565.

OBERDORF. Carried on by a potter named Hans Seltzman; a very fine stove of his, is in the Palace at Fuessen, in Bavaria, with inscription, dated 1514. Many other places throughout Germany were equally famous in the XVIth and XVIIth Centuries, for the manufacture of stoves, as at Augsbourg, Memmingen, &c.

BAŸREUTH. The manufactory of pottery flourished here in the XVIth Century, of a brown stoneware with Renaissance medallions, arabesques, &c. in relief. At a later period, fine fayence was produced, painted in blue *camaieu.* The designs are delicately traced with a brush on a fine paste; the forms are canettes, jardinières, &c. This ware sometimes has the name in full, as on a large vase in the Sèvres Museum. At the end of the XVIIIth Century a *fabrique* of fayence was carried on by a M. Schmidt, who assiduously copied the English ware; there are five specimens in the Sèvres Museum bearing the counterfeit mark of "Wedgwood."

SCHAFFHAUSEN. A common description of earthenware was made here in the XVIIth Century; a specimen is in the Musée de Cluny, with scriptural subjects in white and blue on brown ground, by "Genrit Evers, 1695."

COLOGNE. The stone-ware made here in the XVIth Century is better known throughout Europe than any other description of pottery; its durability for domestic uses and the elegant character of its ornamentation in relief, caused it to be sought for everywhere. The *grès de Cologne* has been confounded with the *grès de Flandres*, which latter name is given erroneously and indiscriminately to all stone-ware of German manufacture, notwithstanding the German inscriptions the pieces bear and the arms of German cities and families. The best and most highly finished decorative *grès* or stoneware cruches were undoubtedly made in Germany, if not at Cologne. The clay for making the Cologne ware came from Langerwche, between Düren and Aix la Chapelle. The manufactory was not actually in Cologne, but in the vicinity, possibly at Newit or Lauenstein, where stone-ware is still made. We know from the following document, that England and the Low Countries were supplied from Cologne. The earliest notice of this fact occurs in a curious petition from William Simpson to Queen Elizabeth, praying that "Whereas one Garnet Tynes, a stranger, living at Acon (Aix la Chapelle), doth buy uppe all the drinking stone pottes made at Culloin (Cologne), and he onlie transporteth them into this realm of England and selleth them, who also serveth all the lowe Countries and other places with pottes. It may please your Majestie to graunte unto the said Simpson full power and onlie licence to provyde, transporte and bring into this realm the same or such like drinking pottes," &c. It will be observed that no allusion is made to any other stone-ware; the *grès de Flandre* or the *grès d'Hollande* are not hinted at. Again Dr. Plot, in 1677, speaking of Jn°. Dwight, of Fulham, says "He hath discovered the mystery of the stone or Cologne wares, heretofore made only in Germany, and by the Dutch brought into England in great quantities." (Chaffers' *Marks and Monograms*, p. 49.)

All the Cologne ware was made in moulds, and it must be borne in mind that the vessels are not always made in the date indicated upon them, for the moulds were used successively through a series of years, and it is no uncommon occurrence to find two different dates upon the same piece. Some of the finest specimens known, bear the name of Baldem Mennicken, a potter, dwelling at Rorren, in Germany; one of these, a ewer, is in the S. K. Museum, the neck is terminated by a lion's head; the subject, in relief round it, represents the three Theological Virtues, the four Cardinal Virtues, and the seven Liberal Arts personified; on each side is a circular medallion, enclosing the arms of England; round the vessel is a German inscription and date 1577. The dates found upon them range from 1550 to 1600, but there is one in the Cologne Museum, dated 1687, which is an extremely late date.

Examples.

Fig. 154. Stone-ware jug, brown glaze with large rosette and other ornaments in relief; XVIth Century. Geological Museum.

Fig. 155. Large *grès* fountain, purple blue and white, the lower part gadrooned, with a central band of figures in niches and openwork wheels; XVIth Century; height 30 inches. S. K. Museum.

Figs. 156, 157. Two Cologne ware canettes of cream colour, arabesques and scrolls, with numerous medallions of figures; dated 1574; height 17¼ inches. S. K. Museum.

Fig. 158. Cologne ware cruche, globular, fluted base, a mask under the spout, grey and blue, with ornaments in relief; date about 1600; height 7¼ inches. S. K. Museum.

Fig. 159. Cruche, of grey and blue stone-ware, with raised masks and rosettes round the neck, and a centre band of arabesques of sphinxes, festoons and scrolls; date circa 1580; height 8¾ inches. S. K. Museum.

BUNTZLAU, in Silesia. *Grès* was made here in the XVIth and XVIIth Centuries. The products of the last century are distinguished by ornaments in relief, flowers, coats of arms, &c., sometimes gilt. At the present time an extensive trade is still carried on in the manufacture of chocolate and coffee pots, usually of brown glaze, lined with white, like our Rockingham ware. The late King Frederick William IV. of Prussia, always used this in preference to more costly ware. In the town hall of Buntzlau, there is preserved a monster coffee pot, 15 ft. high, made at this place in the last century.

HARBURG on the Elbe, opposite Hamburg, is noted as the residence of Johann Schaper, who was born towards the end of the XVIth Century, and flourished here from 1620 to 1670, the date of his decease. His exquisite paintings of landscapes and figures are usually in indian ink or sepia *en grisaille*, the colours being fixed by heat. His fayence mugs are usually painted in brown, shaded, the lights being scratched in with a point, carefully and elegantly drawn. He also painted on glass in the same style, of which there are several examples in the S. K. Museum, and some by his successors.

Fig. 160. Cruche of fine fayence, painted with a landscape in grey *camaieu*; signed "*Joh. Schaper;*" white ground with flowers and fruit in natural colours, mounted with cover and rim in enamel on copper; date about 1640; height 8½ inches. S. K. Museum.

GRENZHAUSEN, in Nassau, about 1780. *Grès* or stone-ware was made here, it is a fine quality and easily mistaken for the more ancient *grès*. The forms are usually plates, dishes and jugs, in which the decoration consists of a fine blue enamel on grey ground, with incuse ornaments executed by hand. There are several specimens of this modern *fabrique* in the Sèvres Museum, and many are frequently seen displayed as specimens of German pottery of the XVIth and XVIIth Centuries.

Fig. 161. Jug of Grenzhausen manufacture, reticulated pattern, engine turned, and enriched with brilliant enamel colours, inlaid in geometrical designs; XVIIIth Century. S. K. Museum.

CREUSSEN, a town of Bavaria, has always been noted for its pottery. The *grès* of the XVIIth Century, called *Creussener Steingut*, is of a dark brown colour, in the forms of cylindrical mugs, tankards, &c., with figures in relief round them, painted in bright coloured enamel. The Apostle mugs, with the Evangelists and Apostles ranged round under arcades, are well known. They sometimes also have coats of arms of the Empire and noble families. It may be observed as a caution, that a great many of these mugs have come from the manufactory of an uniform brown colour, not enamelled: these have been subsequently painted in oil colours, but the fraud is easily detected by scraping them with a knife, which will remove the paint, while the enamel resists.

Fig. 162. Tankard of Creussen ware, chocolate coloured

ground, with coloured enamel ornaments and figures of the Emperor and the Electors of Germany on horseback, dated 1696. S. K. Museum.

SCHERZHEIM, Wurtemberg. The Wintergursts, father and son, were celebrated potters here, and made fayence from the beginning of the XVIIth Century; it is from this manufactory that the table services, of which each piece represents an animal, or vegetable, were made; at the Chateau de la Favorite, at Baden, portions of a service may be seen in the form of a ham, a boar's head, &c.

LAUENSTEIN, near Coblentz. A manufactory was established in 1760; the stone ware made here is of grey and blue, ornamented with incuse patterns; it is still made in large quantities, and carried by the Rhine boats to the markets in Holland, where it meets with a ready sale.

HÖCHST, near Mayence. Enamelled fayence was made here in the beginning of the XVIIIth Century, founded by Gelz of Frankfort. The mark is a wheel, occasionally crowned, in colours or gold. The arms of the Electoral see, first assumed by Wittigis, Archbishop of Mayence, who was the son of a wheelwright. This manufactory ceased in 1794, but a potter named Dahl established one in the vicinity, using a wheel and the letter D. He made statuettes, &c.

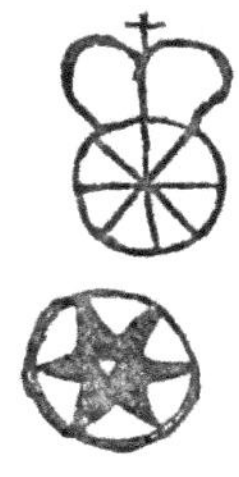

DRESDEN. A manufactory was established at Meissen, on the Elbe, about twelve miles from Dresden, by Augustus II, King of Poland and Elector of Saxony, for the manufacture of hard paste, or true porcelain. The experiments of Tschirnhaus and Böttcher commenced about 1706; to the latter is attributed the invention of hard paste. His first attempt produced a red ware, like jasper, which was cut and polished by the lapidary and gilt by the goldsmith. It was made from a kind of brown clay found at Meissen. This red ware, made by Böttcher, was a fine stone ware, having the opacity, grain and toughness of pottery. A square Böttcher ware coffee pot, cut and polished, with flowers and the head of a boy, are in the S. Kensington Museum; and a bust of Böttcher himself, of the same ware, is in the Right Hon. W. E. Gladstone's Collection. An improvement upon this was a brownish red ware, with a good glaze, on which were placed designs in gold and silver leaf, like the Japanese.

Another sort of pottery was made in the beginning of the XVIIIth Century, in imitation of the Japanese; it was called the red pottery of Dresden. An oval mark, with a horse galloping, and ARV. DE MILDE is frequently found upon the tea pots of this ware.

Fig. 163. Coffee pot and cover, of Böttcher ware, chocolate coloured ground, decorated with gilt scrolls and two medallions of musicians; F under a crown in front; about 1708; height 9 inches. S. K. Museum.

TEINITZ (Bohemia). A manufactory was carried on in this small town, by a potter named Welby, under the protection of Count Trautmansdorf, who has a chateau here. The only specimen we have seen is in the possession of the Rev. T. Staniforth, and is represented in Fig. 164. A fine fayence plate, well painted in bistre *camaieu* with the Discovery of Calisto by Diana; it has an elegant border in grey with alternate square and oval white medallions of richly gilt designs, very much resembling the gilding of Vienna. Its date appears to be about 1800, and bears underneath the annexed mark stamped in the ware.

FRANKENTHAL. Paul Hannong, driven from Strasbourg in 1754, in consequence of the Sèvres monopoly, founded a manufactory here for hard paste porcelain; he also made great quantities of fayence, usually decorated with flowers, as at Strasbourg. It was called "Poterie du Rhin." The letter F stands for Frankenthal, the number relating to the pattern.

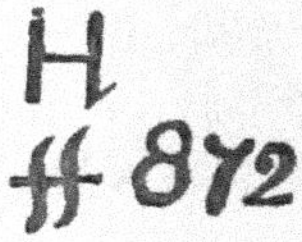

ARNSTADT (Gotha). Established about the middle of the XVIIIth Century. Fig. 165 represents a fayence jug, painted in blue *camaieu*, with St. George and the Dragon, coloured flowers on the sides, purple and green check border; in the possession of Rev. T. Staniforth, marked underneath thus: M. A. Jacquemart (*Merveilles de la Ceramique*, part iii., p. 207) quotes a piece in the possession of M. Gasnault, of Paris, painted with fruit and flowers, inscribed "Pinxit F. G. Fliegel St. Georgen Amsee 3 Noffember 1764;" which he erroneously assigns to St. Georges in Bavaria. By comparison with the mark in the margin, it is clearly Arnstadt, at the sign of St. George, the unintelligible word *Amsee* being actually a false reading of *Arnstadt.*

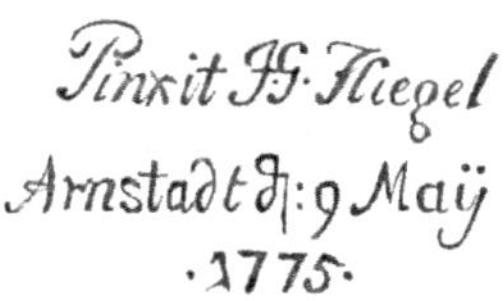

TEYLINGEN, in Holland, has become celebrated in keramic history, from its association with the unfortunate Jacqueline, Countess of Hainault, and the manufacture of an earthenware jug, called after her *Jacoba Kannetje.* This princess, born about 1400, became wife of John Duke of Brabant, and after many severe trials, retired in 1433 to the Chateau de Teylingen, about five hours' journey from Rotterdam; while here, according to the tradition, she employed her leisure in superintending the manufacture of stone pots or cruches, and is said to have thrown many of them into the fosses of the chateau as souvenirs to posterity, that in after ages they might be considered works of antiquity; for this reason these particular cruches found in the foss, and others similar, are called *Jacoba Kannetjes.* Such is the legend in Holland, which is in some degree verified by the actual discovery of a great quantity of them on the spot, proving at least that there was a manufactory there. However, it is probable the same description of pottery was made for common use simultaneously in other parts of Holland and in Germany. This manufacture therefore goes back to the commencement of the XVth Century. Some archæologists are of opinion that these cups were placed before the guests at table, used once, and then thrown into the moat. This stone ware is of a cheap character, common quality and very coarse grain, not enamelled or coloured, but still hard and impermeable. The Jacoba Kannetje, figured by Mr. Marryat in his *History of Pottery*, is a superb Cologne ware canette, with designs and ornaments in relief; nothing less resembles the real *Jacoba* than the specimen there given, which is nearly two centuries later in date.

We may here mention some ornamental red terra-cotta bricks, used formerly in the construction of the large chimney pieces of the XVIth and XVIIth Centuries. The manufacture is unknown, but they are probably Dutch or Flemish. They are unglazed, and ornamented on one side only, in relief, with subjects from scripture history, Renaissance ornaments and designs for borders of continuous patterns, armorial bearings chiefly of Dutch and Flemish origin. In the Cluny Museum is one with the arms of Holland, Zetland and Friesland, 1575. There is a Flemish Renaissance chimney piece in the S. K. Museum, which came from an old house at Antwerp, the back of the fire place is constructed of 168 bricks, with scriptural subjects in relief, and on the top a large triangular headed brick with the arms of Charles V, and motto "Plus oltre," dated 1532.

UTRECHT. There was a manufactory of tiles here, founded in 1760, they were decorated in blue or violet *en camaieu*, in imitation of Delft; the manufactory was closed in 1855.

LILLE. There are documents in the municipal archives of Lille, proving the existence of a manufactory of fayence in 1696. It was founded by Jacques Feburier, of Tournay, and Jean Bossu, of Ghent. They made a ware *à la façon d'Hollande.* The widow of Feburier carried it on after her husband's death, in 1729, with her son-in-law, Francois Boussemart; at his death in 1776, it was continued by M. Petit. There is a specimen in the Sèvres Museum, dated 1716, of Feburier's fayence.

Another important manufactory of fayence was established

in 1711, by Barthélémy Dorez and Pierre Palissier; it continued in active work for nearly a century; a large vase in the collection of M. Houdoy, is signed N. A. Dorez, the grandson of the above, dated 1748. A third fayence manufactory was founded 1740, by J. Masquelier, and was continued in the same family until 1827. A fourth was established in 1744, by M. Chanou, who made a brown earthenware called *terre de St. Esprit*, in the English fashion. A fifth was a manufactory of stoves by a person named Heringle. A sixth was founded in 1773, by an Englishman named William Clarke, for earthenware in the English style. The decree states that he was a native of Newcastle, in England, and possessed the secret of a sort of fayence only made in England, which is nearly equal to porcelain, and which has the property to resist fire without breaking, and that the clay is to be procured in the country.

LUXEMBOURG. This important *fabrique* was established by the brothers Boch, in 1767, who had removed from Audun le Tiche in France. They made various descriptions of earthenware, as well as fine fayence, and largely imitated the English Queen's ware. The mark was B. L. in Roman capitals, sometimes in monogram, and frequently in italics as here shewn. The works are still in existence.

AMSTERDAM. A German jew of Breslau, named Hartog, known as Hartog Van Laun, and another, named Brandeis, established a manufactory of fayence near the gate of Weesp, at Amsterdam. The ware is heavy, not very artistic, and usually in blue *camaieu*. The mark adopted by them was a cock crowing.

Fig. 166 represents a fruit dish, painted in blue with a man and woman seated; in the collection of Mr. C. W. Reynolds.

OVERTOOM. A manufactory of fine fayence was established in 1754, in the parish of Amstelveen, near Amsterdam, in a theatre where French performances were usually given. The Barons, Van Haeren and Van Palland, were the proprietors; Ariel Blankers, director. The fayence though heavy was of a fine white enamel and of good forms; besides table and tea services, they made groups of birds, modelled from nature, statuettes, &c. It ceased in 1764, having lasted ten years; the machinery and materials were removed to the porcelain manufactory at Weesp by Count Van Gronsfeld.

DELFT, a town between the Hague and Rotterdam, was celebrated for its enamelled fayence at a very early period. Haydn, in his *Dictionary of Dates*, says, as early as 1310, but we have no authentic record of its importation into England before the reign of Henry IV. It was probably about the time of the introduction of Chinese porcelain into Europe that the Delft potteries sprang into active existence, although the art was known there long before; and no examples of an earlier date than 1530 have been preserved, or can with certainty be identified. Mr. Marryat says, large services of Delft fayence were presented by Philippe of Austria, Governor of the low countries, to Sir Thomas Trenchard, in 1506; and we are told that Philip and Joan embarking as King and Queen of Castille, at Middleburg, in 1506, took with them a great number of Delft fayence plates and dishes.

The importance of this manufacture went on gradually increasing throughout the XVIth Century, but it is to the commencement of the XVIIth that we must look for its greatest development. Towards the middle of this century there were nearly fifty manufactories of pottery in operation at Delft, employing about 7,000 persons, more than a fourth part of the entire population, and this was the most flourishing period of its existence. In the middle of the XVIIIth Century they were reduced to 24, yet making a considerable quantity of pottery; at the present day of all this number only one remains, and its productions are of inferior character, being a yellowish pipe clay devoid of any attempt at ornamentation.

Savary des Bruslons, about 1720 *(Dictionaire Universel de Commerce)* writes, "The finest fayences made in France are those of Nevers, Rouen, and St. Cloud, but they do not approach, either in quality of the ware, in the enamel, or in the designs, to those of Delft." It may be observed in Delft ware, as well as in the fayence of other countries, that tea and coffee services, such as tea pots, coffee pots, canisters or cups and saucers, are never to be found of an earlier date than towards the end of the XVIIth or even the beginning of the XVIIIth Centuries. In England tea and coffee, although known, through its introduction by the Dutch East India Company as early as 1610-1620, was not used as a beverage until the reign of Charles II. Samuel Pepys, in his Diary, Sept. 25th, 1661, says "I sent for a cup of tea (a Chinese drink) of which I had never drunk before." In 1666 the price of tea was sixty shillings a pound.

The forms of the Delft ware are very varied; among other curious efforts of the potters, they have produced musical instruments. There are four fayence violins extant, all painted in blue *camaieu*, with figures in Dutch costume of the XVIIth Century, dancing and singing, musicians and kermess scenes, in the manner of Gerard Lairesse, with cupids and Renaissance ornaments as borders. According to tradition these violins were made at Delft, by a celebrated modeller, on the occasion of the marriages of his master's four daughters to four young painters, which ceremonies were performed all on the same day, and on the auspicious occasion the painters, modellers, potters and turners of the establishment opened the ball, the four bridegrooms playing their violins, and others accompanying them on musical instruments of the same fragile material, made or painted by themselves. The brides preserved these instruments in their respective families from generation to generation, which had all been painted by the four sons-in-law of the potter. Mr. Champfleury (himself a collector) has written a very entertaining story of an amateur of pottery, who was in search of one of these relics, it is entitled "*Le Violon de Faïence.*"

Fine specimens of Delft have become very scarce. The decorated pieces of Ter Himpelen, although rarely signed, are much prized; he painted fairs and marine subjects on square plaques, about the year 1650. So also are those of Piet Viseer, about 1750, who was a celebrated colourist; and of Van Domelaar, in 1580, who painted Chinese landscapes, &c. The following are among the most celebrated pieces: a large painting on fayence in a cabaret of the village of Lekkerkerk, near Schonhoven, 8 feet high, representing a famous giant who attained that height in the beginning of the XVIIIth Century. In the Museum of La Haye are two fine plaques painted by Ter Himpelen, after Wouvermans and Berghem. At the Chateau de la Favorite at Baden Baden, is a complete service, presented by the King of Holland. There are also some fine specimens at Hampton Court. There was no special mark adopted at Delft; the various manufacturers used their initials or monograms, and occasionally the sign of the *fabrique*, as a hatchet, a rose, a black man's head, a griffin, &c. They are too numerous to be produced in this work, but may be referred to in Chaffers' *Marks and Monograms on Pottery and Porcelain*, 3rd edit., pp. 261-273.

PORCELAIN.

China.

In introducing the subject of Chinese porcelain, we will not trouble our readers with a detailed history of the Celestial Empire from its commencement, when *Pan Kou*, the first man, the Chinese Adam, ninety six millions of years before our era, undertook to settle the disputes of the elements as well as to separate heaven from the earth; nor will we dwell long upon the beings who succeeded him with serpents' bodies, dragons' heads with women's faces, or the dragons with men's heads. It is after these extravagant myths that the Chinese historians place the advent of *Tsang-Kie*, the inventor of letters, in the year 3468 before our era. In 2698 B.C. appeared the prince civilizer of the world—*Hoang-ti*. In his reign were discovered the mariner's compass, the spheres, the kalendar, and the invention of ships for navigation, the use of coins, &c.; the sciences of astronomy, geometry, arithmetic, &c. For these great services he was rewarded by Heaven, who in the words of Garth—

> Allots the Prince of his Celestial line,
> An apotheosis and rights divine.

One day the Emperor, surrounded by his principal ministers, was thinking about the important events of his reign, and how much had been accomplished, when an immense dragon descended from the clouds and placed itself at his feet; the Emperor and those who had assisted him in his wonderful discoveries got upon the sacred reptile's back, which forthwith took its flight to the Celestial regions. Some ambitious courtiers wishing to be associated with their sovereign seized the beard of the dragon, but the appendage giving way, they were precipitated to the earth. *Hoang-ti*, touched with compassion, leant forward, and by the movement dropped his bow; this precious relic has been preserved with care, and is duly honoured on certain days of the year. Such fables as these, with some mixture of historical facts, shew an appreciation of services rendered, which are not confined to the male sex, for the wife of *Hoang-ti*, the Empress *Loui-tseu*, who instructed the ladies of the Empire in the art of raising silk worms, how to wind the cocoons, and afterwards to weave the silk into a cloth, suitable for making dresses; she too is ranked among the good genii, and handed down to posterity, as "the spirit of mulberry trees and silk worms."

This digression brings us to a point which is more immediately connected with our subject, for it was under this same Emperor, in the years 2698 to 2599 B.C., that *Kouen-ou* discovered the first secrets of the keramic art, which discovery was fully appreciated and its development anxiously watched. This pottery of *Kouen-ou* was not the true porcelain, but a sort of stone ware, for the researches of M. Jullien, to which we shall presently refer, place the invention of porcelain to about 185 B.C. A higher antiquity was, for a short time, thought to have been proved beyond dispute some years since, by the discovery of some little Chinese bottles in an Egyptian tomb of the eighteenth or twentieth dynasty, which had never been disturbed or opened before; M. Rosselini added his testimony to the fact of finding the precious relics; they were consequently eagerly sought after as incontestable proofs of the great antiquity of the art of making porcelain. The *savans* at first doubted them, because the character of the inscriptions upon the sides were not like the primitive writing of the Chinese. On closely questioning the Arabs of Cairo, whose particular speciality is the traffic in curiosities, they admitted that they had never found porcelain vases in the ruins or excavations, and that the greater number of the bottles sold to travellers came from some place in the Red Sea. M. Medhurst, Interpreter to the English Government, at Hong Kong, went still further; aided by the Chinese letters, he desired to find the date of the literary fragments on the bottles, and he succeeded. One of the inscriptions ran thus: "The flowers which unfold their blossoms have brought us a new year;" this was found to be the fragment of a sonnet, written by a Chinese poet between the years 702 and 795 A.D. From that moment the reaction was precipitate, and some even ventured to hint they were made to contain snuff, and of quite recent make.

We are indebted to that eminent scholar, M. Stanislas Jullien, for a complete insight into the history of Oriental porcelain, by his translation of a treatise on the fabrication of Chinese porcelain, and a history of the Imperial manufactory of *King-te-chin*, which is prefaced by a valuable essay on the subject, with extracts from other Chinese authors. M. Stanislas Jullien is of opinion, that the porcelain of China was made about 185 B.C. We have said before that the Chinese fix the invention of pottery to the reign of *Hoang-ti*, in the year 2698 before the christian era, but porcelain was first invented under the Han dynasty, between 185 and 80 B.C., or about 1600 years before it was known to the western nations of the globe. Its progress was at first slow, but from the patronage of succeeding Emperors it gradually increased in perfection and beauty.

The word *pourcelaine* has existed in the French language since the XIVth Century, consequently long before the introduction of *Chinese ware* into Europe; the word was applied formerly to the calcareous concretion which lines the interior surface of marine shells, which we call mother of pearl. In the early inventories of the XIVth, XVth and XVIth Centuries, therefore, the word *pourcelaine* has this signification, and certainly does not apply to porcelain in our acceptation of the term. This appellation was probably given to the ware in the beginning of the XVIth Century, from its similarity to these marine shells, and is derived from *porcellana*, a word which the Spaniards apply to cowrie shells, either because it conveyed a good idea of its milky white glossy and translucent appearance, or perhaps from an idea that the ware was actually made from a composition of these very shells. In fact this was a very general impression at that time, for Edoardo Barbosa, who died in 1576, says that it was made from marine shells and egg shells, buried in the earth for eighty or one hundred years. Jerome Cardan and Scaliger both state such was the method of making porcelain adopted by the Chinese. They kept the composition of porcelain a profound secret, and endeavoured to deceive travellers by all manner of wonderful tales.

Let us hear what a writer of the end of the XVIth Century says on the same subject, G. Pancirol:—"In past ages, this porcelain has not been seen; it is nothing more than a certain mass composed of plaster, eggs, shells of marine locusts, and other similar compounds, which being well mixed together is hidden secretly underground by the *pater familias*, who only reveals the place of its concealment to his children; there it remains eighty years without being exposed to the light of day, after which time his heirs disinterring it, and finding it properly prepared for working, they make it into those precious vases, so transparent and so beautiful to the sight, that no architect can find any fault with them. The virtue of them also is admirable, so much so that if poison be put into them they will immediately break. He who once buries this substance never digs it up again himself, but leaves it to his children, nephews or heirs, as a rich treasure of greater value than gold."

There are numerous manufactories of porcelain in China. M. Jullien enumerates fifty-six, but the principal establishment is that of *King-te-chin*. This was established as early as the VIth Century, and was then known as *Nan-tchang-tchin;* but its great importance dates from the time of the Imperial patronage accorded to it in the *King-te* period, when it was called *King-te-tchin* or the borough of *King-te*, this change occurred A.D. 1004. The Pere d'Entrecolles, a Jesuit, who went into China to establish missions in many of the provinces, collected some valuable details of the manufacture of porcelain. These he fully describes in a letter to Pere Orry in Paris, in 1712, accompanied by specimens of the two principal ingredients—*kaolin* and *petuntse.* He visited the Imperial manufactory, and gives the following interesting account:—*King-te-tchin* wants only to be surrounded by walls to deserve the name of a city, and will bear comparison with the largest and most populous cities of China. There are eighteen thousand families, and more than a million of souls, it is situated on the bank of a fine river. The expense of procuring materials is very considerable, for everything consumed has to be brought a great distance; even the wood for the furnaces has to be taken a hundred leagues; provisions are also very dear, yet numerous poor families find employment, who could not subsist in the neighbouring towns. The young and the old, the lame and the blind, all find work, at which they can earn a livelihood by grinding colours or otherwise. Formerly there were only three hundred furnaces, now there are nearly three thousand. *King-te-tchin* is situated in a vast plain, surrounded by high mountains, from which issue two rivers, flowing into each other, which form a wide open basin. Here are seen two or three rows of boats, tied together stem and stern; these are employed either in ascending the river for materials, or in descending it to take the porcelain to *Iao-tcheou.* It is astonishing that in so densely populated a place, so abounding in riches, so much property, and such an infinity of vessels, not surrounded by walls, that it should be governed by only one mandarin, without the least disorder. *King-te-tchin* is distant about a league from *Feou-liang,* and eighteen leagues from *Iao-tcheou;* but the police is admirable: each street is superintended by one or more officers according to its length, and each officer has ten subalterns, who each take ten houses under their especial charge; if they do not keep strict watch, the bastinado is liberally applied. The streets are barricaded, and few if any strangers are allowed to sleep in the town, but must retire to their boats, unless they can find some well known inhabitant to be answerable for their honesty and good conduct.

Lord Macartney, Ambassador to the Emperor of China, in 1792-4, says, that not far from the route taken by the English on their way to Canton, there was an unwalled city, called *King-te-chin*, where three thousand furnaces for the baking of porcelain existed, all lighted at the same time, which at night presented the appearance of a town on fire.

After this interesting account of the grand centre of the porcelain manufacture of China, it is with feelings of regret we close its history by stating that *King-te-chin* is now a heap of ruins: in the course of the recent disturbances which have convulsed the country; those dangerous rebels, the *Tae-pings*, sacked and pillaged the Imperial manufactory, destroying all the kilns and workshops; giving a fatal and irrecoverable blow to this particular industry in China.

Our account of Oriental porcelain would be incomplete, if we omitted to notice the Tower at Nankin. This pagoda is not so ancient as has been generally supposed, but there was a previous tower on the same spot; of what materials it was built we have no record. The porcelain tower of Nankin was constructed by the Emperor *Yong-lo*, 1403-1424; it was outside the town and called by the Chinese *The Temple of Gratitude.* The tower was octagonal, and consisted of nine stages elevated on a pedestal of the same form, the wall was 12 feet thick at the base and 8½ feet at the top; it was built of brick, encased with bricks or tiles of porcelain, enamelled only on the exterior surfaces with white; the frame work of the doors and windows were of yellow or green glaze, ornamented in relief with dragons; the quality of the ware being equal to that of which the ordinary vases are composed; each stage had a projecting cornice of 3 feet, and at each angle was a bell—making eighty in all—when agitated by the wind they produced a sound which at a short distance might have been taken for an Æolian harp; its height was 261 feet, and was ascended on the interior by a spiral staircase of 190 steps.

The Emperor *Khang-hi* visited it in 1664, and caused it to

be repaired. This celebrated structure, once the pride of Nankin, has been completely demolished by the rebels—the *Tae-pings*—who also sacked the town and devastated the whole country round. In Oliphant's narrative of the Earl of Elgin's mission to China and Japan, he gives an account of his visit to Nankin in 1858: "We passed the spot on which formerly stood the porcelain tower, but not a fragment is left to mark the site of this once celebrated monument."

We will take a hasty glance at the curious monsters and genii which so frequently figure upon the porcelain of the Celestial Empire.

The dragons, of which there are various sorts, some may even have been intended for the original monster Saurians, restored by Cuvier from the fossils which have been discovered, and are almost as incomprehensible to our ideas of propriety. These reptiles are generally represented with four legs, armed with powerful claws and a terrific head, scaly and with abundance of teeth. There was *Long*, the dragon of heaven; *Kau*, the dragon of the mountain; and *Li*, the dragon of the sea. The emperor, his sons and princes of the first and second rank, bear as their attributes a dragon with five claws; the princes of the third and fourth rank bear the same dragon with four claws; but those of the fifth rank and the mandarins are only allowed a serpent with claws, called *Mang*.

Khi-lin is an animal with his body covered with scales, his head is branched like that of the dragon, his four delicate feet have hoofs like the stag's, but his looks sadly belie him; he is of good omen and is so gentle and kind, that he would not step upon a worm in his progress.

The Dog of *Fo* must not be confounded with the kylin, he is much more ferocious, his feet are armed with claws, his gaping mouth display his sharp teeth, and he has a curly mane; something like a lion modified by Oriental imagination. He is the guardian of the thresholds of the temples.

The Sacred Horse. History relates that when *Fou hi* sought to combine the characters, so as to express the various forms of matter and produce of things physical and intellectual, a wonderful horse arose from the river, carrying upon his back certain signs from which the philosopher formed the eight emblems, which have retained the name of the source of characters.

Fong Hoang is a singular and immortal bird which lives aloft in the air, and only approaches mankind to announce happy events and prosperous reigns; its crested head and silken plumes on its neck and peacock's tail make it easily known. This bird was anciently the symbol of the sovereign of China, but the dragon with five claws was afterwards substituted, and it has become the emblem of the Empresses.

Many other symbolical animals are found representing months of the year or signs of the zodiac: thus for November, the rat; December, the ox; January, the tiger; February, the rabbit; March, the dragon; April, the serpent; May, the horse; June, the hare; July, the ape; August, the hen; September, the dog; and October, the wild boar. The white stag for longevity, also the crane, which they say prolongs its existence to the extreme limits and bestows the most feeling cares on its aged parents. The mandarin duck, which is so much attached to its mate that he dies in despair if he be separated; thus this duck is the emblem of conjugal fidelity and a happy union.

Cheou lao, the god of longevity, is represented with a venerable head, the upper part monstrously elevated, smiling face and long white beard, sometimes seated on a white stag, he holds in his hand the fabulous tree *Fan tao*, which flourishes for 3,000 years and produces fruit 3,000 years afterwards, and in the other he holds a fan or leaf; if he is surrounded by mushrooms *(ling tchy)*, he is emblematical of immortality.

Pou tai, the god of contentment, is of a more jovial character, leading us from elevated thoughts to physical and material enjoyments; a corpulent man with half closed eyes and open laughing mouth, apparently half inebriated, holding a fan, the divine emblem.

Koung tseu, Confucius, is of a more refined order, who, shocked at the moral disorder of the people, applied himself to improve their social state, in revealing to them ancient laudable customs, making laws, and reviving the sayings of the sages of antiquity.

He is represented seated or standing in a tranquil attitude, with a simple cap worn by literary men, holding a roll of MS. or a sceptre of good omen. He is also seen on many vases as a poet or orator, surrounded by objects relating to his most renowned works.

Pou-tai, the god of contentment just described, is called by some, the god of porcelain. Of this deity, le Père d'Entrecolles relates the following story: "A certain Emperor issued orders for some porcelain to be made after a special pattern given by him. It was represented to the Emperor that the thing was impracticable; but all remonstrances were useless; *it must be done.* The unfortunate potters strove hard, and wasted both their time and money vainly attempting to produce this piece of china, for which they only received blows and reproaches. At length, in a fit of despair, one of them cast himself into the burning furnace, and was instantly consumed. By this human sacrifice the porcelain came from the kiln more perfect than any ever before made, and exactly what the Emperor had desired, and he was appeased. The immolated victim passed afterwards for a hero, and became the god who presides over the porcelain manufacture."

The porcelain of China is composed of two earths, the one a decomposed felspathic rock called *kaolin*, and another rock of the same geological origin, mixed with quartz, called *petuntse.* There being a perfect identity between these elements, they both harmonize so completely that they have an equally resisting power when placed in the kiln. The *kaolin* used in making this porcelain is much softer than *petuntse* when dug out of the quarry, yet it is this which, by its mixture with the other, gives the strength and firmness to the work.

The Père d'Entrecolles relates, that some Europeans having procured a quantity of *petuntse* privately in China, upon their attempting to make porcelain when they returned to their own country, could not succeed for want of the *kaolin*, which the Chinese being apprized of, said humorously that the Europeans were wonderful people to go about to make a body whose flesh was to sustain itself without bones.

The vases of the *Hong-Wou* period, 1368-1398, and those of *Yong-lo*, 1403-1424, are generally rude in design and of imperfect fabrication. Under *Siouen-te*, 1426-1436, a vast improvement is perceptible; the paste and the decoration are of a remarkably fine quality, and they are frequently met with. The best period, however, of Chinese art is the *Tching-hoa*, which continued down to 1487.

The most ancient mode of decoration was the blue *camaieu*, and it is still much esteemed in China; it was executed on the ware, simply dried before the glaze was applied, and then placed in the kiln; being all completed in one baking *au grand feu*, the painting thus executed became imperishable.

It is on this blue ware the greater number of the Chinese characters are found denoting the period in which they were made. The cobalt on the earlier pieces was not so fine as on those of the *Siouen-te* and *Ching-hoa* periods, which are now much sought after. It is extremely difficult to tell even the approximate date of the coloured pieces, especially as there was a conventional method of decorating them which had been practised from time immemorial; the painters worked according to given models or patterns, and the monsters, deities or flowers and landscapes were of the same uncouth and rude designs, placed in successive ages upon the ware.

Le Père d'Entrecolles tells us the manner of painting vases in China, and how the different parts of a landscape on one vase were intrusted to various hands according to their ability to paint special objects mechanically. He says—"One is employed solely to form the coloured circle which is seen round the border of the ware, a second traces the flowers in outline, which a third fills in with colour; another excels only in painting the water and the mountains, while the next is only competent to pourtray birds or animals."

INSCRIPTIONS.

The marks found upon Chinese porcelain are of two sorts; one in Chinese characters or letters designating the period or reign of the Emperor in which it was made, called *nien-hao;* the other by paintings, emblems or words indicating the painter of the piece, its special use, or the place of its manufacture.

It will be needless here to give a full description of the Chinese methods of indicating the dates, which can only be done by a chronological table of all the dynasties and periods. (See Chaffers' *Marks and Monograms on Pottery and Porcelain.*) We will, however, endeavour to explain the meaning of the six marks which are frequently found on porcelain. These marks indicate a period or cycle, and tell the dynasty and the name of the period or motto adopted by the Emperor.

化	大
年	明
製	成

The Chinese characters here given represent the six letters to which we allude, and form the full dynastic inscription. The Chinese invariably read from right to left, downwards; the length of the column is arbitrary, but on vases inscriptions of six words are disposed in three columns of two or in two columns of three words, always commencing at the top right-hand corner downwards; thus—the two first, 1 and 2, *Ta-Ming*, express the dynasty of Ming, which lasted from 1368 to 1615; the two next, 3 and 4, *Tching-hoa*, tell us the period within that dynasty, when the Emperor reigned, namely, 1465 to 1487; the two last, 5 and 6, *Nien-tchi*, signify *made during the period.* These two words are invariable, and are affixed to all the dynasties or periods indiscriminately. In this instance the Emperor's name was actually *Tchun-ti.*

4	1
5	2
6	3

Every Emperor, when he comes to the throne, assumes a distinguishing appellation which denotes at once the Emperor and the period of his reign. This appellation or period is therefore (as we see) placed upon the china instead of the name of the Sovereign. Thus the last reigning Emperor's designation signified literally "The glory of the right way." The present Emperor is designated "Universal abundance."

SEALS OR STENCILLED STAMPS.

These characters of the square seal form (*siao-tchouan*) were from the commencement of the XVIIIth Century either stamped in the ware or stencilled in red, instead of the inscriptions in regular characters (kiai) which we have just described. These signs, composed of rectangular lines, are better adapted for seals or stamps, the lines of the ordinary characters being lengthened and made angular instead of curved to suit the squareness of the seal.

This form of the characters is very difficult to read even by the Chinese themselves, unless they are taught; but there is a certain similitude which will assist us in deciphering them.

Kien Thsing Tai

Tchy Nien Long

This inscription is on a cup belonging to the *Kien-Long* period, 1736-1795, in the seal character; it is in a horizontal line from right to left, which is divided into distinct characters. It reads thus: *Tai-thsing Kien-long Nien-tchy*. The same inscription grouped in its square form would be thus represented.

5 Nien	3 Kien	1 Tai	1736-1795.
6 Tchy	4 Long	2 Thsing	

Various other inscriptions are found upon vases, as "The house of humanity and concord;" "Porcelain of the palace;" "*Ou*, the old man who lives in solitude;" "Riches, high rank, and an eternal spring;" "A fine vase for the use of rich and noble people;" "Curious objects for antiquaries;" "A fine vase of the Hall of Jade;" and various others of similar character, lines or verses from Chinese poets, &c.

Other marks or devices of certain fabriques are given in Chaffers' *Marks and Monograms on Pottery and Porcelain.*

VARIETIES.

A sort of very hard stone-ware, covered with a thick glaze, may be the most ancient description seen at the present day. The surface is covered with a semi-opaque glaze which is called *celadon* by the French, and which varies in colour from a russet gray to a sea green. The glaze of this ware is frequently seen crackled all over in irregular lines, which is termed in England *crackle.* This crackle China is the most esteemed of Oriental porcelain, although it arises from a *defective* cause.

The same effect may be easily produced upon all terra cottas of which the paste is more sensible to the changes of temperature than the exterior coating or glaze. In fayence this accident is of frequent occurrence; the red porous clay being more expansive, draws away the enamel, which, being less elastic, is separated in fragments, the greater the resistance the more they are multiplied. Now one of the qualities of porcelain is precisely to avoid this double action. Its paste is composed of a felspathic rock, decomposed and infusible, called its *kaolin;* cover or glaze comes also from a felspathic rock, slightly crystallized; these melt and assimilate together harmoniously in vitrification, and a complete affinity is evident between the two elements of porcelain. Nevertheless the Chinese, in modifying the glaze, are able to render it more or less expansive and to break the harmony between its own shrinkage and that of the paste or body it covers.

Hence the crackle, at the option of the potter, is made of large, middling or small size.

Various kinds of crackle are thus produced, sometimes upon one and the same piece, as by exposing the porcelain or portions of it when at its greatest heat to a sudden contact of cold or with water, large fissures may be obtained. These cracks are sometimes filled in with black, red, chocolate, or purple colours.

Others may be classed among the curiosities of porcelain—for example, cups or bowls which have an outer reticulated coating, pierced or cut out into arabesques, completely insulated from the inner vessel, except at the rim at top and bottom where it is joined; these have been used for tea or hot liquids, and may be held in the hand *with impunity*, notwithstanding the heat enclosed within it.

Another variety consists in cutting or punching out pieces of the paste or body of the ware before it is baked, in patterns; the pieces so cut out are small ovals like grains of rice placed in stars, rosettes, &c., more or less multiplied. The vase so ornamented is dipped into the glaze which fills up all these small holes, and then placed in the kiln. The pattern, being much more transparent than the body of the ware, is distinctly seen, but especially so when held to the light.

Another beautiful effect is produced by means of the glaze itself, which is of a light or dark shade according to its intensity or thickness; for example: a fish, animal, or other object is stamped incuse on the upper surface of a plate, it is then filled in with a coloured glaze and vitrified, and is consequently shaded according to the thickness of the glaze on each portion of the design, the surface being perfectly smooth.

Vases are sometimes seen separated in the middle into two pieces, (which must have been cut while the clay was soft), completely dividing the upper from the lower half—in arabesques and dove-tail patterns, in such a manner, that although separate, they cannot be altogether removed from each other: the wonder is, that in the baking, the edges in juxtaposition should not have become again cemented together.

The Chinese themselves are great forgers, and endeavour to impose not only upon the Europeans, but upon their own countrymen, many of whom are great amateurs, and are willing to pay extravagant prices for ancient examples of porcelain, especially if made by a celebrated potter; as much as 10,000 francs have been sometimes given at a public sale for a choice example. This talent of counterfeiting works of art has in some instances given such a reputation to the author, that his copies have produced prices equal to the value of the original. M. Stanislas Julien gives an anecdote of an artist named *Tcheou-tan-tsiouen*, who excelled in imitating antique vases. One day he embarked in a merchant vessel at *Kin-tchong*, and landed on the right bank of the river *Kiang;* as he passed onwards to *Pi-ling*, he went to pay a visit to *Thang*, who was the President of Sacrifices, and begged permission to examine carefully and leisurely an ancient porcelain tripod of *Ting*, which formed one of the treasures of his cabinet. With his hand he obtained the exact measurement; he then took an impression of the veins of the tripod by means of a paper which he hid in his sleeve, and returned immediately to *King-te-tchin.* Six months after he came and paid a second visit to Signor Thang. He drew from his pocket a porcelain tripod, and thus addressed him: "Your Excellence possesses a tripod perfume vase in the white porcelain of *Ting*, I also have a similar vase." Thang was struck dumb with astonishment, he compared it with the ancient tripod which he religiously preserved, and could not detect a hair's difference between them. He then applied the foot and cover of his own vase to the counterfeit, but they fitted with wonderful precision. Thang then asked him where he had procured this remarkable piece. "Some time since," said *Tcheou*, "having requested permission to examine your tripod at leisure, I took with my hand all its dimensions. I protest to you that it is an imitation of yours, I do not desire to impose upon you." The false tripod was bought at a high price, and the amateurs of the XVIth and XVIIth Centuries (*Tcheou* lived about 1567 to 1619) did not hesitate to pay a thousand ounces of silver (7,500 frs.) for one of the works of this celebrated potter.

PORCELAIN.

Japan.

THE Portuguese traded with Japan as early as the year 1534; but in consequence of their attempts to convert the inhabitants to Christianity, their intrigues and secret conspiracies against the Government, and last, not least, their interference with the decoration of the porcelain by painting upon it (or rather inducing their proselytes so to do) sacred subjects, such as legends of saints, &c., they were eventually expelled the country in 1641, and some forty thousand of their Christian converts proscribed and massacred.

The Dutch afterwards succeeded in obtaining the confidence of the Japanese, and founded a monopoly of the trade with them, deriving from that source a most lucrative branch of commerce, exporting porcelain to all parts of Europe, to the exclusion of every other European power, which they have retained for more than two centuries.

Our information as to the origin of making porcelain in Japan is very scanty, and we are indebted principally to Dr. Hoffman of Leyden for what we know on the subject; he published a history of the principal porcelain manufactories in 1799, which is appended to M. Stanislas Julien's account of those of China: it was a translation from a Japanese work. He says it was to a Colony of Coræans established in the province of Omi, in the island of Nippo, in the year 27 B.C., that the introduction of this art is attributed. About the same epoch there lived in the province of Idsoumi, situated like that of Omi in the Island of Nippo, a man named *Nomino Soukouné*, who made in pottery and porcelain, vases and notably figures of the size of life, to substitute for slaves, which it had been previously the custom to bury with their masters. *Nomino* received as a recompense authorisation, to take the name of *Fazi*, in the Coræan language *Patsi*, artist workman.

Under *Sei-wa* (859-876 A.D.) the number of fabriques increased considerably.

Under *Syoun-tok* (1211-1221), a Japanese potter named *Katosiro-ouye-mon* commenced the making of small vases to preserve tea, but for want of a better process, he placed them in the kiln on their orifices, which consequently appeared as if they had been used and were little cared for. Desirous of improving himself in the art, *Katosiro*, accompanied by a Bonze or Buddhist monk, visited China in 1211, with orders from his government to make himself acquainted with all the secret processes of the manufacture which was at that time brought to so great perfection there.

On his return, he made such important improvements in the composition and decoration of porcelain that henceforth it became superior in many instances to the Chinese, especially in the fabrication of the best specimens, upon which much time and labour were bestowed. The porcelain of Japan is very much like that of China, but the colours are more brilliant on the fine pieces, a better finish and the designs more of the European character, the flowers, birds, &c., being more natural, and the kylins, dragons, and other monsters less hideous; the paste is of better quality, and a purer white, especially in the XVIIth and XVIIIth Centuries.

Perhaps the most beautiful of all the porcelain made in Japan is the *egg shell*, so called because it is extremely thin and translucent, yet so compact that it can be formed into large vases, as well as plates and bowls or cups.

The small cups without saucers, which are usually placed upon *présentoirs* of lac, are seldom painted on the exterior, but within is frequently found a fillet of gold; and slight sketches in blue or gold indicating the outline of a mountain, then the sun, and clouds, and a line of birds taking flight, or sometimes, animals all in outline. On other pieces are birds, flowers, and animals delicately painted in colours.

The art has been continued to the present day; those beautiful and extremely delicate cups and saucers, thin as paper itself, are frequently seen covered on the outside with a casing of bamboo threads woven together, and the larger basins and covers of the same thin texture.

All these are produced now, as well as in ancient times, at Imari in the province of Fizen. It is not in the village itself where these manufactories are established, but as many as twenty-four or twenty-five are situated near the mountain of *Idsoumi-yama,* whence the kaolin is obtained of which the vessels are made. M. Hoffman enumerates twenty-five of these fabriques which were celebrated in the last century, being all in the island of *Kiou-siou.*

LAC.

The Japanese excel in a particular fabrication which is almost peculiar to them: the *lac*, usually called *Lac Japan.* This *lac* is a resinous gum which exudes from certain trees, especially the *Rhus vernix*, and it is called by them *Ourousi-no-ki.* This varnish is applied by them to a great variety of materials, with an incontestable superiority to other nations; and is sometimes inlaid with delicate pieces of mother-of-pearl, artificially coloured, to vary the lustrous effect in landscapes and flowers, birds of rich plumage, &c., the leaves of the trees and feathers of the birds in many instances being separately inlaid. The usual colours are red, brown, and black of various shades, and gold is used upon it with wonderful effect. *Lac* is frequently applied to porcelain vases, either entirely covering the surface, or only partially, in gold lac in relief.

Crackle china was made in Japan as well as in China from a very early period, and frequently painted with flowers, landscapes, and birds. An early writer says, "The ancient crackle vases are much esteemed in Japan. To obtain a veritable crackle vase, amateurs do not hesitate to give a thousand ounces of silver (£300). It is not known under what dynasty they commenced to fabricate the crackle perfume vases; under the foot of some there is a bright iron nail which never rusts."

What few marks are found upon this porcelain are not understood, but they much resemble the Chinese characters.

There are, however, some indications upon the Japanese porcelain which are never met with upon the Chinese; these consist of three, five, seven, or more dots or points in relief on the backs of large dishes or plates, which are caused by the points of support on which the pieces rested in the kiln.

SATSUMA in Japan, which was bombarded by the English some few years since, produces a peculiar description of pottery; numerous specimens were brought to this country by the officers, but our attention was more particularly directed to this fine pottery at the Exposition in Paris in 1867. The paste is hard and compact, of yellowish white, slightly tinted with rose colour; the glaze which is transparent is cracked here and there, which gives it a particular and harmonious appearance. The paintings are highly finished in the European taste with landscapes and flowers, but still with the Chinese peculiarity of avoiding regularity as to centres and balance of subjects in their designs.

Figs. 171 and 172 represent a bottle and a bowl of this ware of recent manufacture, now in the South Kensington Museum.

PORCELAIN.

Italy.

PORCELAIN has this distinguishing characteristic, that when held up to a strong light it appears translucent, unlike fayence, which is perfectly opaque. Its fracture is hard and white internally, like a broken piece of alabaster.

Porcelain of soft paste has the appearance of an unctuous white enamel like cream; it is also to the touch of a soft, warm and soapy nature, something like the surface of fine fayence. The *pâte tendre* is also soft in another sense, being unable to bear so great a degree of heat in the furnace as hard porcelain. The soft paste may therefore be easily cut or scratched with a steel point or a file, which would have no effect upon the hard paste; it is consequently liable to become much scratched by frequent use. The hard paste or true porcelain is of the whiteness of milk, and feels to the touch of a hard and cold nature, and is somewhat heavier than the soft; underneath the plates and other pieces the rim or edge is left unpolished, or without glaze.

The painting upon porcelain is executed after the ware has been baked, whilst in a biscuit state, the piece to be painted is dipped into a diluted glaze, which readily absorbs the water, leaving on the surface a thin coating of components which quickly dries into a solid shell, uniformly thick over all its parts, and sufficiently firm to bear handling without being rubbed off during removal into the seggar or case which protects it in the kiln.

The amateur must be upon his guard in collecting porcelain, and not place too much reliance on the marks which he may find upon the ware. When the mark is not indented on the paste, or baked with the porcelain when at its greatest heat (*au grand feu*), it gives no guarantee for its genuineness. The mark was nearly always affixed before glazing. It is necessary in forming a correct judgment of the authenticity of a piece of valuable china, such as Sèvres, that many things be taken into consideration. First, above all it is most important to be satisfied whether the porcelain be of hard or soft paste, and whether such description of paste was made at the particular epoch represented by the mark; then, if the decoration be in keeping with the style adopted at the time indicated; the colours, the finish, the manner of decoration, and various other *indicia* must also be taken into consideration.

FLORENCE.

The first successful attempt in Europe to imitate porcelain was made at Florence as early as 1580, under the auspices of Francesco I. de Medici, but it was not so hard as that of china; that is to say, composed of *kaolin* and *petuntse*, but a soft paste and *translucent*, which is one of the principal tests of porcelain. For some reason, the manufacture of this porcelain was abandoned after the death of the inventor. This Medici porcelain is now very scarce; there are not more than thirty pieces known. The mark found underneath these pieces represents the cathedral at Florence painted in blue.

Examples in the South Kensington Museum.

Fig. 173. Plate, deep centre, painted in blue with flowers; flowers also on the reverse, and a device of a ball with three flaming rays and short spikes between. Marked at the bottom in blue with the cathedral of Florence and the letter F. About 1600.

Fig. 174. Bowl, painted inside and out with blue flowers. Marked with the cathedral and the letter F. About 1600.

Fig. 175. Cruet for oil and vinegar, scroll ornament in blue; on each spout A and O (Aceto and Oleo). About 1600.

DOCCIA.

The manufactory of Doccia was founded in 1735 by the Marquis Carlo Ginori, contemporaneously with the Imperial manufactory at Sèvres. About 1760 it rose to great importance, and large groups were executed from the models of the most celebrated sculptors. In 1821 the moulds of the Capo di Monte porcelain were transferred to Doccia.

During the last ten years, the fabrication of the imitative Capo di Monte ware of the XVIIIth Century, in coloured *mezzo-relievo*, has been brought to great perfection, as well as the successful imitation of the maiolica of Xanto and Maestro Giorgio of the XVIth Century, by the invention and introduction of the metallic lustres in the colouring. These important results were obtained and perfected by Giusto Giusti, a pupil of the Doccia school, to whom honourable mention was accorded in the London Exposition in 1851, as well as in that of Paris in 1855. He died suddenly in 1858.

The Doccia manufactory is particularly distinguished by the variety of its productions and successful imitations of the maiolica of the XVIth Century, of the Capo di Monte porcelain bas-reliefs, the reproductions of Luca della Robbia, and Chinese and Japanese porcelain.

The marks employed are a star or the word GINORI printed or stamped on the ware. Fig. 176 is a tea pot, painted with flowers, in the possession of Lady Charlotte Schreiber.

NAPLES.—CAPO DI MONTE.

This manufactory was founded by Charles III. in 1736. It is considered of native origin, as the art, which was kept so profound a secret in Dresden, could, at that early period, have scarcely had time to be introduced here, the character of its productions being also so essentially different. The King himself took great interest in it, and is said to have worked occasionally in the manufactory. The beautiful services and groups in coloured relief are of the second period, *circa* 1760.

The earliest mark is a fleur-de-lis, generally roughly painted in blue, as in the margin. These marks have been hitherto considered as denoting the ware made at Madrid only, but the fleur-de-lis was used both at Capo di Monte and Madrid.

The mark of the second period under the patronage of Ferdinand IV, 1759, is N for NAPOLI under a crown, graved in red or blue on the moist clay.

A later mark used about 1780 is composed of the initials of Ferdinandus Rex, either in monogram or separately under a crown.

Some pieces of a later date are marked with the name, stamped, of GIUSTINIANI, mostly in the Etruscan style, after paintings or forms of specimens found at Herculaneum.

Examples.

Fig. 178 is a cup and saucer painted with the signs of the zodiac, blue and gold borders. The saucer has a figure of Time, and the motto, "Mon amitié lui survivra ;" mark F. R. crowned ; in Rev. T. Staniforth's collection.

Fig. 179 is a Capo di Monte vase, with green ornaments, on gold ground, and medallions of figures ; mark a fleur-de-lis. One of a pair in the possession of Mr. Chas. Dickins.

Fig. 180. Saucer, with portrait of Ferdinand IV. and legend; mark N crowned ; Lady C. Schreiber's collection.

Fig. 181. Cup, painted with flowers ; Rev. T. Staniforth's collection.

Fig. 182. Cup and saucer, landscape and figures ; mark N and crown : Mr. C. W. Reynolds's collection.

Fig. 183 is a coffee pot, with classical subjects.

Fig. 184. A milk pot, with lake *camaieu* landscapes.

Fig. 185. A cup and saucer, view of the Bay of Naples; these are in the collection of Mr. Walker Joy.

TREVISO.

There was a manufactory of soft porcelain here, probably established towards the end of the last century, carried on by the brothers Giuseppe and Andrea Fontebasso. Sir W. R. Drake has in his collection a coffee cup of soft porcelain inscribed "*Fabbrica di Giuseppe ed Andrea Fratelli Fontebasso in Treviso. Gaetano Negrisole Dipinse,* 1831."

F.F.
Treviso. 1799

Fratelli Fontebasso, marked in gold on a porcelain écuelle, blue ground, with gold fret borders and oval medallions of Italian buildings, landscapes and figures; in the possession of the Rev. T. Staniforth, of Storrs, Windermere. See fig. 186.

G.A.F.F.
Treviso.

The marks are on a porcelain coffee cup and saucer, the cup painted with a garden scene, with a man and woman holding flowers, the former holding a bird, the latter a cage; at bottom "Gesner, Id. xiii." The saucer gilt only, and marked underneath "Treviso," in blue, the other is red; in the collection of Mr. C. W. Reynolds. See fig. 187.

TURIN.—VINEUF.

This manufactory was established about 1770. Vittorio Amedeo Gioanetti was born in Turin in 1729; he was a professor of medicine, and took his degree as doctor in 1751, and a public testimonial was accorded to him in 1757. He was subsequently elected Professor of Chemistry in the Royal University, and was a successful experimentalist. It was about 1770 that he established a manufactory of porcelain at Vinovo or Vineuf. Attempts had been previously made, but they were unsuccessful, and it was not until Gioanetti applied himself to the manufacture that it succeeded perfectly. In the "*Discorso sulla fabrica de porcellana stabilita in Vinovo. Turin*, 1859," will be found a description of the various earths and clays of Piedmont as described by Gioanetti himself. It was noted for its fine grain and the whiteness of its glaze, as well as the colours employed. The cross alone in brown, is on a cup and saucer, painted with the arms of Sardinia and gilt borders; in Mr. A. W. Franks' collection.

TURIN. Vineuf. The letters sometimes found on this porcelain stand for Dr. Gioanetti. These marks are usually graved in the paste, but occasionally coloured.

Fig. 188 is an écuelle, ornamented in gold, with initials and the Royal arms; Mr. C. W. Reynolds' collection.

VENICE.

Porcelain of soft paste was made here probably about 1720. The first proclamation we have any record of, was made in 1728, offering facilities and privileges to any persons who would undertake such works, and all subjects or foreigners who desired to introduce into the city of Venice manufactories of fine earth or porcelain and fayence in use in the East or West, were invited to compete. At the date of this proclamation a porcelain manufactory did actually exist in Venice, but the exact time of its establishment is not known.

The "Casa excellentissima Vezzi" was founded by Francesco Vezzi, a goldsmith of Venice. He invested the sum of 30,000 ducats in a porcelain company, amongst whose shareholders were Luca Mantovani and others, including, there is reason to believe, Carlo Ruzini, who reigned Doge from 1732 to 1735. Francesco Vezzi died on the 4th May, 1740. The site of the Vezzi manufactory was at St. Nicolo in Venice. How long after Vezzi's death the manufactory of porcelain was carried on does not appear, but judging from the statements made to the Senate in 1765, it did not long survive him, and the secret of his process for making porcelain had evidently not been disclosed.

It is recorded that the cause for that manufactory not being permanent, but sinking "into inactivity and decay," was the fact that it was dependent on the purchase of porcelain paste in foreign countries.

Materials for making porcelain were to be obtained in the Venetian dominions, but not such as to produce the *hard* or Oriental porcelain; they therefore procured it from Saxony, and probably also some of the workmen, which will account for the fact that the "Casa excellentissima Vezzi" produced both *hard* and *soft* paste.

To the Vezzi manufactory we must refer all the pieces marked in red or blue with Ven^a, or other contractions of the word VENEZIA. They are painted with masquerades, grotesque Chinese figures and decorations in relief, flowers, birds, arabesques and geometrical patterns in colours, statuettes, &c., especially the Venetian red which pervades all the decorations, the handles, borders and mouldings being sometimes covered with silver or platina, producing the effect of oxidized metal mountings. Another striking peculiarity in the decoration of porcelain of this period is a border of black or coloured diaper work formed by crossed lines, and in the interstices small gilt points or crosses bordered by scrolls. These specimens are mostly of hard paste in form of bowls, platės, tureens, &c., and by some connoisseurs have been taken for Dresden, whilst others have hesitated between Venice and Capo di Monte; but they are doubtless of Venetian make and decoration; being unmarked, our only means of judging is by comparison. One fact is, however, clear, which has hitherto been doubted by some, viz., *that both hard and soft paste were made not only by the Vezzi, the Hewelckes and Cozzi at Venice, but by the Antonibons at Nove.*

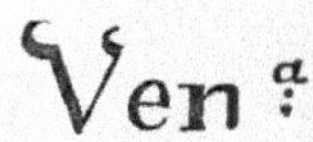

A beautiful example of this porcelain is represented fig. 193. A vase and cover of hard paste painted in lake *camaieu,*

heightened by gold, with a continuous landscape; the peculiar border, noticed above, with marks and interlaced bands, is shown on the cover; the edges, knob and flutings are raised and plated with silver or platinum, which when tarnished can be cleaned with a leather; in the possession of Mr. W. Chaffers.

The signature of Ludovico Ortolani, a Venetian, painted at the porcelain manufactory in Venice. This was the Vezzi *fabrique, circa* 1740. It occurs on a saucer painted in lake *camaieu*, with a lady seated, holding a bunch of grapes and a tazza, and Cupid (symbolical of autumn), border of leaves, scrolls and birds; in Mr. Reynolds' collection. See figure 189.

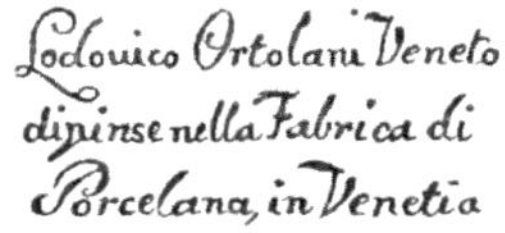

After the Vezzi manufactory had ceased to exist we have no documents to prove that any efforts were made to introduce the manufacture of porcelain into Venice until December, 1757, when a petition was presented to the Venetian College by Frederick Hewelcke and Co., who stated that the sale introduced and directed by them in Dresden of Saxon porcelain had been carried on in a very flourishing manner, but that in consequence of the then existing war (the seven years' war which commenced in 1756), they had been obliged to abandon Saxony and to seek in a foreign country "a peaceful refuge convenient for the exercise of their art." They prayed that exclusive permission for twenty years might be accorded them to manufacture in some convenient spot Saxon porcelain (*Porcellana di Sassonia*) of every kind, form and figure, with exemptions from taxes, for the exercise of their art during that period.

On the 18th of March, 1758, the decree granted to the Hewelckes the privileges they had requested. It seems to have proved eventually *unfortunate*, and at the termination of that war, which had brought them to Venice in 1753, they returned to their native country.

In 1765, the Senate granted to Giminiano Cozzi, in the Contrada di San Giobbe, Venice, protection and pecuniary assistance in carrying out a manufacture of porcelain. Cozzi's first efforts were directed to imitate the Oriental ware; he states in his petition that he founded his anticipations of commercial success mainly on the fact that he had discovered at Tretto in Vicentina, in the Venetian territory, clay suitable for the manufacture.

A very large trade was carried on for nearly fifty years. The pieces produced at Cozzi's manufactory were marked with an anchor in blue, red or gold, and are still frequently met with, although specimens of his best products have become scarce. They consist of statuettes

in biscuit, in glazed white porcelain, and of coloured groups, vases, &c. The gilding on Cozzi's porcelain is especially fine, the pure gold of the sequin having been used in its decoration. We have imitations of the porcelain of other countries, Saxony, Sèvres, Chelsea and Derby; the imitations of the Oriental are astonishing. The Marquis D'Azeglio possesses some examples of the coloured groups as well as the glazed white figures; in fact, specimens of nearly all the varieties of Venetian porcelain we have been describing are to be found in his historically interesting collection.

Cozzi's manufactory ceased in 1812. Since that date there does not appear to have been any porcelain made in Venice, but at Nove they still continued making porcelain for more than twenty years later. Lady Charlotte Schreiber has a splendid set of five porcelain vases of the Cozzi period, the centre being 17 inches high, the others 13½, beautifully painted with bouquets of flowers, mask handles with festoons of fruit in relief. All these pieces are marked with the red anchor. See fig. 190.

Fig. 191 is a cup and saucer, painted with fruit, belonging to Mr. Walker Joy.

Fig. 192. A pair of small figures of the Seasons; Lady C. Schreiber's collection.

NOVE.

The manufacture of porcelain at Nove may be traced back as far as the 12th January, 1752, at which time Pasqual Antonibon brought from Dresden a certain Sigismond Fischer to construct a furnace for making porcelain in the Saxon style.

From this time forward he continued his experiments, and must have made great progress in the art, for in February, 1761, he had three furnaces, of which one was for Saxon (*ad uso Sassonia*), the other two for French porcelain (*ad uso Francia*).

In 1762, Antonibon submitted to the Board of Trade specimens of his porcelain, and petitioned that the patent rights which had been conceded to Hewelcke should be extended to him. At that time, the report states, Antonibon had at Nove a manufactory, rich in buildings, machinery and tools. The capital embarked in it was estimated at 80,000 ducats, and he gave employment to 150 men and their families, in addition to 100 people employed in his retail business, carried on at his three shops in Venice, so great was the sale of his products. This extensive manufactory was, however, principally for maiolica.

On the 7th April, 1763, a decree was made in his favour; and he appears to have set earnestly to work in his manufacture of porcelain. His competitor, Hewelcke, shortly after, deserted Venice; but he had a more formidable rival in Giminiano Cozzi, who obtained a decree for making porcelain in 1765, in which Pasqual Antonibon's manufacture is noticed, the Senate declaring it to be the duty of the magistrate to make such arrangements as would lead to an amicable understanding between the rival manufacturers and their workmen.

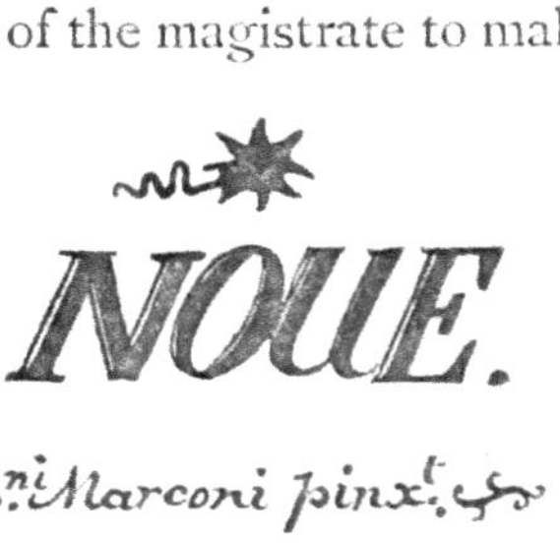

This curious mark of Antonibon's manufactory is on the centre of a set of three Eventail jardinières of porcelain, beautifully painted with mythological and classical subjects and garden scenes, elaborately gilt borders, and the arms of Doge Tiepolo. The comet is uncommon; the painter's name is Giovanni Marconi; in Mr. Reynolds' collection. One of these vases is figured No. 196.

Pasqual Antonibon and his son Giovanni Battista continued the fabrication of porcelain until the 6th February, 1781, when they entered into partnership with Signor Parolini, always continuing the same manufacture, *con sommo onore dell'arte*, until the 6th February, 1802. It was then leased to Giovanni Baroni, and he produced some very charming pieces both in form and decoration; but in a few years, from being badly conducted, it began to fall off, and by degrees it went to decay and was abandoned. The "Fabbrica Baroni," however, lingered on more than twenty years.

On plate xxxiii., page 45, we have given two examples of the Baroni *fabrique*, one in maiolica, the other in porcelain, with female figure handles, painted with classical subjects, both of which are in the Reynolds' collection.

On May 21, 1825, the old firm of "Pasquale Antonibon and Sons" resumed the works, the actual proprietors being Gio. Batt Antonibon and his son Francesco; they continued making porcelain until 1835, but all their efforts to sustain it were ineffectual; they could not compete with the porcelain manufactories of France and Germany, so they were compelled to abandon the manufacture. Since which time to the present they confine their attention to *terraglia* (*terre de pipe*), *majoliche fine* (*faïence*), and *ordinarie* (ordinary wares), which are all monopolized by Rietti, a dealer at Venice.

The mark on the porcelain of Antonibon is usually a star of six rays in blue or red, sometimes in gold. Lady Charlotte Schreiber has a milk pot, fig. 195, on which the star is impressed, and also a vase and cover, painted in lake *camaieu*, of St. Roche, with N stamped in the clay; another star by its side, painted red, fig. 194.

Sometimes the word Nove is written in full, accompanied by a star of six or eight points.

Spain.

MADRID.

This manufactory (*Soft Paste*) called "*La China*," was founded by Charles III. in 1759, in the gardens attached to his palace of El Buen Retiro, in Madrid. It was organized by workmen whom he brought with him from Naples. The early ware produced here consequently resembles that of Capo di Monti.

The Royal manufactory and every thing connected with it was destroyed by the French, and the place converted into a fortification, which surrendered with 200 cannon on the 14th August, 1812, to the Duke of Wellington. It was subsequently blown up by Lord Hill when the misconduct or perfidy of Ballasteros compelled him to evacuate Madrid. "It has been," says Major Byng Hall, "one of the calumnies against the English that from jealousy all the finest specimens of china were destroyed by them, whereas the French destroyed every thing, and converted the manufactory into a Bastille which, and not the china, was destroyed by the English."

Ferdinand VII. on his restoration, recreated *La China*, removing what was left to La Mancha, once a villa of the Alva family on the Manzanares; but this also has ceased to exist, at least as regards artistic merit.

The mark is usually a fleur-de-lis, painted in red, blue or gold (as on the Capo di Monti china), irregularly formed. On the very early pieces we

occasionally meet with the two C's crowned. Sometimes the letters O. F. L. are added.

Examples.

Fig. 198. Group of two children with a goat, of coloured porcelain; height 14 inches.

Fig. 199. One of a pair of vases, with scenes from *Don Quixote;* height 17 inches.

Fig. 200. One of a pair of vases, painted with children; height 22 inches. These are in the possession of Signora Donna Emilia de Riano.

Fig. 201. A pair of groups of boy bacchanals, seated on wine casks; Mr. C. W. Reynolds' collection.

ALCORA.

The Comte de Laborde, in his *View of Spain*, as recently as 1808, says, "On ne fait de porcelaine (en Espagne) qu'a Alcora et à Madrid: celle d'Alcora est très commune, on en fait très peu." In confirmation of this assertion, M. Chas. Davillier, in a visit to Spain, saw an engraving of a furnace for baking porcelain with this inscription: "Modele de four pour la porselene naturele, fait par Haly pour M. le Comte d'Aranda. Alcora, 29 Juin, 1756." It is also noticed by Don Antonio Ponz, *Viage de Espana*, in 1793.

Two large plaques of porcelain of the latter half of the XVIIIth Century, from the Comte d'Aranda's manufactory, both very well painted, are in Mr. Reynolds' collection. One represents Christ bearing his cross, in colours; the other, painted in sepia, of costumes of three Spanish provinces, with figures at a fountain, is here given, fig. 202.

Saxony.

DRESDEN.

THE celebrated porcelain manufactory at Dresden, or rather at Meissen (in its vicinity), was established by Augustus II., Elector of Saxony, for the manufacture of true porcelain, that is, hard paste. The experiments of Tschirnhaus and Böttcher commenced about 1706, and to the latter is attributed the invention of hard paste. His first attempt was a red ware, like jasper, which was cut and polished by the lapidary, and ornamented by gilding; it was a fine stoneware, having the opacity, grain, and toughness of pottery. In 1708 Tschirnhaus died, and, shortly after, Böttcher succeeded in discovering the mode of making true porcelain by the accidental detection of the kaolin necessary for the purpose. Böttcher was born at Schleiz, in Vogtland, in 1682, and died in 1719. At an early age, he was sent by his father to Berlin to study alchemy, and was considered a great adept in this occult science, and was even supposed to have discovered the secret of the philosopher's stone. After remaining some time in the service of William I. of Prussia, he became annoyed at the insupportable surveillance to which he was subjected, and fled; but he was arrested in Saxony, and the Elector detained him as a state prisoner; partaking of the credulity of the age as to the possibility of discovering the philosopher's stone, he resolved to test the powers of Böttcher, and sent him to the fortress of Königstein; subsequently he was removed to the Castle of Albretchtsberg, at Dresden. While there he continued his experiments, not altogether in the attempt to make gold, but in discovering the means of making true porcelain, and was, by a fortunate chance, enabled to discover the secret. The story is thus told:—John Schnorr, a rich iron-master of the Erzegebirge, in the year 1711, riding on horseback at Aue, near Schneberg, observed that his horse's feet stuck continually into a soft white clay, which impeded his progress. Hair-powder for wigs (made principally from wheat flour) was at that time in general use, and a careful examination of this earth suggested to Schnorr the substitution of it for the more expensive material, which was sold in large quantities at a cheap rate in Dresden, Leipsic, and other cities. Böttcher, among others, used it, but, finding it much heavier, desired to ascertain the deleterious ingredients, and analysed it, when, to his great astonishment, this ingenious chemist found the identical properties of the kaolin, which was the only thing required to complete his discovery of true porcelain. It was known in commerce as "Schnorr's white earth of Aue," and was used secretly at the manufactory until the Aue kaolin was exhausted in 1850. In consequence of this important discovery, Augustus II established the great manufactory at Meissen, of which Böttcher was appointed Director in 1710, and about 1715 he succeeded in making a fine and perfect white porcelain. The first attempts to paint upon this ware were very imperfect, consisting of a blue colour under the glaze, in imitation of Nankin blue porcelain. It was under Horoldt's direction, in 1720, that paintings of a superior character, accompanied by gilding, and medallions of Chinese figures were introduced, and magnificent services completed. In 1731, Kandler, a sculptor, superintended the modelling of animals and groups, vases, &c., and other artists painted birds, insects, and copies of paintings principally of the Flemish school. From 1731 to 1756 the best productions emanated from the Dresden manufactory.

A Dresden china figure of a Dutch skipper, of stout build,

with a pointed hat, has in front the initials I. F. and the date 1738. In Lady Charlotte Schreiber's collection, see fig. 206. Another figure from the same model has I. F. 1752; marked in blue underneath with the crossed swords, in the Rev. T. Staniforth's collection.

Kändler modelled men and animals of the natural size, as well as peacocks, herons, pelicans, and other birds. Among the pieces produced about this time, by or under the direction of Kändler, at Meissen, was "The Tailor of Count Bruhl," mounted upon a goat, with all the implements of his trade about him. This vain man had a great desire that his likeness should be executed in porcelain at the royal manufactory, and his request was complied with, but not probably so as to gratify his vanity, for not only the tailor but his wife were thus immortalised, *aere perennius*, in porcelain. In 1754 Dietrich became Director, and he was succeeded in 1796 by Marcolini, whose beautiful productions are well known. His period is always known by a star underneath the crossed swords. In spite of the precautions taken at Meissen to prevent the secret becoming known—the penalty being death, or perpetual imprisonment in the Castle of Königstein—some workmen escaped to reveal it elsewhere.

This white porcelain was sometimes ornamented by private persons, especially by a Baron Busch, Canon of Hildisheim, who was the only person possessed of the secret of engraving with a diamond on china.

In an advertisement of a sale by auction at Golden Square by Mr. Owen in June, 1767, we find "a tea set of the beautiful snow white Dresden, with the hunt of the heron and falcon most curiously engraved by Baron Busch. The valuable service now at Saltzdal belonging to the Duke of Brunswick, esteemed at £10,000., was made a present to that prince by the Baron, as were also the other curious pieces in the cabinets of most of the princes of the Empire. This set was brought into England by the secretary of a sovereign prince, also some plates framed as pictures, engraved by the same hand after Rembrandt, &c."

Lady Charlotte Schreiber has a sucrier, dish, cup and saucer, etched with birds, trees, and ruins, by Busch. The etching does not appear to penetrate beneath the glaze, but it is unsigned, see figs. 203-205. Busch also etched on glass, and some pieces we have seen have his name written on them.

In the Marcolini period we sometimes find portraits, formed by the outlines of flowers and leaves, leaving the profile on the white ground of the piece. The Rev. T. Staniforth has a cup and saucer, *gros bleu* ground, with medallions in the centre of bouquets of flowers, containing profiles of celebrated characters, five in each piece, see fig. 213.

The first mark used was the monogram A. R., signifying Augustus Rex, and was affixed to all pieces intended for Royal use. It is found upon many imitations of the Oriental porcelain; used from 1709 to 1712. This mark has been recently placed upon modern Dresden, but is easily distinguished from the ancient.

The caduceus mark was used from 1712 to 1720, and is said to have been placed upon pieces intended for sale. It is found on specimens in the Chinese style, as well as others.

DRESDEN. The mark for Royal pieces. The letters K. P. M. stand for *Koniglichen Porzellan Manufactur:* marked in blue under the glaze.

The common mark was the crossed swords, which is still in use, but on the pieces of the King's period, 1770, a dot or ring was placed underneath, and Marcolini's period of about 1796 is known by one or more stars below the handles.

Examples.

Fig. 207 is a lofty white vase with flowers and birds in full relief. Lady C. Schreiber's collection.

Fig. 208. A vase and cover, tureen shaped, perforated and gilt, raised cartouches, and cupids, painted with views of public buildings in Dresden, the cover surmounted by a crown. South Kensington Museum.

Fig. 209, 210. Busts of a boy and girl in white porcelain. South Kensington Museum.

Fig. 211, 212. Tea pot, cup and saucer, pink ground, painted with landscapes and figures. Mr. Walker Joy's collection.

Austria.

VIENNA.

THIS manufactory (*hard paste*) was founded about 1717. There are several traditions as to its origin: one is that a musician named La France, and a billiard marker, named Dupuis, brought with them to Vienna in October, 1717, a certain Cristofle Conrad Hünger, who had been employed at Meissen as an enamel painter and gilder, and in the following year they were joined by a man named Stolzel of Meissen, who was possessed of the secret, and became director. It was a private enterprize set on foot by Claude du Pasquier, who obtained from the Emperor Charles VII a privilege for twenty-five years. Major Byng Hall (*Adventures of a Bric-à-Brac Hunter*) says that it was established by Claude Innocenz de Blaquier, who engaged one Stenzel or Stolzel to co-operate with him. With this object in view De Blaquier proceeded secretly to Meissen, where he contrived to scrape acquaintance with the arcanist in a coffee-house. He engaged with Stenzel in a game of billiards, taking care to lose, and thus he secured his object. Stenzel after some slight hesitation, accepted an offer of a thousand dollars to be paid yearly, and a carriage at his disposal, and proceeded forthwith to Vienna. De Blaquier obtained a patent for twenty-five years, granted by Charles VI., signed by his Imperial Majesty at Luxemburg 27th May, 1718. In this patent it was distinctly notified that the factory was to receive no pecuniary aid from Government; but an exclusive privilege was granted for the sale of porcelain, wholesale and retail, throughout the whole empire.

The patent further stipulated that the ware should consist of the highest material, and should display the most elegant and well selected forms and colours, to which end neither labour nor expense was to be spared in the endeavour to produce patterns of original forms and fancy. This done, Blaquier entered into partnership with Henrich Zerden, a merchant named Martin Peter, and an artist named Howard Hünger. De Blaquier had many difficulties to contend with, and the productions not being equal to the Chinese, and inferior even to those of Meissen, both as regards beauty and material, taste and decoration, and the sale consequently moderate, he was compelled to produce coarser articles; added to which De Blaquier not being possessed of the secret, and the arcanist Stenzel not having been paid regularly according to his contract, returned to Meissen, having maliciously destroyed many of the models. The works were, therefore, suspended at the end of the second year without a knowledge of the secret or material. De Blaquier being a man of energy and determination endeavoured by numerous experiments to discover the porcelain mixture, and his efforts were finally crowned with success.

"The factory was at first established in a small house belonging to Count Kufstein, and he worked with only ten assistants and one kiln. But in the year 1721 it was removed to a house belonging to Count Breuner. Here the workmen were increased to twenty hands, and more kilns were erected. Nevertheless, the factory was not successful, and after twenty-five years' labour De Blaquier decided in 1744 to offer it to the Government. The establishment was then in good working condition, and the workmen for the most part very efficient, and he proposed to take on himself the direction and management.

"The young Empress Maria Theresa resolved to support the factory, which promised to give occupation and profit to her subjects, honour and gain to the State. She, therefore, commanded that it should be taken by State contract from its owner, that its debt of 45,449 florins should be paid off, and De Blaquier receive the direction with a salary of 1500 florins a-year. Modelling of groups and figures appears to have commenced when the factory became the property of the Government in 1747. Niedermeyer was the master modeller. Count Philip Kinsky and Count Rodolph Cholert took great interest in the development of the factory, and in 1760, under Government control, it advanced rapidly to that perfection of art it subsequently maintained."

Major Byng Hall, to whom we are indebted for this information, tells us that in 1750 the workmen only numbered forty; eleven years later that number had increased to 140; in 1770 to 200, and in 1780 to 320. From 1747 to 1790 was the best period for figures and groups, while from 1780 to 1820 painting on china became celebrated, the subjects being taken from Watteau, Lancret, Boucher, Angelica Kauffman, and others, as well as allegorical subjects.

In 1785 the most important improvements were made under the Baron de Lorgenthal or Sorgenthal; artists of the highest talents being employed, and a first-rate chemist named Leithner was engaged to prepare the colours and gilding, and the chefs d'œuvre of the early masters were copied, while the gilding was brought to a perfection which has never been surpassed.

After the death of the Baron in 1805, M. Niedermayer became Director. It continued its flourishing condition until about 1815. Leithner used the finest gold, which brought the gilding to the utmost perfection; moreover, he discovered a rich cobalt blue, and a red-brown colour, which no other factory could imitate. From the year 1784 to the date of its extinction, it was the custom to mark every piece with the number of the year, which circumstance may be of great service to the connoisseur who seeks early specimens of Vienna porcelain. It is stamped without colour underneath the piece—or rather indented, the first numeral being omitted; thus the number 792 stands for 1792; 802 for 1802; 835, and so on.

From 1827, under the direction of Scholtz, who followed Niedermayer, it was on the decline, and economy, indifferent workmen, bad artists copying from French models, its doom was sealed. The splendid and expensive gilding, the exquisite painting, &c., gave place to cheaper and less refined productions, and it dwindled down to a second-rate factory, and became a burden to the State.

The imperial manufactory at Vienna was in consequence of the great annual expense discontinued in 1864, and all the implements and utensils sold, the house being now used for other purposes. Some of the principal workmen, however, still continue to decorate porcelain as a means of subsistence.

The books on art, and all the drawings of its most successful period, many of the models, the library, and the Keramic collection, were given to the Austrian Museum recently established in Vienna, to be retained as a lasting memorial of its celebrity.

The mark used from 1744 was a shield of the arms of Austria, painted in blue, occasionally impressed; and this simple mark has been continued to the present day.

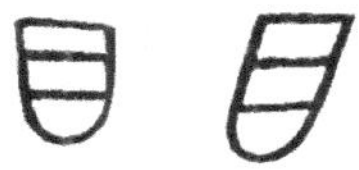

SCHLAKENWALD. *Hard Paste.* This is one of the oldest porcelain manufactories (except Vienna) in Austria; it was established about the year 1800. George Leppert was the owner in 1842, and much improved this industry in the State. Some pieces are marked "Leppert & Haas."

Fig. 214 is a cup and saucer painted with costume figures. Mr. Walker Joy's collection.

HEREND (Hungary). There was a manufactory of porcelain here towards the end of the XVIIIth Century, but we are not informed of its origin. The author has in his possession a porcelain cafétière, or set of four covered pieces, viz.: coffee and milk pots and two sugar vases, fitting into a stand, which has as many holes to receive them; painted with large red carnations, gold edges; marked as in the margin in incuse letters; date about 1800. Sometimes we find the word HEREND impressed and the arms painted.

HEREND.

Herend.

HERIND. Porcelain manufactory, carried on by Morice Fischer. The mark used by them is the shield of arms of Austria. Established in 1839.

Prussia.

BERLIN.

THIS manufactory (*Hard Paste*) was established by William Gaspar Wegely in 1751, in the Neue Frederick Strasse. His invention is thus alluded to in the *Gentleman's Magazine* for 1753: "There has been discovered here (at Berlin) the whole art of making china ware, without any particular kind of earth, from a kind of stone which is common enough every where. The fine glossy outward coat is prepared from this, as well as the substance of the china, over which, after it is painted, they throw a kind of varnish, which fixes the colouring, and makes the figures look as if enamelled, without any mixture of metallic ingredients." The manufactory was carried on for about eight years, but never remunerated the originator, and he abandoned it in 1761, when Gottskowski, a celebrated banker, became the purchaser, and removed the works to Leipsiger Strasse; assisted by his capital, it was brought to great perfection.

John Ernest Gottskowski obtained the secret of porcelain from Ernest Heinrich Richard, who had been employed by Wegely, for which he received 4,000 dollars, and was made Director, with a salary of 1,200 dollars. Gottskowski did not personally manage the manufactory, but placed it under the management of the Commissioner Grunenger, which led to his employment from the year 1763 to 1786 as the head of the Royal porcelain manufactory at Berlin.

In 1763, Gottskowski gave up to the king the whole of his fabric of porcelain, receiving 225,000 dollars, entering into a contract for the sale of his secrets. "Grunenger has recorded in his chronicle his labours to obtain the men best adapted for the different departments, among them Richard Bowman and others of some note. From the specification and inventory drawn up on the occasion some idea may be formed of the magnitude of his enterprise. There were 7 administrators, 1 artist, 1 model master, 2 picture inspectors, 6 furnace men, 3 glaze workers, 5 lathe turners, 3 potters, 6 mill workers, 2 polishers, 6 sculptors, 6 embossers, 6 founders, 11 designers, 6 earthenware moulders, 13 potter-wheel workers, 3 model joiners, 1 girdler, 22 porcelain painters, 22 picture colourers, 3 colour makers, 4 packers and attendants, 8 wood framers, making altogether 147 persons. The attendant expenses were 10,200 dollars. It is calculated that 29,516 red and coloured earthenware, 10,000 white vessels, and 4,866 painted porcelain—many of them of grotesque form, and many of the fashion of the day—were fabricated; articles of every description, groups, vases, flacons, statuary, snuff boxes, fancy articles, ear-rings, lamps, and every thing that the artist could suggest and the potter carry out. It is satisfactory to know that there exist at the present day 133 models from which these articles were fabricated; and the results of the labour, the energy, and the taste brought into play a hundred years ago, may easily be studied." (*Major Byng Hall.*) It was in September, 1763, that Frederick the Great appeared for the first time in his manufactory, and Grunenger has recorded his attentive examination of even the minutest details, and conversed with him on the improvements which might be made. Commissioner Grunenger, Mauritius Jacobi, Nogel, Eichman, Richard, Meyer, Clauce, Böhme, and Klipsel continued at the head of the establishment and directed the different departments. A sum of 140,000 dollars was devoted to the improvement of the *fabrique.*

We read in the *Gentleman's Magazine* for 1764, that "The King of Prussia has at a great expense introduced a porcelain manufactory into his dominions, and has already brought it to such perfection as to rival that at Meissen, near Dresden, which his Majesty, during the late war, in a manner ruined." With a view to encourage the manufacture in his kingdom, he made presents of superb services of Berlin china to several German princes in the year 1766. When Frederick the Great occupied Dresden, in the seven years' war, he expatriated many of the best modellers and painters to form his Royal manufactory; among these were Meyer, Klipsel, and Böhme. The King also transported great quantities of the clay and a portion of the collection. Independent of this, and the better to insure employment for the five hundred persons engaged in the processes, he restricted the Jews resident in any part of his dominions from entering into the marriage state, until each man had obtained a certificate from himself, which was only granted on the production of a voucher from the Director of the manufactory, that porcelain to a given amount had been purchased, and that there was reasonable cause for granting the indulgence. Of course the Jews more readily disposed of their purchases than the general dealers, and the device was attended with much success. To insure its success and extend its operations, he embraced every opportunity that was presented; and the establishment was so well supported that in 1776 seven hundred men were constantly employed, and it is said that three thousand pieces of porcelain were made daily.

In 1769, an order was published permitting a lottery company to purchase annually to the amount of 90,000 dollars.

"In 1771, in the neighbourhood of Brackwitz, not far from Halle, a superior clay was discovered, from which a porcelain of exquisite whiteness and beauty was obtained. Somewhat later discoveries were made at Beerdersee and at Morland Seumwitz of material of the highest quality sufficient for consumption during a century, and from thence, at the present day, the Royal manufactory derives its most valuable material." (*Major Byng Hall.*)

In 1787, Frederick William II. appointed a commission,

under the direction of the Minister Von Stemitz and Count Reden, and great improvements in the management were carried out. (*Ibid.*)

Up to the present period the manufacture has not ceased to deserve the admiration of the public.

The Berlin Royal Porcelain Manufactory now works seven kilns, and employs three hundred workmen; the annual produce amounts on an average to half a million of finished articles, value 150,000 Prussian dollars. The superintendence is entrusted to M. Kolbe (who succeeded M. Frick in the direction), under whom are Dr. Elsner as chemist, M. Mantel as master modeller, and M. Looschen as head painter.

The porcelain manufactories of Berlin and Charlottenburg are both under the direction of M. Kolbe, Counsellor of State, employing at the present time sixteen furnaces and about five hundred workmen. At Berlin wood is used for fuel, at Charlottenburg coal.

BERLIN. The mark of Wegely from 1751 to 1761, two strokes of the W being longer and crossing each other.

BERLIN. In 1761, when it became a Royal establishment, the sceptre was used, on painted and gilt porcelain in brown, on white china it was marked in blue. The letters K. P. M. are sometimes placed below it.

BERLIN. A special mark, in blue, first used about 1830 on small richly decorated pieces. The letters represent Königlichen Porzellan, or Preussiche, Manufactur.

HÖCHST. Mayence. *Hard Paste.* Founded in 1720, by Gelz, a *faïencier* of Francfort, assisted by Bengraf and Lowenfink, but they were unsuccessful, and called in Ringler, of Vienna, who had escaped from the manufactory. In 1740, during the Electorate of Jean Frederic Charles, Archbishop of Mayence, their porcelain ranked among the first in Europe. About 1760 the celebrated modeller Melchior was engaged, and some very elegant statuettes were produced, and elegant designs for vases, &c. He left the manufactory about 1785, but his successor, Ries, was not so skilful, and all his figures having disproportionate heads, the so-called "thick-head" period commenced. Christian Gottlieb Kuntze is another celebrated enamel painter of this fabrique. On the invasion of the French under General Custine, in 1794, all the materials were sold by auction.

HÖCHST. Mayence. The mark is a wheel,—the arms of the Archbishop of Mayence,—sometimes surmounted by a crown; in gold, red, or blue, according to the quality.

HÖCHST. Mayence. Sometimes the wheel is used without the crown.

Fig. 217-8. Tray and sucrier, painted with birds, harlequin borders.

Fig. 219, Sucrier, painted with conversation subjects. In Mr. Walker Joy's collection.

Fig. 220. Lamp, lake *camaieu*, landscape, &c. Mr. C. W. Reynolds' collection.

Bavaria.

FRANKENTHAL.

The manufactory of porcelain at Frankenthal was established in 1754, by Paul Hanüng, who, having discovered the secret of hard porcelain, offered it to the royal manufactory at Sèvres, but not agreeing as to the price, the offer was declined, and they commenced persecuting him—for in that year a decree forbade the making of translucent ware in France except at Sèvres—and Hanüng was compelled to go to Frankenthal, leaving his fayence manufactory at Strasbourg in charge of his sons. In 1761 it was purchased by the Elector Charles Theodore, and it attained great celebrity, which it maintained until he became Elector of Bavaria, in 1798, when it greatly declined, and all the stock and utensils were sold in 1800 and removed to Greinstadt. The following chronogram denotes the year 1775:—

VarIantIbVs·fLosCVLIs·DIVersI·CoLores·fabrICæ·
sVb·reVIVIsCentIs·soLIs·hVIVs·raDIIs·eXVLtantIs.
In·frankenthaL·

It occurs on a porcelain plate, having in the centre the initials of Carl Theodor, interlaced and crowned, within a gold star of flaming rays; radiating from this are thirty divisions, and on the border thirty more, all numbered and painted with small bouquets, *en camaieu*, of all the various shades of colour employed in the manufactory. On the back is the usual monogram, in blue, and "*N.* 2" impressed. In the collection of the Rev. T. Staniforth, see fig. 221.

Fig. 222 to 225. A dejeuner painted with fête champêtre scenes, &c. Mr. C. W. Reynolds's collection.

Fig. 226. Cup and saucer, painted with animals. Mr. Walker Joy's collection.

The early mark under Hanüng was a lion rampant, the crest of the Palatinate, from 1755 to 1761; marked in blue. This monogram, the mark of Joseph Adam Hanüng, is often found with the lion.

Second period, when it became a Government establishment. The initials of Charles Theodore under the crown. A specimen in the S. K. Museum—a vase and cover, painted with a mythological subject—has this and the preceding mark of Hanüng both together.

NEUDECH, on the Au, and NYMPHENBURG. Established in 1747, by a potter named Niedermayer. The Comte de Hainshausen became patron in 1754, and in 1756 he sent for Ringler, who organized the establishment, and it was then placed under the protection of the Elector Maximilian Joseph. On the death of Charles Theodore, his successor, in 1758, the Frankenthal manufactory was abandoned, and transferred to Nymphenburg, which is still a Royal establishment, and well supported. The pieces are manufactured in white at Nymphenburg, but chiefly decorated at Munich and elsewhere; that is the reason why the mark is frequently found impressed, and the mark of some other factory painted in colour.

Fig. 228 is a caddy painted with cattle, marked with the double triangle. Mr. C. W. Reynolds' collection.

The following marks were used at Nymphenburg:—

The arms of Bavaria impressed, without colour, on hard paste, the shield is frequently of a squarer form than here given.

This is an early mark, painted in blue, consisting of two interlaced triangles, with mystic characters at each point of the angle, which vary on different specimens; probably Masonic.

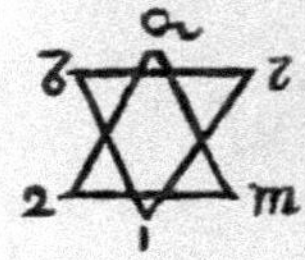

ANSPACH.

1718. A town which belonged to the Margraviate of Anspach and Bayreuth. The mark of an eagle with wings displayed, is in blue. Specimens in the Sèvres Museum.

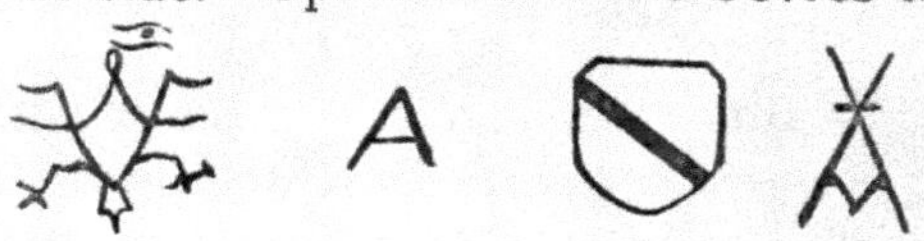

Fig. 229 is a sucrier and cover, painted with flowers. In Mr. C. W. Reynolds's collection.

Thuringia.

VOLKSTEDT.

The porcelain manufactory of Sitzerode was transferred here in 1762, where it was farmed by a merchant named Nonne, of Erfurt, who greatly enlarged and improved the works. About the year 1770 it was carried on by Greiner. The mark is C. V. or G. V., sometimes with a shield of arms, which may be the initial letters of Greiner, Volkstedt. In 1795 more than 120 workmen were employed. The letters C and V are sometimes interlaced.

Fig. 236. A tea pot, painted with flowers; Mr. Reynolds' collection.

RUDOLSTADT.

Established 1758, originally at Volkstedt, and afterwards removed to Rudolstadt, near Jena. The mark was R, for the name of the place. Gotthelf Greiner had the direction of several of the Thuringian manufactories; he died in 1797. This establishment still exists, but only common blue and white ware is made. The mark is in blue. The hay fork is part of the arms of Schwartzburg (a hay fork and curry comb).

The letters T. R. under a crown were used from 1806 to 1818; W. R., under a crown, from 1818. The mark of a stag's horn, from the arms of Wurtemberg, was used at a later period.

Fig. 230 is a coffee pot, painted in lake *camaieu*, with a landscape and buildings after Claude, gilt, arabesque and scroll border; from the Bernal collection, S. K. Museum.

FULDA. Hesse. Established about 1763 by Arnandus, Prince-Bishop of Fulda, for the manufacture of porcelain. The mark (in blue) signifies Fürslich Fuldäish, (belonging to the Prince of Fulda). Sometimes a cross was used on groups and figures. The best artists were employed, and many grand vases, figures and services produced, of a fine white paste, and handsomely decorated.

Examples.

Fig. 231. Coffee pot, with sea view and figures.

Fig. 232. Tea pot, painted with urns and insects.

Fig. 233. Cup and saucer, painted with birds; in the possession of Mr. Walker Joy.

Fig. 234-5. Pair of figures of peasants, well modelled; in Mr. Chas. Dickins' collection.

Brunswick, Wurtemburg, etc.

FURSTENBURG.

THIS manufactory was established in 1750 by Bengraf, who came from Höchst; he died the same year, and Baron von Lang, a distinguished chemist, undertook the direction of the works, under the patronage of Charles Duke of Brunswick. The manufactory has been carried on by the Government up to the present time.

In 1807 the Sèvres Museum obtained from the manufactory a plate, painted with classical subjects by Brüning, a coffee cup, decorated in gold, by Heinze, and other specimens. Mr. Stunkel, director of the *fabrique* in 1840, also presented other pieces. The mark is an F., of various forms, pencilled in blue.

LUDWIGSBURG.

LUDWIGSBURG, called also KRONENBURG porcelain. This manufactory was established by Ringler in 1758, under the patronage of Charles Eugene, the reigning Duke. It was celebrated for the excellence of its productions and the fine paintings on its vases and services, as well as for its excellent groups. The mark is the double C, for the name of Duke Charles, ensigned with a high German Ducal crown, surmounted by a cross. The mark of two C's with a Count's coronet, which is frequently attributed to this town, belongs to Niderviller.

Fig. 237. Milk pot, painted with flowers; mark a hay fork.

Fig. 238. Cup and saucer, with pastoral figures; mark R. Mr. Walker Joy's collection.

REGENSBURG (RATISBON)

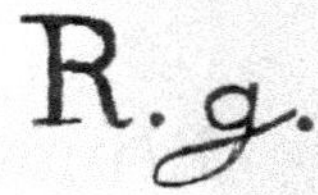

was established about 1760. The mark consisted of the first and last letters of the name.

Fig. 239 is a cup and saucer with landscapes in sepia. Mr. Walker Joy's collection.

GROSBREITENBACH.

Established about 1770 by Greiner. The demand for his porcelain was so great, that not being able to enlarge his works at Limbach, he purchased this as well as Weilsdorf and Volkstedt.

This mark is frequently imperfectly formed, and hardly to be recognized as a trefoil leaf.

Fig. 240 is a cup and saucer painted with flowers. Mr. Walker Joy's collection.

LIMBACH.

Saxe Meiningen. This manufactory was also under the direction of Gotthelf Greiner. Established about 1762.

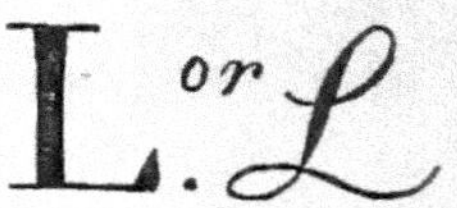

The marks are said to be a single or a double L; but there appears to be some confusion in the appropriation, for the same letters are also assigned to Ilmenau and Breitenbach.

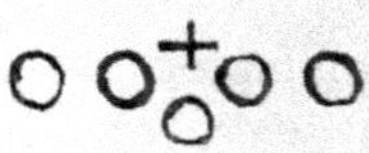

Another mark, attributed to Limbach, as well as two L's crossed.

Fig. 241. A cup and saucer with sepia landscapes. Mr. Walker Joy's collection.

GERA

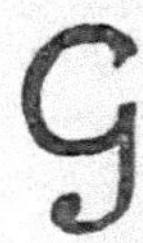

A manufactory was founded here about 1780. The usual mark is G as in the margin.

Fig. 242 is a cup and saucer, with black profile portrait. Mr. Walker Joy's collection.

GOTHA.

Founded in 1780 by Rothenberg, and afterwards (1802) conducted by Henneberg. The mark G, for the name of the town, of this form.

G
G

Fig. 243 is a cup and saucer, painted with a view of the town. Mr. Walker Joy's collection.

RAUENSTEIN, in Saxe Meiningen. Established 1760. *Hard Paste.* Marked in blue. This mark is on a cup and saucer, painted with flowers, in the collection of the Right Hon. W. E. Gladstone.

R—n

WALLENDORF. Saxe Coburg. *Hard Paste.* Established by Greiner and Haman in 1762. This mark is given by Marryat, but there are so many W's that it is difficult to identify their localities with any degree of certainty.

W

Fig. 244 is a tea pot painted with blue sprigs. Mr. Walker Joy's collection.

BADEN-BADEN. *Hard Paste.* Established in 1753 as a porcelain manufactory by the widow Sperl, and workmen from Höchst, with the patronage of the reigning Margrave, under Pfalzer. It ceased in 1778. The mark is an axe, or the blade of an axe, in gold.

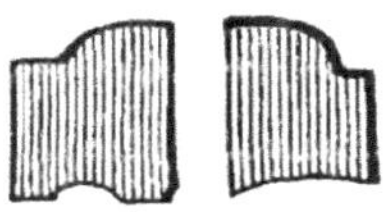

Switzerland and Holland.

NYON.

A MANUFACTORY was in full work here towards the end of the XVIIIth Century. It is said to have been established by a French flower painter named Maubrée, and several Genevese artists painted on the porcelain, occasionally marking it with a "G" or "Geneva" in full; sometimes with and sometimes without the fish. There never was a manufactory of china at Geneva.

Fig. 245 is a cup with two handles, cover and saucer, a portrait in the centre. The Rev. C. Staniforth's collection.

ZURICH. *Hard Paste.* Established about 1750, by one of the workmen from Höchst, perhaps Ringler; after a few years it was abandoned, and left under the direction of Sprengler and Hearacher from 1763 to 1768. In 1775 it was conducted by Trou. It has much the character of German china. The mark is in blue.

Fig. 246. A cup and saucer painted with fruit. Mr. Walker Joy's collection.

Fig. 247. A group of a Soldier trampling on a Turk and unveiling a lady, martial and love trophies on the ground. Mr. C. W. Reynolds's collection.

The first manufactory for porcelain in Holland was at Weesp, near Amsterdam. It was established in 1764 by the

Count Gronsveldt-Diepenbroek, who had by some means obtained the secret of the composition of hard paste. Having bought the materials of the old fayence works of Overtoom, he proceeded to make porcelain, and produced some fine white and transparent specimens; it only lasted seven years, was closed in 1771, and the materials publicly sold. Notwithstanding the unsuccessful result in a commercial point of view, it was reopened by a Protestant minister, the Rev. De Moll, of Oude Loosdrecht, associated with some capitalists of Amsterdam, but the next year it was removed to Loosdrecht. The decorations are very much of the Saxon character. The marks are a W, and two crossed lines, or swords, with dots, in blue. The latter has been assigned to Arnstadt, but is now authenticated as belonging to this manufactory.

Fig. 248 is a large ewer painted with a basket of flowers; marked W. Mr. C. W. Reynolds' collection.

Fig. 249. A coffee pot with figures after Teniers. Mark a cross and dots. Mr. Walker Joy's collection.

LOOSDRECHT, situated between Utrecht and Amsterdam, was the next town, where porcelain was successfully made. It sprung from the ashes of Weesp, and in 1772 became a proprietary, with the Rev. De Moll at its head; after his death, in 1782, the concern passed into the hands of his partners, J. Rendorp, A. Dedel, C. Van der Hoop, Gysbz, and J. Hope, and was by them removed, in 1784, to Amstel. The ware is of fine quality, decorated in the Saxon style; specimens are frequently met with, having gilt borders and a light blue flower between green leaves. The letters M. o. L. stand for "*Manufactur oude Loosdrecht*," marked in blue or impressed on the ware; the best pieces have a star also. By a singular coincidence it happened that the establishment was under the direction of the Rev. De Moll. Sometimes the letter M is divided from the two last letters by two dots, which may mean "*Moll: oude Loosdrecht.*"

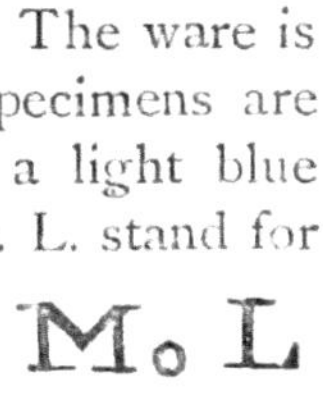

Fig. 250. A vase perforated and painted with birds. South Kensington Museum.

AMSTERDAM. M. Jacquemart places this mark to Amsterdam, being the ancient crest of the united provinces,—the Batavian lion, traced in blue,—and quotes a specimen in the Museum of Sèvres. Mr. Reynolds has a pair of elegant bottles, painted in lake *camaieu* with birds and trees, the mark in blue. See fig. 251.

OUDE AMSTEL. In the year 1782, on the death of the Rev. De Moll, the manufactory of Loosdrecht was removed to Oude Amstel (Old Amstel), near Amsterdam, and carried on with redoubled zeal by the same Company, directed by a German named Daeuber, about 1784. It flourished under his direction for a few years, and a fine description of porcelain was produced, but it was not encouraged in Holland, and gradually declined, in consequence of the large importations from England which inundated the country. It was again offered for sale in 1789, and came into the hands of J. Rendorp, C. Van der Hoop, and Gysbz, still remaining under Daeuber's direction, but was entirely demolished at the close of the last century. Sometimes the initials of the director, A. D., are found.

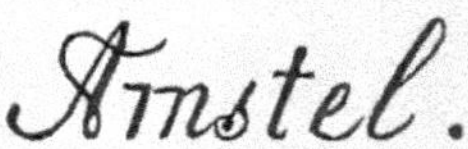

Fig. 252, 253. A tea pot and sucrier with views in Holland.

Fig. 254. A sucrier painted with birds. Mr. Walker Joy's collection.

LA HAYE (THE HAGUE).

About the year 1775, a porcelain manufactory for both hard and soft paste was opened at the Hague, under the direction of a German named Leichner or Lynker; it was first situated in the *Bierkade*, and later in *Niewe Molstraat*. The *fabrique* was not very important, there being only one furnace, employing from fifty to sixty workmen and painters. The works ceased in 1785 or 1786. The mark is a stork, a symbol of the town, in grey or gold.

Fig. 255. A milk jug painted with flowers. In the Rev. T. Staniforth's collection.

Lille. This porcelain manufactory was established in 1711 by Sieurs Barthélémy Dorez, and Pierre Pelissier, his nephew, natives of Lille. The porcelain (*pâte tendre*) of this time was like that of St. Cloud, but in the Delft style, the favourite ornamentation being Chinese designs, but no mark is known. At a later period (in 1784) a manufactory of hard porcelain was established by Leperre Durot, under the patronage of the Dauphin ; it was styled " Manufacture Royale de Monseigneur le Dauphin." The porcelain of Leperre Durot is richly adorned with gold and carefully painted bouquets of flowers.

In 1790 the manufactory changed hands, and several attempts were made to insure its success, without avail, and about 1800 it altogether ceased. M. Roger succeeded Leperre Durot, and in 1792 he sold his interest in the works to Messieurs Regnault and Graindorge, who were ruined, and the establishment soon closed. The mark on the hard porcelain of Leperre Durot, is a crowned dolphin, the emblem of the Royal protection ; it is in red, either pencilled or stencilled.

On a cup, cover, and saucer, with gold ornaments on white, and landscapes painted in Indian ink ; in Mr. Reynolds' collection. See fig. 256.

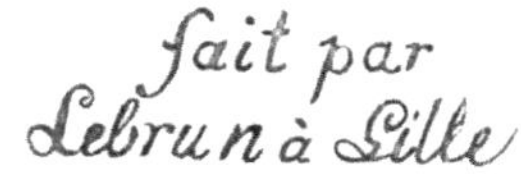

TOURNAY.

Established in 1750 by Peterinck. In 1752 one hundred workmen were employed, which in 1762 increased to as many as two hundred. For some time previous to 1815 the works were carried on by M. Maximilian de Bettignies, who, in consequence of the annexation of Tournay to Belgium, ceded it in that year to his brother Henri, and established another at St. Amand-les-Eaux. Soft paste, which has been discontinued many years in every other *fabrique* in France, is still made at both places, and they consequently produce the closest imitations of old Sèvres *pâte tendre.*

This mark is in gold on a cup and saucer, painted with animals and birds, illustrating Fontaine's Fables; in the collection of the Rev. T. Staniforth. See fig. 257.

This mark was used after 1755; in gold for the best quality, in blue or red for inferior specimens.

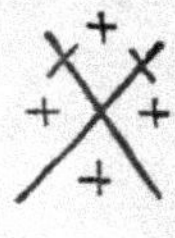

Fig. 258 is a basin in lake *camaieu*, landscapes and figures; in Mr. Walker Joy's collection.

BRUSSELS. *Hard Paste.* There was a manufactory of porcelain here towards the end of the last century. This mark is on a tea pot, with a band of roses in the centre and two belts of silver, with gold borders; on the cup and saucer of the same service is the name "*L. Cretté*," painted in red. These are in Mr. Reynolds' collection.

BRUSSELS. This name is on a service, some pieces of which have only the name "*L. Cretté*." Portions of another service, with the name and address, are in the collection of the Rev. T. Staniforth, (see fig. 259,) a milk pot. Two other marks; the latter is the mark of L. Cretté.

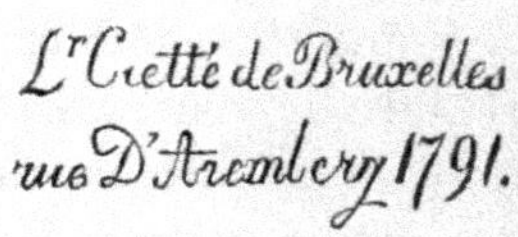

Fig. 260 is a tea pot, painted with roses, &c., gilt borders; in Mr. Reynolds' collection.

LUXEMBURG. *Hard Paste.* Established at Sept Fontaines about 1806, by M. Boch. Both pottery and porcelain were made here; plates, vases, figures, &c.

B. L

LUXEMBURG. M. Boch. On a specimen in the Sèvres Museum, attributed by M. Riocreux to this manufactory.

Figs. 261 and 262. Four figures, marked B. L.; Mr. Chas. Dickins' collection.

Russia and Poland.

At St. Petersburg, an Imperial china manufactory was established in 1744, by the Empress Elizabeth Petrowna, with workmen from Meissen. Catherine II. patronized the works, and in 1765 enlarged them considerably, under the direction of the minister, J. A. Olsoufieff, since which this *fabrique* has held a distinguished place among European manufactories; an artist named Swebach superintended the decorations, and in 1825 two workmen were sent from Sèvres to assist in the manufactory. The paste is hard and of a blueish cast, finely glazed. It always betrays its Dresden origin, and the imitations of the china of Saxony are wonderful in making up portions of sets which have been broken.

The mark of the Empress Catherine II. (*Ekaterina*), from 1762 to 1796. Those of later periods are the initials of the Emperors in Russian capitals under crowns, Paul, Alexander I., Nicholas, and Alexander II.

Fig. 265 is a cup and saucer, with the Imperial arms, and the mark of the Emperor Paul. Mr. C. W. Reynolds' collection.

Fig. 266. A verriere, with views of buildings; in the same collection.

Moscow. 1720. The potter, Eggebrecht, who had undertaken a manufactory of Delft at Dresden, by direction of Bottcher, had, after that was discontinued, left to go to Moscow, and, being acquainted with some of the processes for making porcelain, commenced manufacturing it at Moscow. The Russians, had, in 1717, endeavoured to entice one of Bottcher's best workmen, named Waldensten, and were unsuccessful; but, it is said, another workman, a few years after, named Richter, assisted them in their operations, but no traces are to be found of their subsequent history.

MOSCOW. A porcelain manufactory was established at TWER, by an Englishman named Gardner, in 1787, and another by A. Popoff. Fig. 267 is a cup and saucer, painted with a view of Moscow, bearing his initials, as in the margin. South Kensington Museum.

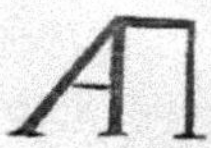

KORZEC (Wolhynie). POLAND. About 1803, Mérault, a chemist of the Sèvres manufactory, went to direct the *fabrique* at Korzec, taking with him an assistant in the laboratory named Petion After carrying it on for a few years, Mérault abandoned the direction, and returned to France. The mark is an eye within a triangle, in blue, beneath the glaze; it occurs on a *pâte dure* cup and saucer, the cup painted with a medallion portrait of a lady, *en grisaille*, richly gilt borders and ornaments, doubtless executed by one of the Sèvres decorators taken there by Mérault; in the possession of the Rev. T. Staniforth. See fig. 268.

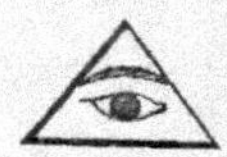

Sweden and Denmark.

MARIEBERG. This manufactory produced porcelain (*soft paste*), as well as fayence, and a great many specimens have recently come under our notice; the marks on some are similar to those on fayence. The quality of the porcelain as well as the decoration are like that of Meneçy Villeroy in France. It was established by M. Ehrenreich, under the patronage of Count Scheffer, Councillor of State, in 1750, and altogether ceased about 1780.

This mark is on a porcelain compotier and cover in the possession of Mr. Louis Huth. Above are the three crowns of Sweden. The M. B. for Marieberg, and F, probably the name of the decorator.

The next mark occurs on a porcelain compotier and cover, painted in pink camaieu with roses and china-asters, gilt leaf borders, in the possession of Mr. Horace Marryatt; and another is in the S. K. Museum, presented by M. Christian Hammer of Stockholme.

RÖRSTRAND is a suburb of Stockholm, and the porcelain manufactory is now carried on by Messrs. B. R. Geyers & Co.

COPENHAGEN. This manufactory was commenced by an apothecary of the name of Müller, in 1772. The Baron Von Lang, from the Furstenburg manufactory, is said to have been instrumental in forming this at Copenhagen; it is at least known that he entered the Danish service about the same time. Among the artists employed in painting porcelain about the time of its first establishment were Gylding, Seipsius, and Ruch. The capital was raised in shares, but, not being successful, the Government interfered, and it became a Royal establishment in 1775, and has ever since been maintained at considerable loss. The mark is in blue, of three parallel wavy lines, signifying the Sound and the Great and Little Belts. There is a fine tea service of Copenhagen china—the plateau has a beautifully executed portrait of Raphael, the other pieces painted with portraits of all the most celebrated painters; in the possession of the Rev. T. Staniforth, of Storrs. See fig. 269.

Fig. 270 is a cabaret, with medallions of landscapes; in Mr. Walker Joy's collection.

France.

ST CLOUD was established about 1695 for the manufacture of porcelain, at which time M. Morin was proprietor, and Chicanneau director of the works. About 1700 Morin died or retired, and Chicanneau became sole proprietor, but he died shorly after.

In the letters patent of 1702, granted to the heirs of Chicanneau, we find that his widow, Barbe Courdray, and her children Jean, Jean Baptiste, Pierre and Genevieve Chicanneau, were interested in the works; that their father had applied himself many years past in the fabrication of fayence, which he had brought to a high state of perfection, and had made many experiments and attempts to discover the secret of true porcelain, and from the year 1696 had produced some nearly equal to the porcelain of China. His children, to whom he imparted the secret, had since his death successfully continued the fabrication, and they were permitted individually or collectively to fabricate porcelain at St. Cloud, or any other part or parts of the kingdom, except Rouen and its faubourgs; this privilege was for ten years. In 1712 a renewal took place for ten years, and in the meantime the widow Barbe Courdray had married a M. Trou.

In 1722 letters patent were granted for twenty years more to Jean and Jean Baptiste Chicanneau, Marie Moreau, the widow of Pierre Chicanneau (third son) and Henri and Gabriel Trou, children of Barbe Courdray by her second marriage.

About this time serious disagreements occurred between the two families, and they separated, Gabriel and Henri Trou remaining at St. Cloud, patronised by the Duke of Orleans; and Marie Moreau opened another establishment in the Rue de la Ville l'Eveque, Faubourg St. Honore, directed by Domenique François Chicanneau. In 1742 another arrêt granted privileges for twenty years to both these establishments, and Marie Moreau dying in 1743, left Domenique her business.

The manufactory at St. Cloud was destroyed by fire (the act of an incendiary) in 1773, and the manufacture ceased, the proprietors not being able to raise sufficient funds to rebuild it.

The earliest mark on the ware was the sun, in compliment to Louis XIV. From 1730 to 1762 the marks were St. C. for St. Cloud, and T for Trou the director, either traced in blue or graved in the ware.

The examples here given are:—Figs. 271 and 272. Two jugs and covers of quilted china in the S. K. Museum; and fig. 273 is a statuette of Astronomy seated, holding the sun, in Lady C. Schreiber's collection.

Rouen. Louis Poterat, Sieur de St. Etienne, of St. Sever, at Rouen, obtained letters patent in 1673, stating that he had discovered processes for fabricating porcelain similar to that of China, and wares resembling those of Delft, but the former was of a very rude character and never arrived at any perfection.

After the establishment at St. Cloud had commenced selling porcelain, the proprietors of the Rouen manufactory appear to have revived their porcelain in the hopes of competing with them, but with no good result.

M. Pottier, of Rouen, has a specimen of what he considers to be Rouen porcelain; and there is another so classed in the Sèvres Museum, but both being unmarked the attribution is very conjectural.

Chantilly. This manufactory was founded in 1725 by Ciquaire Cirou, under the patronage of the Prince de Condé, as appears by letters patent dated 1735, who was succeeded by Antheaume and others. The porcelain was highly esteemed, and there was hardly any object which they did not produce, from the lofty vase to the simplest knife handle. The Chantilly pattern was a great favourite for ordinary services, called "Barbeau," a small blue flower running over the white paste. The mark is a hunting horn in blue or red, frequently accompanied by a letter, indicating the pattern or initial of the painter. Sometimes the horn is impressed and marked in blue on the same piece.

Fig. 274 is a cup and saucer, painted with Chinese flowers, in the S. K. Museum.

MENECY-VILLEROY. This important manufactory was established in 1735 by François Barbin, under the patronage of the Duc de Villeroy. The early specimens are similar to the *porcelaine tendre* of St. Cloud, of a milky translucid appearance.

He was succeeded about 1748 by Messieurs. Jacques and Jullien, and the manufactory continued in a flourishing state until 1773, when on the expiration of the lease it was removed to Bourg la Reine. The mark is usually D V impressed, sometimes traced in colour.

DV

Examples.

Fig. 275 is a sugar basin and spoon, painted with flowers, in the S. K. Museum. Fig. 276, a basket and cover with flowers in relief; Lady C. Schreiber's collection. Fig. 277, a pair of white vases, with flowers in relief; Mr. C. W. Reynolds' collection.

SCEAUX PENTHIEVRE, near Paris. This manufactory was established in 1750 by Jacques Chapelle; it was situated opposite the Petit Châtelet, under the patronage of the Duc de Penthièvre. It was carried on by Glot in 1773. These letters are engraved on the soft clay, and are the usual porcelain marks. The Prince-Pro-

SX

tector died in 1794, but the production of *pâte tendre* ceased before that time. Sometimes the mark of an anchor with the name underneath was used: the Duke being High Admiral of France.

Fig. 278 is a cup and saucer marked with the anchor, and fig. 279 a milk pot painted with poultry, marked S. X. In the collection of Mr. C. W. Reynolds.

ARRAS. Established 1782, by the Demoiselles Deleneur, under the patronage of M. de Calonne, Intendant de Flandre et de l'Artois; it only lasted a few years. The mark is A R, in blue, under the glaze. In 1785 they adopted coal instead of wood for baking the ware.

AR

Fig. 280 is a *seau*, painted with flowers, in the S. K. Museum.

BOULOGNE. A few years since a manufactory of porcelain was established here by M. Haffringue with the kaolin of Limoges. The mark is a square tablet with an anchor and letters in the angles.

Figs. 281 and 282 are two specimens in white biscuit, with bird and cupids in relief. Lady C. Schreiber's collection.

ETIOLLES (Seine et Oise), near Corbeil. *Soft Paste.* Established 1768; Monnier manufacturer. The mark deposed by him at Sèvres was that adjoined. It lasted only a short time.

MP

A service lately in Mr. Reynolds' collection was inscribed on each piece "Etiolles, 1770, Pellevé," the last word being probably the potter's name.

BOURG LA REINE. Established in 1773 by Messieurs Jacques and Jullien, who removed thither on the expiration of their lease at Menecy, and the fabrication was continued, only changing the mark of D.V. to B.R. It was in active existence, making china purely of an industrial character, in 1788.

BR

CLIGNANCOURT. Established in 1775 by Pierre Deruelle,

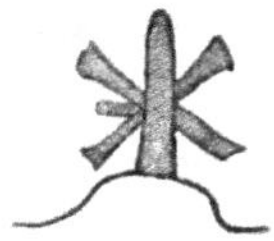

under the patronage of Monsieur le Comte de Provence, brother of the King (afterwards Louis XVIII). The first mark was a windmill, in blue, which is rarely met with, being used so short a time.

This is a later stencilled mark, in red, erroneously supposed to be that of Deruelle, used on pieces in the Chinese style, in hard paste, from 1775 to 1780. In more perfect marks we can trace the letters L. S. X., for the Prince's names, Louis Stanislas Xavier.

Sometimes the letter M and a crown were used for Monsieur the King's brother. It ceased about 1790.

Figs. 283 and 284 are specimens in Mr. Reynolds' collection, and fig. 285 a milk pot, in that of Mr. Walker Joy.

Orleans. This manufactory was established by M. Gerréault in 1753, under the protection of the Duc de Penthièvre, and the porcelain first made here was of the soft paste, but they subsequently produced hard paste. It is marked with a label of three points (*lambel d'Orléans*), in blue, graved in the moist clay. Gerréault was succeeded in the direction of the manufactory of Orleans by Bourdon *fils*, about 1788; Piedor; Dubois; and lastly, Le Brun, from 1808 to 1811. The mark on the *pâte tendre* is composed of a *lambel* of three points, in outline, and a G beneath; on hard porcelain, the *lambel* is filled in with colour. From 1808 to 1811 Benoist Le Brun marked the ware with his initials, in blue or gold, in form of a cipher.

Fig. 286 is a sucrier with medallions of roses, in Mr. Walker Joy's collection.

Luneville. Established 1731, called "Manufacture Stanislas." It lasted only a short time, but a later manufactory, founded about 1769, was celebrated for its productions.

Paul Louis Cyfflé, sculptor, obtained, in 1768, letters patent for fifteen years, by virtue of which he established another manufactory for superior vessels of the material called *terre de Lorraine*, and in the following year a new privilege was granted for making groups and statuettes with his improved paste, under the name of *pâte de marbre*. Cyfflé was born at Bourges in January 1724, and resided at Lunéville as early as 1746, so that it is probable he may have worked at the Stanislas manufactory at Lunéville, his own not being established until 1768. The works of Cyfflé were of biscuit, that is, not covered with glaze, so that the delicacy of the work for which he was remarkable was not destroyed, and gave it a greater resemblance to marble.

There were some very important groups made here stamped "Terre de Lorraine," probably the same as noticed by Horace Walpole, in his Catalogue of Strawberry Hill, as the "Biscuit de Nancy."

NIDERVILLER. This important manufactory was established about 1760 by Jean Louis, Baron de Beyerlé. After successfully carrying on this branch for several years, he attempted hard porcelain in 1768, and procured potters and artists from Saxony. In his new enterprise he was equally successful, sparing no expense to procure the best modellers, both in fayence and porcelain, assisted by Paul Louis Cyfflé, of Lunéville, and others. Three or four years before his death, which happened in 1784, the estate was bought by General de Custine. This new proprietor continued the *fabrique*, under the direction of M. Lanfray, who paid especial attention to the production of fine porcelain; the fabrication of statuettes was greatly increased, the best of which were modelled by MM. Lemire and Favot, from Lunéville.

After the decapitation of the unfortunate M. de Custine, his estates, being forfeited to the Republic, were sold on the 25 Germinal, An X (1802), to M. Lanfray, and carried on by him until his death in 1827. His marks during this time on painted pieces and figures were the name of the town stamped, or his own initial stencilled. On the 25th Nov., 1827, the manufactory was sold to M. L. G. Dryander, of Sarrebruck, who is the present proprietor. For many years he continued to make porcelain, as well as fayence groups and statuettes, but the distance of his *fabrique* from the kaolin of St. Yrieix prevented him competing successfully with those of Limoges, and this branch was abandoned.

The marks used here were various, sometimes on the early pieces we find B. N. for Beyerlé, Nidervillers, but usually two C's crossed, sometimes surmounted by a Count's coronet. On late specimens Lanfray placed his initials F. C. L. in monogram, stencilled in blue.

Fig. 287 is a cup and saucer, in Mr. Walker Joy's collection.

Boissette, near Melun. Established in 1777 by Jacques Vermonet *père et fils*, which lasted only a short time. A tea pot, painted with bouquets of flowers, is in Mr. Reynolds's collection; see fig. 288.

Caen, Normandy. This manufactory was established, and supported by some of the principal inhabitants, at the time of the French Revolution (about 1793), when several workmen from Sèvres came to join it. It was carried on for a few years in the Rue Montagne près les Moulins, at Caen, but finding no market for the china, the manufacture was discontinued in the commencement of the present century, and the stock divided among the parties concerned; as it never became an article of commerce, it is rarely met with. The china is hard paste, and equal to that of Sèvres, and of the same forms. A tea cup and saucer, delicately painted with gold and green festoons, and small square medallions of landscapes in Indian ink, with the word "Caen" stencilled in red, is in the collection of the Rev. T. Staniforth, Storrs, Windermere, represented in fig. 289.

Valenciennes (Nord) 1785. By an Order of Council, dated 24th May, 1785, Mons. Fauquet is permitted to carry on a manufacture of porcelain at Valenciennes. In 1775 he married a lady named Lamoninary. The initials of their names, as well as the letter V, appear on some specimens. M. Fauquet

was originally established at St. Amand in the manufacture of fayence as early as 1775, and probably carried on both simultaneously.

ST. AMAND LES EAUX. Founded by M. Maximilian De Bettignies in 1815, for the manufacture of porcelain *pâte tendre*, like the old Sèvres. He was formerly proprietor of the Tournay manufactory, which he ceded to his brother Henri when that city became re-annexed to Belgium. Of all the manufactures of *pâte tendre*, these are now the only two in Europe which continue the specialty, and from the nature of their products they more closely resemble the *vieux Sèvres* than any other. Some specimens of modern manufacture were sent to the London Exposition in 1862.

STRASBOURG, 1752. Established by Paul Hanong. About the year 1752 he obtained the secret of true porcelain from Ringler, but in consequence of the monopoly of Sèvres he was compelled to relinquish it, and in 1753 removed to Frankenthal, where he was received with open arms, and in 1761 greatly flourished under the protection of the Elector Palatine Carl Theodore. The Strasbourg marks are those of Hanung, as in the margin.

Fig. 290 is a milk pot with landscapes; Mr. Reynolds' collection.

MARSEILLES. An important manufactory of porcelain was established here by Jacques Gaspard Robert about 1766, and was in full activity on the visit of the Comte de Provence in 1777, who especially noticed a large vase, finely modelled, a complete service expressly made for England, and porcelain flowers delicately copied from nature, like those of Sèvres. The order from England, where so many important china manufactories already existed, shows it was renowned at that time. Porcelain was made also by Honoré Savy and Veuve Perrin, but was only of secondary importance. It was closed about the period of the French Revolution in 1793.

PARIS. Rue Thiroux. 1778. André Marie Lebeuf manu-

facturer; called "Porcelaine de la Reine." The mark is A. under a crown, for Antoinette (it was under the protection of Marie Antoinette), stencilled in red.

Fig. 292 is a sucrier, in the possession of Mr Walker Joy.

PARIS. Rue de Bondy. 1780. Dihl and Guerhard manufacturers, under the patronage of the Duc d'Angoulême; called "Porcelaine d'Angoulême." The name of the fabrique is sometimes written or stencilled at length.

Fig. 293 is a cup and saucer. Mr. Walker Joy's collection.

PARIS. Rue de Fontaine au Roi, called "De la Courtille." Established 1773 by Jean Baptiste Locré, afterwards joined by Russinger in 1784, who during the Revolution was sole director. The mark is composed of two flambeaux crossed, in blue, and not two arrows as usually given.

Fig. 294 is part of a tea service in the S. K. Museum.

PARIS. Pont aux Choux. *Manufacture du Duc d'Orleans.* On the 22nd of April, 1784, Louis Honoré de la Marre de Villars opened an establishment for the manufacture of porcelain in the Rue des Boulets, Faubourg St. Antoine. The mark deposited was M.J. It was afterwards disposed of to Jean Baptiste Outrequin de Montarcy and Edme Toulouse, who in Aug., 1786, obtained a brêvet from the Duke of Orleans, Louis Philippe Joseph, and authority to sign the productions with the letters L. P. and take the title of "Manufacture de M. le Duc d'Orleans." They were afterwards established in Rue Amelot, *au Pont-aux-Choux*, by which name the porcelain is generally known.

This mark ceased in 1793, with the condemnation of the Duke of Orleans, and the works subsequently produced were inscribed merely "*Fabrique du Pont-aux-Choux.*" These letters are marked in blue beneath a porcelain tea pot, painted with sprigs of flowers, in the Rev. T. Stainforth's collection, see fig. 295.

PARIS. Rue de Crussol. Established 1789 by Charles Potter, an Englishman; called the "Prince of Wales's China;" the mark is *in red*. The next is a similar mark *in blue*, the top letter being B, is on a canary coloured cup and saucer, painted with flowers and butterflies; in the collection of the Rev. T. Staniforth, see fig. 296. These two marks are on separate pieces of the same service, one marked in red, the other in blue; in Mr. Reynolds' collection.

R
C·P
1

B
Potter
42

PARIS. Formerly Belleville, and now Fontainebleau; established 1790 by Jacob Petit. The mark is blue, in the moist clay. This manufactory is still carried on at 54, Rue Paradis Poissonnière, and the Depôt, 32, Rue de Bondy. The products of the first period were much esteemed, being well painted and well modelled, bearing his mark, but recently the proprietor has unwisely altered his original plan and imitates Dresden, counterfeiting also the mark of the crossed swords, a practice which cannot be too much reprehended, as it is the cause of much deception. Jacob Petit also makes biscuit figures, birds' nests, flowers, &c. In 1853, he patented in England some improvements in porcelain, which consisted in having raised surfaces and painting the same, the combination being claimed.

J.P.

PARIS. Fabrique du Charles Philippe Comte d'Artois, afterwards Charles X, 1769. We read in the *Guide des Amateurs*, printed in Paris, 1787:—"This manufacture in the Rue du Faubourg St. Denis is the most ancient of all those established in Paris. Hanüng of Strasbourg, who brought into France the secret of hard porcelain, formed the first establishment in 1769. Having obtained the protection of Charles Philippe, Comte d'Artois, it is called by his name." It belonged actually to Bourdon des Planches, who continued the fabrication of hard porcelain, &c., and it was discontinued in 1810.

VINCENNES. 1786. There was a porcelain manufactory here, directed by M. Le Maire, probably the same who founded that in Rue Popincourt, which was ceded to M. Nast in 1783. M. Jacquemart thinks the L. P. under a crown belongs to this *fabrique*, and that it was under the protection of Louis Philippe Duc de Chartres, afterwards King of the French. There were four establishments at Vincennes; the first by the brothers Dubois, subsequently transferred to Sèvres; the second by Maurin des Aubiez, in 1767; the third by Pierre Antoine Hannong; and the fourth that described above.

SEVRES.

The history of the celebrated manufactory at Sèvres must be traced back to that of St. Cloud, which, we have seen, was founded as early as 1695. Here Louis XIV. accorded his patronage and favour by granting exclusive privileges. In 1735 the secret of the manufacture was carried, by some of the workmen, to Chantilly, and for a time continued there by the brothers Dubois. They left in a few years, taking with them their secret, and settled at Vincennes, where a laboratory was granted them, but after three years they were dismissed.

In 1745, a sculptor, named Charles Adam, formed a company, and the scheme was approved of by the King, privileges being accorded them for thirty years, and a place granted for their works in the Château de Vincennes. In 1753 the privilege of Charles Adam was purchased by Eloy Brichard, and Louis XV. took a third share; hence it became a Royal establishment. Madame de Pompadour greatly encouraged the ceramic art, and it arrived at great perfection. The buildings were found too small to meet the increasing demands for their beautiful productions, and in 1756 they removed to a large edifice at Sèvres, built expressly for the company.

The Vincennes porcelain is now much esteemed; a

favourite decoration was flowers and birds, on a beautiful *bleu de Roi* ground, and cupids painted in *camaieu* of a single colour. The mark at first was the double L, without any letter denoting the date, and after 1753 (when the dating commenced) the letters A B and C are found enclosed within the cipher, after which it merges into the Sèvres category.

In 1760 the King became sole proprietor, and M. Boileau was appointed director. By a decree of council, made in this year, Sèvres had the exclusive privilege of making porcelain, plain or painted, gilt or ungilt, ornaments in relief, sculpture, flowers or figures. Certain *fabriques*, which had already privileges granted them, were allowed to continue their works of white porcelain painted in blue, with Chinese patterns only; the employment of any other colour, especially gilding and making figures and flowers, was strictly prohibited. Even the makers of fayence were prohibited using coloured grounds in medallions or otherwise, or gilding.

About 1761 the secret of making hard porcelain was purchased of Pierre Antoine, the son and successor of Paul Hanüng, for an annuity of 3,000 livres (£120.), and the manufacture of the *pâte tendre* being expensive, and liable to accidents in the furnace, it was deemed important to substitute hard paste. Although possessed of the secret they had not the means of producing it, being unable to procure the *kaolin* necessary, until accident led to the discovery of some quarries yielding it in abundance at St. Yrieix, near Limoges.

In 1769, after Macquer had brought the ware to perfection. the manufacture was successfully established at Sèvres, and both descriptions of china continued to be made until 1804, when, Brongniart being director, soft paste was altogether discontinued, and declared to be "useless in art, of expensive manipulation, dangerous to the workmen, subject to great risk in the furnace, &c."

It is a remarkable fact that the Sèvres Museum, so rich in specimens of other *fabriques* of France, possesses no collection of the grand vases or groups made at the Royal manufactory in the latter half of the last century, but the moulds are preserved, and many of the choicest pieces have been reproduced in plaster.

The principal colours used in decorating the ground of the Sèvres vases were—

1. The *bleu celeste*, or turquoise, invented in 1752 by Hellot.

2. The rich cobalt blue, called *bleu de Roi*, of which there were two varieties, the darker being designated *gros bleu*.

3. The *violet pensée*, a beautiful violet from a mixture of manganese, one of the rarest decorations of the *pâte tendre*.

4. The *rose Pompadour* (called in England *rose Du-Barry*), a charming pink or rose colour invented in 1757 by Xrhouet of Sèvres.

5. The clear yellow or "jonquille," a sort of canary colour.

6. The *vert pré*, or bright grass green.

7. The *vert pomme*, or apple green.

8. The *rouge de fer*, a brilliant red; and the *œil de perdrix* was at a later period a favourite ornament for the grounds of vases.

The forms are exceedingly varied, but names are assigned to each, either from the designers of the models or their special shapes or ornamentation; these may be found at length in *Marks and Monograms on Pottery and Porcelain*, 3rd edit.

This beautiful ware, *pâte tendre*, was always much esteemed, and never could have been produced at a reasonable price even at the time it was made, the expensive decoration as well as the risk in firing being so great, and manufactured for Royal presents or occasionally sold by express permission at exorbitant prices, and they bore a more approximate value to the present exorbitant prices than is generally supposed. There might have been and were opportunities of buying specimens of *vieux Sèvres* during the turmoils of the Revolution at reasonable prices, and in the first quarter of the present century they were to be obtained. It was during that period that George IV. when Prince Regent formed the magnificent collection now the property of Her Majesty. But those times are past, and anybody desiring to possess choice specimens must not object to pay £1,000. for a fine vase, or from £50 to £100. for a cup and saucer.

There are doubtless finer collections of Sèvres china in England than any other country of Europe; and the specimens exhibited at the South Kensington Museum in 1862 must have much astonished the foreign visitors who came over to the International Exhibition, although that was only a small portion of the Sèvres keramic treasures existing in this country.

The decree of 1753 directs the use of letters to denote the date of manufacture of every piece, to be placed within the double L; thus the letter A signifies that it was made in 1753; when the alphabet was gone through, double letters were used, as A A for 1778, ending with R R in 1795.

Then came the first Republican epoch, 1792 to 1804, in which the letters F. R. were substituted. Next the first Imperial epoch from 1804 to 1814; and the second Royal epoch,

1814 to 1848, during this the King's initials were adopted. Then the second

Republican epoch, 1848 to 1851; and lastly, the second Imperial epoch in 1852 up to the present time.

In addition to this date-mark the initial or signs adopted by the painter and gilder were placed upon the ware; we can therefore not only tell the exact year in which any piece was made, but the name of the decorator, from books in the Sèvres manufactory, where the signs and names were entered. These are given, *in extenso*, in Chaffers' *Marks and Monograms on Pottery and Porcelain*, third edition, pages 454 to 466.

Examples.

Fig. 297. An ecuelle, dated 1771; (Bernal collection) S. K. Museum.

Fig. 298. A biscuit group, Cupid and Psyche; S. K. Museum.

Fig. 299. A boat-shaped vase, painted with cupids; in Her Majesty the Queen's collection.

Fig. 300. A vase (*vaisseau à mat*), painted with landscapes and figures; in Her Majesty the Queen's collection.

England.

POTTERY.

THE earthenware vessels previous to the XVIth Century were of a very coarse description, rudely fashioned and devoid of ornament, but occasionally covered with a yellow or green glaze, sometimes cast in a mould in grotesque forms. Numerous specimens of early English cups are found in excavations in London, and other parts of England, which may be identified by comparing them with the vessels in Norman and Mediæval manuscripts.

But many other materials were fashioned into drinking cups; in wood we find a curious square drinking vessel called the mether, which required some dexterity in handling lest the liquor should be spilled: this was used in Ireland. A very interesting specimen called the Dunvegan cup, in the possession of Colonel Macleod, is of this form, mounted in silver, and bearing an inscription of the Xth Century.

In England the peg tankard was much used, so called from a number of pegs inside, at equal distances, to regulate the quantity to be taken by each person when passed round a table; these were frequently handsomely carved with religious subjects. Another description of wooden drinking cup was the mazer bowl, so called from the German word *mæser*—maple.

Leather bottles and jugs called black jacks were much used in England; the bottle was generally barrel-shaped, and carried by travellers; its praises are recorded in the old English ballad of the XVIth Century, each verse concluding with the couplet—

> "I wish in heaven his soul may dwell
> Who first found out the leather bottell."

The gourd, pumpkin, cocoa-nut, and other fruits with a hard rind or shell were undoubtedly the most primitive vessels, being formed ready for use, and were frequently mounted in silver.

During the XVIth and XVIIth Centuries glass was used by the rich, especially that which came from Venice, but from its fragile nature was very expensive wear. For plates and dishes a harder and more durable material was required, and wooden trenchers or pewter platters were generally in use.

A French writer in 1558, named Etienne Perlin, in his description of England, says: "The English drink beer not out of glasses but from earthen pots, the covers and handles made of silver for the rich; the middle classes mount theirs in tin, the poorer sort use beer pots made of wood."

The earthen vessels made in England, although inexpensive, were badly burned, and not very durable; and the German stone ware with a salt glaze was eagerly sought after throughout the XVIth Century, and imported in large quantities. These stone pots were usually impressed with the arms of German towns; a rose or other device in front, and a ferocious bearded visage under the spout. They were called Bellarmines, after the celebrated Cardinal Bellarmin, who in the XVIth Century made himself so conspicuous by his zealous opposition to the Reformed religion, and were derisively called after him.

These bellarmines were in general use throughout England in the XVIth and beginning of the XVIIth Centuries at inns and public houses to serve ale to the customers; they were of various sizes, the galonier which held eight pints, the pottle pot four pints, the quart and the pint. The importation of these stone pots was almost monopolized by the Cologne potters, near which city they were made. In the reign of Queen Elizabeth we find one William Simpson presenting a memorial that he may be allowed to bring "the drinking stone pottes made at Culloin" into this country, and requests permission to make such like stone pots in England; but he was not successful in his suit.

In 1626, however, two other potters, named Rous and Cullyn, merchants of the city of London, obtained the exclusive privilege of making stone pots and jugs in this country, and a patent was granted them for fourteen years; the preamble states that "heretofore, and at this present, our kingdom of England has been served with stone pottes, stone jugges, and stone bottells, out of foreign parts, from beyond the seas."

STAFFORDSHIRE.

When Dr. Plot wrote his natural history of this county in 1686 there were very few manufactories of pottery; he only speaks of one at Amblecott and another at Wednesbury; but he says: "The greatest pottery they have in this country is carried on at Burslem, near Newcastle-under-Lyme." The earthenware made here towards the end of the XVIIth Century was of a very coarse character, and the decoration extremely rude, consisting merely of patterns trailed over the surface in coloured clay, technically termed *slip*, diluted to the consistence of syrup, so that it could run out through a quill. The usual colours of these slips were orange, white and red, the orange forming the ground and the white and red the paint. After the dishes were thus ornamented they were glazed with lead ore, beaten into dust, finely sifted, and strewed over the surface, which gave it the gloss but not the colour. The vessels remained twenty-four hours in the kiln, and were then drawn for sale, which was principally to poor cratemen, who carried them at their backs all over the country for sale.

The forms of these vessels were tygs or mugs, with two

or more handles for passing round a table, candlesticks, dishes, &c. The earliest names we find upon them are Thomas and Ralph Toft, William Talor, Joseph Glass; all names still known in Staffordshire.

Examples.

Fig. 301. A tyg, with four handles, dated 1621.

Fig. 302. A mug, with two handles, dated 1682.

Figs. 303 and 304. Two tea pots; all of these are in the Geological Museum.

Fig. 305. A plateau, with Charles II. and his Queen in relief, by Ralph Toft, 1677.

WEDGWOOD.

The family of Wedgwood was of long standing at Burslem, and many members of it were engaged in making pottery long before the birth of the great potter, Josiah Wedgwood. His father, grandfather, and great-grandfather were all engaged in the trade, as well as many of his relations. Josiah Wedgwood was born in 1730, at Burslem; he was the youngest of thirteen children; his father, Thomas Wedgwood, died when Josiah was only nine years old. His eldest brother, Thomas, succeeded his father as a potter, and Josiah was bound apprentice to him in 1744. During his apprenticeship he was seized with a violent attack of the small-pox, which left its effects in his system, and settled in his legs, and this disorder continued with him until manhood; an accidental bruise, however, resulted in the amputation of his leg in the thirty-fourth year of his age. A short time after the expiration of his apprenticeship he left his brother's house to make knife handles, imitation agate, and tortoiseshell small wares, at Stoke, where, in 1752, he entered into partnership with John Harrison, but in two years they separated.

In 1754 Josiah Wedgwood went into partnership with Thomas Whieldon of Fenton Low, one of the most eminent potters of his day, and they remained together five years, the principal manufactures being tortoiseshell plates and dishes, cauliflower jugs, tea pots with crab-stock handles, agate knife handles, and small wares generally; while here he also produced that fine green glaze which covered his dessert services, in imitation of leaves.

In 1759 the partnership expired, and he returned to Burslem, and in his twenty-ninth year commenced business on his own account at the "Churchyard" works, where he was born. Here he set himself earnestly to work, improving the manufacture of pottery, and soon became so successful that he was compelled to enlarge his establishment, and took the "Ivy House" works. He engaged the services of his cousin, Thomas Wedgwood, who had gained his experience at the Worcester works, and in 1765 he took him into partnership. The first ware which gained him reputation was his fine cream-coloured ware, which remained a staple article from 1762 down to the time of his decease, and after Royalty had approved of it the name was changed to Queen's ware. His cousin Thomas had the superintendence of this particular department, which he designated the *useful* branch. In 1768 Josiah took into partnership Thomas Bentley, and to him was entrusted the *ornamental* branch, both departments being kept perfectly distinct (as far as the interests of his partners were concerned).

Wedgwood also produced, about this date, a sort of red ware, formed of the same ochreous clay used by the Elers nearly a century before; it required no glaze except what it derived from friction on the wheel and lathe, and was covered with engine-turned ornament; and in 1766 a black ware, which he called basaltes or black Egyptian. These manufactures were not confined to his works; other potters made vast quantities of it; but Wedgwood made great improvements in the bodies and forms of the ware, and was rewarded by a vast accumulation of business; so much so that he was compelled to open a new manufactory at Etruria. Having shortly before taken out his patent (the only invention he ever secured by patent) for encaustic painting on copies of Etruscan vases, his first essays at the new works were a set of these, now preserved in the family, inscribed "One of the first day's productions at Etruria in Staffordshire, by Wedgwood and Bentley, June 13, 1769." These were of black basaltes, with encaustic paintings of classical subjects. Wedgwood himself threw these vases, while Bentley turned the lathe.

In 1773 he made "a fine white terra cotta of great beauty and delicacy, proper for cameos, portraits and bas reliefs;" this was the forerunner of the jasper ware, which became by constant attention and successive improvements the most beautiful of all his wares. In 1776 the solid jasper ware was invented, which, however, attained its greatest perfection ten years later.

In the manufacture of this elegant ware Wedgwood largely employed sulphate of barytes, and for many years derived great profits, none of the workmen having any idea of the nature of the material upon which they were operating, until a letter containing a bill of parcels of a quantity of the article fell into the hands of a dishonest servant, who told the secret, and deprived the inventor of that particular source of emolument; for when the same article was made by those who employed inferior workmen, to whom they only paid one-fourth of the salary given by Wedgwood, the price of jasper ware became so reduced that he was unable to employ those exquisite modellers whom he had formerly engaged to superintend that branch of the manufacture.

The celebrated service made for the Empress Catherine of Russia was of Queen's ware; it was commenced in 1773, and had upwards of 1,200 views of seats of the nobility and gentry of England, and being for the Grenouilliere Palace each piece had upon it a green frog. The price paid for this service was £3,000.

In 1780 Thomas Bentley, the friend and partner of Josiah Wedgwood, died, and in 1781 the stock in London, so far as related to their partnership, was sold at Christie's; the sale lasted twelve days.

In 1785 a "jasper dip" was introduced, in which the white clay vessels were dipped, and received a coating of jasper, instead of being jasper throughout, which was considered a great improvement, and caused an increase of 20 per cent. in the price.

In 1787 the Portland Museum was sold by auction, and the gem of all others Wedgwood coveted was the celebrated Barberini vase, made of glass of two strata, dark blue and opaque white, the ornaments on the surface being cut from the solid, in the same manner as an onyx cameo. This vase was of Roman work, of the IInd or IIIrd Century of our era. Wedgwood desired to become the possessor, but finding he would be opposed by the Duke of Portland, it was arranged that the Duke should buy the vase, and lend it to Wedgwood for the purpose of copying. It was sold for £1,029. He was restricted from moulding it, lest any injury should result, and it was therefore modelled by Webber after the original. The material in which it was produced was black jasper, which was apparently black, with the slightest possible tinge of blue; in Wedgwood's own words, "a mixture of blue and black, and then dipped in black," the figures being in white relief. Fig. 306 represents one of these vases in the Geological Museum.

The principal inventions of Wedgwood, as enumerated in his Catalogue of 1788, were—

1. The cream-coloured table ware, afterwards Queen's ware.
2. Terra cotta, made to represent porphyry, granite, &c.
3. Basaltes or black Egyptian ware, imitation bronzes, &c.
4. White porcelain biscuit.
5. Bamboo, a cream-coloured porcelain biscuit.
6. Jasper, a porcelain that would receive throughout its whole substance, from the mixture of metallic oxides, the same colours as they would communicate to glass or enamels in fusion, very applicable to the production of cameos, portraits, &c., that require to be shown in bas-relief, since the ground can be made of any colour while the raised parts are pure white.
7. A porcelain biscuit, exceedingly hard, resisting the

strongest acids or corrosive substances, very useful in laboratories and for mortars.

The modelling bills from 1773 to 1775 inclusive, are still preserved among the Mayer MSS., which, although but a small portion of the whole, permit us to individualize many well-known and interesting objects. Messrs. Hoskins and Grant's bills for plaster casts, prepared to mould from, contain the names of the busts, and the prices paid for them :—Zeno, Pindar, Faustina, Germanicus, Antoninus Pius, Seneca, Augustus, Cato, Marcus Aurelius, Homer, Antinous, Solon, and Plato, at 21s. each; Inigo Jones, Palladio, and others, at 25s.; Venus de Medicis, 15s.; large Marcus Aurelius, 31s. 6d.; four ovals of the Elements, 36s.; small busts in pairs, of Swift and Milton, Virgil and Horace, Locke and Newton, Beaumont and Fletcher, &c., at 10s. 6d. and 12s. each; Harvey and Newton, 50s. the pair; and many others.

Wedgwood, in a letter to Bentley, August, 1774, says :—"These busts are much better finished than the plaster casts or models we take them from. Hackwood bestows a week upon each head in restoring it to what we suppose it was when it came out of the hands of the statuary. Pray do not let our labour be unobserved when they are under your care. It is a fortnight's work to prepare and mould one of these heads."

Webber, a modeller of uncommon ability, was recommended to Wedgwood by Sir W. Chambers and Sir Joshua Reynolds, and shortly after the death of Mr. Bentley he took the management of the ornamental department; many fine bas-reliefs are by his hand.

Flaxman was engaged by Wedgwood and Bentley as early as 1775, and he continued furnishing them with drawings and models up to the time of his departure for Rome in 1787. After Bentley's death in 1780 Flaxman's fame as a sculptor obtained him more important work, but still, as time permitted, he worked for Wedgwood.

When Flaxman went to Italy in 1787 he arranged to execute occasionally some models, but principally to suggest.

overlook, and give finishing touches to the works of the Italian artists who were employed in copying from the antique under the direction of Angelo Dalmazoni. Pacetti's works were numerous, as well as those of Angelini. Fratoddi and Mangiarotti were cameo engravers; they copied on shells some of the finest antique gems. Manzolini and Cades were also employed in Italy for Wedgwood.

The tablets, friezes and other subjects in bas-relief were modelled by the artists in red wax, being a composition of bees' wax and a few drops of turpentine, coloured with vermilion, on slabs of fine slate.

From these originals, casts were taken in plaster of Paris for ordinary use, but subsequently the working casts were made of clay, and baked, which made them everlasting; but as they shrank considerably in the firing, the originals had to be made proportionately larger to allow for it.

These models were packed in wooden boxes and sent to England *via* Leghorn, and to guard against accidents they were forwarded by one ship, and casts of them by another. With so many artists employed, these models were very numerous, and many of them have been erroneously attributed to Flaxman.

Josiah Wedgwood died on 3rd of Jan., 1795 in his 65th year.

Examples.

306. The Portland vase of black and white jasper.

307. Vase of blue jasper, the Muses.

308. Tripod of black Egyptian, supported by three figures.

309. Tea pot, caddy and plate, printed transfer.

310. Card of jasper cameos; in the Geological Museum.

311. Vase of basaltes, subjects in relief; S. K. Museum.

312. Jasper plaque, Bacchanalian Sacrifice, 24 in. by 10 in.; in Mr. John J. Bagshawe's collection.

313. Three vases, granite ground, with gilt festoons and handles of female figures; in Mr. John J. Bagshawe's collection.

313*. Ewer of agate ware, by Wedgwood and Bentley; in Mr. Emerson Norman's collection.

In 1773, RALPH SHAWE of *Burslem* made great improvements in the manufacture, and took out a patent for chocolate coloured ware, striped with white and lined with white, glazed with salt.

RALPH WOOD was established at Burslem about 1730, and was succeeded by his son AARON WOOD about 1750; he served his apprenticeship to Dr. Thos. Wedgwood, and was a very clever cutter of moulds for stoneware plates and dishes, with raised pattern borders, &c., which have been erroneously termed Elizabethan. A large collection of his ware, with the moulds, &c., are in the S. K. Museum. Cream ware is said to have been invented by him. He was succeeded by his son ENOCH WOOD about 1770, who was a sculptor, and made many busts of eminent men. His successors were Wood and Caldwell, who continued the manufacture of busts and groups.

Examples—Fig. 314 is a granite obelisk by Ralph Wood, about 1730, in the Geological Museum. Fig. 315, a fine statuette of Chaucer by the same; in the possession of Rev. T. Staniforth. Figs. 316 to 318, a tea set of white crouch ware, by Aaron Wood.

ASTBURY of *Shelton*, early in the 18th century, made red, crouch, and white stone ware. It is said he derived his knowledge of mixing the clays by pretending to be an idiot, and obtained employment at the Elers manufactory at Bradwell, and after gaining their secret, he set up in business against them.

The discovery of using calcined flints as an ingredient in the composition of pottery is attributed to the younger Astbury, which led to the manufacture of fine fayence, and paved the way for the great improvements afterwards achieved by Wedgwood. The story is thus told: While travelling to London on horseback, he had occasion to seek a remedy for a disorder in his horse's eyes, when the ostler of the Inn by burning a flint reduced it to a fine powder, which he blew into them. The potter observing the beautiful white colour of the flint after calcination, instantly conceived the use to which it might be employed in his art, and this is said to have been the origin of the first white flint stone ware.*

The potter to whom Staffordshire was indebted for great improvements in the ware was JOHN PHILIP ELERS, who about 1690 came over from Holland and settled at Bradwell. He was descended from a noble family of Saxony; his father, Martin Elers, married the daughter of a rich Burgomaster of *Amsterdam;* his daughter married Sir W. Phipps, ancestor of the Marquis of Normanby, and John Philip Elers' grand-daughter, Maria Elers, married Richard Lovell Edgeworth, (father of the authoress Maria Edgeworth).

John Philip Elers was a clever chemist, which enabled him to discover the art of mixing the clays of the neighbourhood to greater perfection than had ever been attained in *Staffordshire*, and by carefully levigating them, and sifting through fine hair sieves, he manufactured to a considerable extent an improved kind of red pottery, in imitation of that of Japan, and by the addition of manganese to the clays, he made a fine black ware, which a century afterwards was adopted and improved by Wedgwood, and termed Black Egyptian, or Basaltes.

The specimens yet preserved, by their excellence in grain, texture, and shape, will ever manifest the skill and success of Elers. They were ornamented in relief, with sharp and well designed flowers and leaves, especially the tea leaf—by copper moulds, and afterwards turned on the outside upon the lathe in tea services, &c.

Fig. 320 is a tea pot of red ware, with flowers in relief by Elers, in the Geological Museum.

MOSES STEEL was a manufacturer at *Burslem* in 1715. The name of a descendant is found on a vase, blue ground with white figures in relief, in the style of Wedgwood, in the Geological Museum, fig. 319.

---

* John Dwight, of Fulham, used "calcined, beaten and sifted flints" in the composition of his wares, nearly fifty years before Astbury is here stated to have made the discovery.

SAMUEL HOLLINS of *Shelton*, established about 1760 a manufactory of fine red ware tea pots, he procured the clay from Bradwell. He was succeeded about 1777 by T. and J. HOLLINS. In the Geological Museum is a green bowl with ornaments in relief, signed "S. Hollins" (fig. 321), and a basin in the same collection (fig. 322) is of white ground with blue figures in relief, similar to Wedgwood, stamped T. and J. Hollins.

At SHELTON the New Hall China Works owe their origin to the purchase of Champion's (Cookworthy's) patent by a company of potters in 1777, and was the first porcelain manufactory in Staffordshire. In despite of the opposition of Wedgwood and the potters of that county, the patent had been extended, and the new company consisted of Messrs. Samuel Hollins, of Shelton; Anthony Keeling, of Tunstall; John Turner, of Lane End; Peter (or Jacob) Warburton, of Hot Lane; William Clowes, of Port Hill; and Charles Bagnall, of Shelton. The ware made here was not of a fine character, and inferior artists were employed, and was never in great estimation. It consequently soon fell to decay, after many changes. The mark is the name of the works in a double ring. Fig. 323 is a cup and saucer painted with flowers; S. K. Museum.

Shaw mentions a Mr. MILES, of Miles's Bank, *Hanley*, who produced the brown stone ware about 1700. There is in the Geological Museum a fayence barrel supported by four Cupids, of brown glaze with gilt hoops, resting on a stage with four supports; of good work, apparently the first half of the XVIIIth century, impressed with the name of Miles; see fig. 324.

ELIJAH MAYER, of *Hanley*, was a contemporary of Wedgwood. He was noted for his cream coloured ware and brown line ware, but he produced many other varieties. In the Geological Museum is a vase of unglazed drab terra cotta, with festoons, &c., in relief, coloured; see fig. 325.

The basaltes or black Egyptian ware tea services, with animals, &c., in relief, are well known. Another popular service was one made to commemorate Nelson's victories of the Nile and Trafalgar, with crocodiles, pyramids, Britannia, Fame, and monument inscribed, "Pro patria," and tablet with Nelson, &c. These are usually impressed with E. Mayer's name.

PALMER, of *Hanley*, was a great pirate of Wedgwood's inventions, and Mrs. Palmer, who seems to have been the active manager of her husband's business, engaged persons surreptitiously to obtain Wedgwood and Bentley's new patterns as soon as they arrived at the London warehouse, for the purpose of copying them. Palmer had a London partner of the name of NEALE. They imitated his black Egyptian vases and other inventions, and eventually his Etruscan painted vases, but these being secured by patent, (the only one Wedgwood ever took out), an injunction was served upon them for an infringement, which ended in a compromise—Palmer purchasing a share in the patent. In 1776 he failed, and the business was carried on by Neale & Co., who by some means discovered the secret of the jasper body. From specimens we have seen, they were formidable rivals of Wedgwood.

Fig. 326 is a punch barrel by Neale, of fine fayence, painted in flowers and musical instruments, resting on a square pedestal, with nymphs and satyrs in relief, the cover surmounted by Silenus; in the S. K. Museum.

Fig. 327. A square jardinière of blue and white jasper; in the Geological Museum.

J. VOYEZ, of *Hanley*, was a clever artist, he was in the employ of Wedgwood, and afterwards with Neale and Palmer.

Fig. 328 is a fayence vase of good form, with leaves, masks and festoons in relief; in the collection of the Rev. T. Staniforth.

Fig. 329 is a fine black basaltes vase, with a sculptured medallion of Prometheus, signed by J. Voyez, 1769; in Sir T. W. Holburne's collection.

THOMAS WHEILDON, of *Fenton*, established a pottery in 1740; besides the common household articles, he made fancy marbled ware, such as agate knife handles, chimney ornaments, tortoiseshell and melon dessert services, black glazed tea and coffee services, &c. Aaron Wood was his apprentice, and made models for pickle leaves, crabstock handles, cabbage leaf spouts for tea pots, &c. Josiah Spode was also his apprentice, and Josiah Wedgwood was in partnership with him until 1759.

ENOCH BOOTH, of *Tunstall*, and WARBURTON of *Cobridge* in the same county, were extensive potters, and first made the cream coloured pottery on the improvement of Booth's fluid glaze.

JOHN TURNER, of *Lane End*, made a fine description of ware, and his is the most successful imitation of Wedgwood's jasper, with ornaments in relief, and only second to his in excellence; he also made a fine white stone ware.

Fig. 330 represents a sugar basin of yellow clay, with figures in relief; Geological Museum.

Fig. 330A. A tea pot, with medallion of figures in relief; Mr. E. Norman.

WILLIAM ADAMS, of *Tunstall*, was a favorite pupil of Wedgwood, and while with him, executed some of his finest specimens of jasper ware. He afterwards went into business on his own account, and by his great care, and the knowledge he had attained in Wedgwood's service, carried on an extensive trade, for the knowledge of the mixture of the clays by the introduction of sulphate of barytes in the making of Wedgwood's jasper, was very generally known long before his death.

Fig. 334 is a jug of blue jasper in imitation of Wedgwood, in the Geological Museum.

Fig. 335. A beautiful jasper plaque, with Diana in relief, belonging to Mr. Jno. J. Bagshawe.

The Messrs. DAVENPORT, of *Longport*, made great improvements in the manufacture of earthenware, they were celebrated especially for their stone china; the manufactory was established in 1793, and has been successfully carried on up to the present day in the same family.

Figs. 331 and 332 are examples of his ware, in the Geological Museum.

Miles Mason, of *Lane Delph*, early in the present century produced some fine ware. The ironstone china was brought to great perfection by Charles James Mason, and the forms were of a high character, very much resembling porcelain.

Fig. 336 is a cup, cover and saucer, by Mason, in the Geological Museum.

Thomas Minton established a manufactory at *Stoke-upon-Trent* in 1791, he was apprenticed to Turner of Caughley as an engraver. His productions were of the useful kind, viz.: services for the table, and he made porcelain very much in the style of Worcester. He died in 1836, and was succeeded by his second son, the celebrated Herbert Minton, who brought the potter's art to the greatest perfection, He died in 1861, and was succeeded by Michael Daintry Hollins and Colin Minton Campbell, his nephew and heir. Recently Mr. Hollins left the concern, and it is now carried on by Mr. Campbell in conjunction with his cousins Thomas William and Herbert Minton, great grandsons of the founder, who have greatly extended the works by the application of steam and machinery.

This mark was used by Thomas Minton, the double S. for Stoke and M. for Minton, the numerals refer to the pattern.

Fig. 333 is a porcelain bowl, blue and gold, painted with flowers; in the S. K. Museum.

LIVERPOOL.

Early in the XVIIIth century, and probably much before that, Liverpool was noted for the manufacture of pottery. Little is known of its early history, and it was not until Mr. Jos. Mayer rescued from oblivion many interesting particulars that anything like a succinct account was published. In his interesting notice of the Art of Pottery in Liverpool, we learn that the most celebrated of the early potters was Alderman

Thomas Shaw, who had a bank for making pottery in the beginning of the XVIIIth century; several large plaques and monumental slabs of his make are in existence, dated from 1716 to 1756. About this time, there seems to have been a large demand for punch bowls, and as these formed the principal ornaments on the sideboards of the middle classes, and especially on board the ships, which were constantly going and coming in the port, considerable pains were taken in decorating them, and many are still in existence painted with ships, convivial mottoes, and inscriptions; one of these, which will hold at least two gallons, is in the Geological Museum, Jermyn Street; another has "Parliament bowl, free without excise," 1736, alluding to the taking off the duty on spirits by "Walpole's Bill." A third praises the fine quality of the tin used for making the glaze, from Luxillion in Cornwall, the name of the owner of the mine (and date 1731) being thus immortalized:—

"John Udy of Luxillion
His tin was so fine,
It glidered this punch bowl
And made it to shine.

Pray fill it with punch,
Let the tinners fill round,
They never will budge
Till the bottom they sound."

Another important establishment was founded by Mr. John Sadler, the son of a painter, who had learned the art of engraving.

He was the inventor, about 1752, of the method of transferring prints from engraved copper plates upon pottery, and in conjunction with Mr. Guy Green, proposed to take out a patent in 1756, the draft of which is still preserved, but they preferred keeping the invention secret to the doubtful security of patent rights.

Wedgwood availed himself of this new mode of decoration, and sent his Queen's ware weekly to Messrs. Sadler and Green to be printed.

Examples.

Fig. 337. Mug, printed with Freemason's arms, by Sadler.

Fig. 338. Punch bowl, printed with a ship; Geological Museum.

Fig. 339. Porcelain mug, with transfer portrait of General Wolfe, signed by J. Sadler.

Fig. 340. Mug, with transfer portrait of Lord Chatham.

Fig. 342. Four printed tiles by Sadler; these are in Lady C. Schreiber's collection.

Fig. 341. A tea pot with portrait of Wesley, and a tortoise-shell mug; S. K. Museum.

Mr. RICHARD CHAFFERS was the principal manufacturer of Liverpool; he served his apprenticeship with Alderman Shaw, and in 1752 established a bank for the manufacture of blue and white earthenware and fine porcelain. His dinner and tea services, punch bowls, jugs, mugs, and decorative vases, gained him great reputation, and they were largely exported to our American Colonies, (now the United States). A very useful little article in particular, which had a great run there, was a pepper-box of the hour glass shape, inscribed with the maker's name at length and the date 1769, it was so well known, that it was a common saying of an ill-tempered person that "he was as hot as Dick's pepper box."

His porcelain works were established about the same time as those of Worcester and Derby, and his productions had a great sale in England.

In the *Liverpool Advertizer* of 1756, we find his China manufactory thus advertized:—"The porcelain or china ware made by Messrs. Richard Chaffers & Co. is now sold here in the town, but at their manufactory at Shaws Brow, considerable abatement is made for exportation and to wholesale dealers." Several specimens are preserved in Mr. Mayer's collection, obtained from members of his family in the neighbourhood.

Mr. Mayer gives an interesting account of an expedition Mr. Chaffers made into Cornwall, as early as 1756, to search for kaolin or soap stone, which our limits will not allow us to give at length. Suffice it to say, that this eminent potter greatly advanced the art in Liverpool, and his excellence was frankly acknowledged by Wedgwood himself, to whom he presented a tea set of his china ware, and who, on admiring the body and examining the colours used in the decoration, exclaimed, "This puts an end to the battle. Mr. Chaffers beats us all in his colours, and with his knowledge he can make colours for two guineas which I cannot produce so good for five." At his death many of his best potters entered the service of Mr. Wedgwood.

The Liverpool establishments of Mr. PENNINGTON, Mr. PHILIP CHRISTIAN, and RICHARD ABBEY, were on an extensive scale, but towards the end of the XVIIIth century only one of any importance survived, and that belonged to Messrs. WORTHINGTON, HUMBLE and HOLLAND, who in 1796 established a large manufactory on the south bank of the Mersey. As Wedgwood had christened his settlement Etruria, they called theirs Herculaneum. A larger capital being required, in 1806 an increase of proprietors took place. The first wares made here, were Queen's ware, and blue printed. About 1800 they commenced making porcelain—the mark used was "Herculaneum," or "Herculaneum Pottery." About 1836, when it came into the possession of Messrs. Case, Mort & Co., the mark used was a bird called the liver, which forms the crest of the Borough of Liverpool.

JACKFIELD, in *Shropshire*, was a very old pottery, and there are some pieces extant with the dates 1634. In 1713 it was carried on by RICHARD THURSFIELD. The ware made here was of a red clay, with a brilliant black glaze, sometimes with scrolls and flowers in relief. Tea services are frequently seen. The jugs were known in the locality as "black decanters." About 1780 the works were taken by Mr. John Rose, and subsequently removed to Coalport.

Fig. 343 is a black glazed tea pot inscribed, "Richard and Ruth Goodin, 1769;" in the Geological Museum.

FULHAM.

The first successful imitation of the *grès de Cologne* was made by JOHN DWIGHT, an Oxfordshire gentleman, which in course of time almost entirely superseded the importation from abroad. This great potter took out his first patent in 1671, and established a manufactory at Fulham in that year, which was successfully carried on through two patents of fourteen years each. Dr. Plot, in his *History of Oxfordshire*, published in 1677, thus eulogizes him:—"The ingenious John Dwight, formerly M.A. of Christ Church, Oxon, hath discovered the mystery of the stone or Cologne wares, heretofore made only in Germany, and by the Dutch brought over into England in great quantities, and hath set up a manufacture of the same, and hath brought it to greater perfection than it has attained where it has been used for many ages, insomuch that the Company of Glass Sellers of London, who are the dealers for that commodity, have contracted with the inventor to buy only of his manufacture, and refuse the foreign." After speaking of his invention of white and transparent porcelain, he concludes:—"In short, he has so advanced the art plastic, that 'tis dubious whether any man since Prometheus have excelled him." The Fulham stone ware is frequently seen at the present day in collections. It is of exceedingly hard and close texture, very compact and sonorous, covered with a salt glaze, of gray colour, ornamented with a brilliant blue enamel in bands, leaves, and flowers, having medallions of Kings and Queens of England in front, with Latin names and titles, or their initials only. Mr. Baylis, of Prior's Bank, obtained a curious collection of the varieties of ware made at the Fulham works, consisting of about twenty-five specimens which had been preserved (by the Dwight family) since the period of their manufacture, and were purchased by him from the last representative of the family. They next passed into the possession of Mr. Reynolds, who sold them by auction, and they are now unfortunately dispersed. Among these were some beautifully modelled busts in the grès or stone ware, of Charles II. and James II., figures of heathen deities from 7 in. to 13 in. high; but the most interesting relic was a half-length female figure of a child lying upon a pillow with its eyes closed, clasping a bouquet of flowers, evidently modelled from the child after death. It tells its own tale, for on the back is inscribed—"Lydia Dwight, died March 3, 1672." This is now in the S. K. Museum.

There is a large fayence plateau, covered with the rich *bleu de Perse* enamel, decorated in white, with the Royal arms and monogram of Charles II. In looking over this collection we are astonished at the variety of Dwight's productions, and the great perfection to which he had brought the potter's art. The figures, busts and groups are exquisitely modelled, and will bear comparison with any contemporary manufactures of Europe. A careful inspection will convince any unprejudiced mind of the erroneous impression which exists, that until the time of Wedgwood the potter's art in England was at a very low ebb, and that none but the rudest description of pottery was made, without any attempt to display artistic excellence. Here, however, we have examples of English pottery a century before Josiah Wedgwood's time, which would do credit to the atélier of that distinguished potter himself. John Dwight died in the year 1737, and with him also departed the glory of his manufactory at Fulham.

Fig. 344 is a Bellarmine of the time of Charles II., with a medallion of C. R. and crown and fleur-de-lis.

Fig. 345 is a jug, with Hogarth's Midnight Conversation in relief.

Fig. 346. Two fragments of blue and purple stone ware jugs; all these were found in an excavation at the Fulham works; in the possession of Lady C. Schreiber.

LAMBETH.

The next important pottery in England was that of Lambeth. In the *History of Lambeth* it is related that about 1650 some Dutch potters established themselves here, and by degrees the manufacture became important, for the village contained no less than twenty manufactories, in which were made the glazed pottery and tiles used in London and various parts of England. The ware was very much of the character of Delft, with a fine white creamy glaze, painted with landscapes and figures in blue.

The white bottles or jugs, upon which are written the names of the wines, accompanied by dates ranging from 1642 to 1649, were made here. In 1676 a number of potters obtained a patent on the 27th of October of that year, the preamble to which grant states, "Whereas John Ariens Van Hamme hath humbly represented unto us that he is, in pursuance of the encouragement he hath received from our Ambassador at the Hague, come over to settle in this our kingdom with his family, to exercise his art of making tiles and porcelain and other earthenwares, after the way practised in Holland, which hath not been practised in this our kingdom."

The trade flourished here for more than a century, until about 1780 or 1790, at which time the Staffordshire potters, by the great improvements they had made in the quality of their ware, and having coal and clay ready to their hand, they were enabled to produce it at a cheaper rate, and eventually beat the Lambeth potters out of the field.

The Lambeth potters, about the end of the XVIIth Century, appear also to have copied the forms of the Palissy ware, especially in large oval dishes with initials and dates. They also made, among other articles, apothecaries' slabs, which were used for mixing conserves, pills, &c., and hung up in their shops; these slabs were in form of a heart or escutcheon, generally painted in blue *camaieu*, with the apothecaries' arms and the motto, "Opifer que per orbem dicor."

YORKSHIRE.

In Yorkshire, pottery of coarse character was made in the XVIIth century. An ancestor of Josiah Wedgwood was established at Yearsley, about the year 1700; and on the estate of Sir George Wombwell pancheons, pitchers and fragments of pottery, of a coarse brown ware, with lead glaze, have been frequently found on the site of the old manufactory, the existence of which has been handed down in the district by the traditionary distich—

> "At Yearsley there were pancheons made
> By Willie Wedgwood, that young blade."

There was also a manufactory established at the Manor-house, York, about 1665, of which little is known except the mention of its existence by Ralph Thoresby and Horace Walpole; although it is by the former erroneously called porcelain, the ware is actually a fine stone ware, with a salt glaze. Lord Orford says: "I have a coffee cup of Mr. Place's ware; it is of gray earth, with streaks of black, and not superior to common earthenware." This specimen was sold at Strawberry Hill, and is now in the Geological Museum, presented by Mr. A. W. Franks. It is very similar to the small specimens of Dwight's early Fulham ware.

There was a pottery on the river Don, near Doncaster, called the *Don Pottery*, established by Mr. John Green, of New-hill, who came from the Leeds pottery about 1790. In 1807 some other memhers of his family joined, and the firm was for a short time "Greens, Clark & Co."

Mr. John J. Bagshawe of Sheffield has a pattern book containing designs of nearly 300 specimens; the title is as follows:—Designs of sundry articles of Queen's or cream-coloured earthenware, manufactured by Greens, Clark and Co., at Don Pottery, near Doncaster, with a great variety of other articles. The same enamelled, printed, or ornamented with gold or silver, to any pattern, also with coats of arms, cyphers, landscapes, &c." The Don Pottery was very similar to that of Leeds, frequently producing pierced work baskets, vases, dinner, dessert, and tea services, &c.

Fig. 348 is a canister of octagonal form, of yellow clay, ornamented with chocolate brown appliqué, musical trophies, and medallions of female figures in relief, and very fine work, in emulation of Wedgwood; in the possession of Mr. E. Norman.

The well-known Leeds ware was made by Messrs. Hartley, Greens and Co. in 1770. This ware is of a sort of cream colour, beautifully made, and has much perforated or basket work, sharply cut out of the borders in various patterns. Important centre pieces with figures were also made here, and are easily distinguished from the Staffordshire cream-coloured earthenware. The pieces are frequently stamped "Leeds Pottery;" sometimes with the makers' names. This manufactory is still carried on by Messrs. WARBURTON. BRITTON and Co.

Fig. 349 is a perforated chestnut bowl and cover; and fig. 350 a plate printed with a portrait; in the Geological Museum.

At *Castleford*, about 12 miles from Leeds, DAVID DUNDERDALE established works for the finer kinds of pottery, especially Queen's ware and the black Egyptian; his pottery is usually marked "D D & Co., Castleford."

Fig. 351 is a tea pot, with ornaments in relief, of white ware edged with blue; in the Geological Museum.

Fig. 352. A candlestick, similar; in the Geological Museum.

At *Yarmouth* a potter named ABSOLON decorated pottery of the cream colour. The arrow is found impressed on many pieces, others have the name of Turner. The favourite subjects are single flowers and plants, with their names on the back of the piece.

Fig. 353 is a plate painted with a flower; in the Geological Museum.

A very important manufactory was initiated by Mr. EDWARD BUTLER in 1757, at *Swinton*, near Rotherham, on the estate of the Marquis of Rockingham. In 1765 it was carried on by Mr. William Malpas, and in 1778 by Messrs. Bingley, Brameld & Co., who enlarged the works, and made earthenware of a very superior quality. The well-known Rockingham tea pots, of a mottled chocolate colour, glazed inside with white, were in great repute for extracting the full flavour of the beverage "which cheers but not inebriates."

These vessels are higher, and more like coffee pots, which was considered an improvement. One agent, Mortlock, the china seller of Oxford Street, paid for that article alone for one season's demand, upwards of £900. These are usually stamped "Rockingham," but the names of "Brameld" and of "Mortlock" are occasionally found. But the aims of the Messrs. Brameld were of a higher character, and some exquisite works of great artistic merit were produced, and which (although not generally known) are occasionally seen. A favourite pattern was a large flower vase, called the lotus vase, formed of upright over-lapping leaves, with birds and butterflies in relief, all enamelled in colours. These may easily be mistaken for Oriental. When the Rockingham works were closed in 1842 many of the moulds were purchased by Mr. John Reed, and transferred to the Mexborough Pottery. Among them was the lotus vase, and the keep of Conisborough Castle, a Norman structure near Swinton.

Newcastle. There were some extensive manufactories here for making Queen's ware, some of which are perforated like that of Leeds, and wicker pattern borders. Some of the earthenware mugs have a pink metallic lustre, and are ornamented with transfer engravings. On these we have a view of the new bridge over the Weir, and on the inside a toad in relief, which, when filled with beer, is unseen, but when the liquor is half drunk becomes visible, much to the horror of a person who is drinking it. One similar, in the Geological Museum, is inscribed—

> "Though malt and venom seem united,
> Don't break my pot, or be affrighted."

Fig. 353A. A dish of Queen's ware, with fruit in relief, stamped, "Fell, Newcastle."

Fig. 362. A mug, with printed monument of Lord Nelson, inside is a toad; in the Geological Museum.

Fig. 354. A jug, with lustre and subjects in relief; in the Geological Museum.

St. Anthony's, about 2½ miles from Newcastle-upon-Tyne; makers, Sewell and Donkin. Queen's ware and pink metallic lustre, also printed subjects; sometimes Sewell alone, the name stamped. A jug of his make has cupids in relief, coloured with pink metallic lustred clouds and bronzed borders ; in the Geological Museum (see fig. 355). He also produced ware like that of Leeds, pierced wicker baskets, &c.

The stone ware made at Nottingham in the first half of the XVIIIth Century is well known; it has usually a dark brown glaze, with a slightly metallic lustre, and is very hard and durable, and frequently ornamented with outlines of stalks and flowers, especially the pink. Tobacco jars in form of a bear, puzzle jugs, &c.

Fig. 356 is a brown stone ware mug, inscribed "Made at Nottingham the 17th August, 1771."

Fig. 357 is a jug in form of a bear; Geological Museum.

At *Cadborough*, near Rye in Sussex, is a pottery established by Mr. MITCHELL for common sorts of pottery. He has, however, produced some vases of elegant forms of glazed ware.

Fig. 358 is a curious vessel, used at weddings, in form of a pig; and fig. 359 is a small green vase; both are in the Geological Museum.

Lowesby, Leicestershire. Established by Sir FRANCIS FOWKES, *circa* 1835. The mark, sometimes without the fleur-de-lis, is stamped on red terra cotta with black enamelled ornaments, in imitation of Wedgwood.

Fig. 360 and fig. 361 represent a garden pot and a vase; in the Geological Museum.

A manufacture of earthenware was established at *Swansea* about 1750, which was greatly enlarged by Mr. GEORGE HAYNES in 1780, who styled it the "Cambrian Pottery." In 1802 the works were purchased by Mr. Lewis Weston Dillwyn, for the manufacture of pottery; but about 1810 an improvement was made which was termed *opaque porcelain*, and, with the assistance of Mr. Young, the draughtsman employed in delineating natural history, the ware became remarkable for its beautiful and truthful paintings.

The early Swansea ware was elegant in form, as ornaments in form of lamps, &c., frequently covered with a deep blue glaze.

BRISTOL. At REDCLIFFE BACKS a manufactory of Delft ware was carried on in the last century by a Mr. Frank. There is in the Geological Museum a slab composed of twenty-four tiles, with a view of Redcliffe Church, painted by him about 1738. He was preceded by a potter named Read.

At TEMPLE BACKS Mr. Joseph Ring, son-in-law of Cookworthy (after the porcelain works had been relinquished in 1777), opened a manufactory called the "Bristol Pottery." It was carried on for many years, and about 1820 it was occupied by Messrs. Pountney and Allies. The articles produced were similar to those of the superior potteries in Staffordshire, and the mark used was a cross.

PORCELAIN.

THE manufacture of porcelain in England was much earlier than has been generally supposed, and the invention was patented in England by John Dwight of Fulham, in 1671, while that at St. Cloud was not patented until 1702, nearly 30 years afterwards. The words, in Dwight's patent are as clearly indicative of this fact as they can be; it was for "the mistery of transparent earthenware, (commonly known by the name of porcelaine or china.)" Dr. Plot, in his History of Oxfordshire, written in 1677, corroborates the fact. "He," (Dwight) "hath found ways to make an earth, white and transparent as porcellane, and not distinguishable from it by the eye, or by experiments that have been purposely made to try wherein they disagree." The principal test of porcelain being its transparency, there can be no doubt about the nature of the ware here spoken of.

WORCESTER.

Although this manufactory originated more than a century ago, and has always been carried on by private enterprise, it is still in a flourishing state. It was established, in 1751, chiefly through the exertions of Dr. Wall, a physician and a good practical chemist, who in conjunction with others formed the "Worcester Porcelain Company." The early productions were principally of the useful description, and sold at a cheaper rate than the wares of Bow and Chelsea. A writer in the Annual Register in 1763 says, "We have, indeed, many other manufactures of porcelain which are sold at a cheaper rate than any that is imported, but except the Worcester, they all wear brown, and are subject to crack, especially the glazing, by boiling water." About the year 1757, the important method of multiplying designs upon the biscuit ware by means of transferring impressions of engraved copper plates to the surface, was adopted almost simultaneously with Liverpool; the invention being in fact claimed by both, but we will not wait to discuss the question of priority, for specimens of both, are found bearing the names of Sadler and Green of Liverpool, and Richard Holdship and Robert Hancock of Worcester, dated in the same year. The mark used by Holdship was his initials R. H. and an anchor, being a rebus upon his name; he also printed china for the Derby works, in

that case substituting the word Derby for Worcester under his initials. Hancock's name was usually written at length. The garden scenes and tea parties printed upon the Worcester ware are well known. Bat printing succeeded the printing from engraved or etched plates. This new style, instead of being first printed upon paper and then transferred, was accomplished thus: the plate was stippled with a fine point by London artists after designs by Cipriani, Bartolozzi, Cosway, and Angelica Kauffman, so fashionable about the beginning of this century,—landscapes, shells, fruit, flowers, etc. The copper plate being carefully cleaned, a thin coating of linseed oil was laid upon it, and removed by the palm of the hand from the surface, leaving the oil in the engraved spots; instead of paper, bats of glue were used, cut into squares of the size of the engraving; one of these bats was pressed on to the plate, so as to receive the oil out of the engraved holes, and laid on to the china, transferring the oil to the surface; it was then dusted with the colour required, the superfluous colour being removed carefully with cotton wool, and then placed in the kiln.

The porcelain made from 1760 to 1770 was of very superior quality, and the colours used upon some of the ornamental pieces and services approached very closely to those of Chelsea, the patterns were usually in imitation of Japanese. There are some Worcester vases finely painted with classical figures and subjects by Donaldson, but as he was not attached to the works, and painted also for Chelsea, the vases were probably purchased in the white state, and decorated in London, a very common occurrence. In 1772 the works were sold and another proprietary formed, Dr. Wall still having the superintendance.

In 1783 the Worcester porcelain works were purchased by Mr. Thomas Flight, from whom it afterwards passed to Messrs. Flight and Barr; the principal painters at this time were: Pennington, who painted figures; Astle, flowers; Davis, exotic birds in the Chelsea style; Webster, landscapes and flowers; Barker, shells; Brewer of Derby, landscapes; and Baxter, an accomplished artist, painted figure subjects.

The marks upon Worcester porcelain are of great variety, but they still historically denote the changes that have occurred in the direction of the manufactory, and we are thereby better able to ascertain the dates of particular specimens. The proprietors seem to have copied the marks of all the celebrated fabriques in their turn. A few of those most frequently used are here given, from *Marks and Monograms on Pottery and Porcelain*, by W. Chaffers.

The Worcester works remained with Messrs. Flight and Barr until 1840, when the two principal manufactories of Worcester—that of Flight and Barr, and that of the Messrs. Chamberlain, were amalgamated; the plant and stock removed to the premises of the latter, and it was styled Chamberlain and Co. The last-named works were established by Robert Chamberlain in 1786; he was the first apprentice at the Old Worcester Porcelain Company, and he and his brother Humphrey took premises in High Street. At first they only decorated porcelain, which they bought of Turner of Caughley;

but afterwards manufactured largely on their own account, and their business increased to a great extent, being patronized by the Royal Family. A full-dress service for the East India Company at Madras, was supplied at £4190; another for the Prince Regent cost £4000. The well-known breakfast service made by them, by order of Lord Nelson, but which is supposed to have been presented by the ladies—in some way passed out of the family. To give an idea of the prevailing taste for showy china in the beginning of this century, Mr. Binns says that Messrs. Chamberlain paid on an average for wages £4500 per annum; and the amount for gold alone to decorate the porcelain was £900. per annum. The usual mark was simply "Chamberlain's Worcester."

These two works were united in 1840, and remained so until 1852, when Messrs. Kerr and Binns became the ostensible proprietors. In 1862 another Joint Stock Company was formed, Mr. R. W. Binns having the direction of the artistic department, and Mr. Edward Phillips being general superintendent.

Examples.

Fig. 362. Plate, decorated with blue and gold, by Chamberlain. Fig. 363. Mug with transfer, The King of Prussia. Fig. 364. Sucrier and milk jug, with transfer of garden scenes. Fig. 365. Jug, blue ground, with painted medallions of flowers and birds. These are in the Geological Museum.

Fig. 366. Cup and Saucer, dragon pattern, S. K. Museum.

Fig. 366A. Portion of a service, Japan pattern, blue, red and gold; in Mr. Chaffers' collection.

Fig. 366B. Portions of a service, transfer coloured views and figures, partly gilt; in the possession of Mr. W. Chaffers.

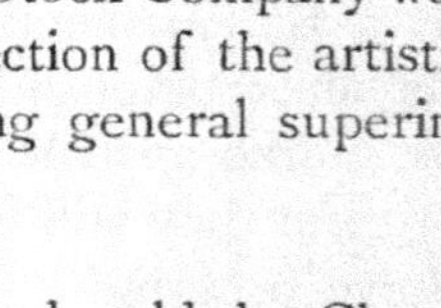

SWINTON, near Rotherham. The manufacture of porcelain at the Rockingham works was introduced about the year 1823 by Mr. Thomas Brameld, who spared no expense in endeavouring to bring it to perfection, under the patronage of the Earl Fitzwilliam. The china was of a superior description, and the painting and decoration of high character. The ordinary services were marked BRAMELD, the ornamental pieces were stencilled with a griffin. In 1826 the proprietor became embarrassed, but the works were continued by the Earl's assistance until 1842. In 1832 they succeeded in obtaining royal patronage, and a magnificent service was ordered by King William IV.; instead, however, of placing the firm in a more flourishing condition, it was actually the cause of their ruin, for the expense incurred by the engagement of first-class artists, and the superabundance of gold employed in decorating it, resulted in so great a loss that the manufacture was totally discontinued a few years after.

Fig. 367 is a pattern plate in the Geological Museum, and fig. 368 a vase or centre piece of the service made for William IV. in the possession of Mr. E. Norman.

DERBY.

The earliest manufactory was called "the Derby Pot works," and was carried on at Cock Pit Hill by Messrs. John and Christopher Heath for pottery and porcelain. It is said to have been on an extensive scale, but little is known of its operations. The proprietors, who were bankers in Full Street, became bankrupt in 1780, when the stock was sold and the works discontinued.

The "Derby porcelain manufactory" was founded in 1751 by William Duesbury; the first productions were chimney ornaments, lambs, sheep, and services for the table, but it was not probably until he purchased the Chelsea works in 1769 that any great reputation was acquired, and few if any specimens can be identified. On this occasion the pieces were marked with a D and an anchor across it, denoting the union of the Derby and Chelsea works; these are called Derby-Chelsea porcelain. Some beautiful examples

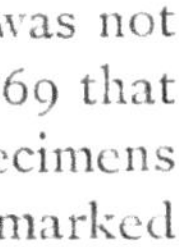

of porcelain painted in the Chinese style were produced about this time, but as the rage for Oriental seemed so prevalent, the proprietor to insure the sale of his china, copied the Chinese marks as well as the style of decoration; and the

Dresden mark of the crossed swords is also sometimes found upon them. But their ordinary trade mark was the D and anchor. Subsequently, after royal patronage was accorded, the mark was altered to an italic *D*, with a cross above, and three dots in each side angle, surmounted by a crown. This china is termed Crown-Derby, and was adopted from 1780, and continued by Mr. Bloor his successor as late as 1830. After the purchase of the Chelsea and Bow works, the Derby porcelain manufactory rose to great importance; the proprietors having of course retained the best workmen who had been engaged there. In fact, with all the models and moulds, the mixers, throwers and painters of those two great establishments, it may be considered as the Chelsea and Bow works continued in another locality. Upon the death of Mr. William Duesbury, in 1785, his son William still remained there, and a third William Duesbury succeeded in the beginning of this century. Robert Bloor, about 1815, took the works, which were altogether closed in 1848. An offshoot, however, is still carried on by Messrs. Stevenson and Hancock.

Examples.

Fig. 369. Crown-Derby scent vase, with flowers in relief.

Fig. 370. Plate, painted with flowers, by Billingsley; and

Fig. 371. Crown-Derby cup, cover and saucer; in the Geological Museum.

Fig. 372. Chelsea-Derby vase with painted medallions; and

Fig. 373. Pair of groups, lovers in alcoves; Lady C. Schreiber.

Fig. 374. Porcelain cup of the early Cock Pit Hill works; Mr. Alfred Wallis.

Fig. 375. Pair of Chelsea-Derby vases, view of Kedleston Hall, etc., with gold stripes; Lord Scarsdale.

Figs. 376 to 378. Three cups and a saucer; Lord Scarsdale.

Fig. 379. "The Derby prentice plate," kept for sixty years

at the works as a pattern, painted by Billingsley, c. 1785; Mr. John Haslem.

Fig. 380. "The thistle plate," painted by W. Pegg, c.1800; Mr. John Haslem.

Fig. 381. "The Rodney Jug," painted by E. Withers, c. 1782, used by a club of china painters at Derby for 70 years; Miss Ward.

Fig. 382. Pair of cups, painted with views near Derby; Mr. John Haslem.

Fig. 383. Chelsea-Derby tea pot, and cup and saucer, painted with flowers and gold lines; Mrs. Nixon.

Fig. 384. Chocolate cup, gilt border, with feather sprig; Major J. Evans.

Fig. 385. Chocolate cup, blue and gold border; the Earl of Chesterfield.

Fig. 386. Cup and saucer, blue and gold, jewelled; Captain F. N. Smith.

Fig. 387. Crown-Derby cup, painted with the smugglers and flowers on gold ground; Mr. J. Sanders.

Burton-on-Trent. A manufactory of earthenware was established here early in this century, and about 1839 porcelain was made and carried on for seven years: a specimen of the ware is here given. Fig. 388, a porcelain comport, painted with flowers and fruit, belonging to Mr. W. Bemrose, jun.

Wirksworth. A china manufactory existed here about 1770, as well as pottery, established by a Mr. Gill, and continued for about 20 years, but no mark is known.

Fig. 389 is a cup and cover assigned to this place; Mr. W. Bemrose, jun.

Pinxton. A manufacture of porcelain was established at Pinxton in Derbyshire, about 1795, by Mr. Billingsley in partnership with Mr. John Coke; the former was a practical potter, having been engaged at the Derby works as a flower painter, in which he excelled; he brought with him a staff of workmen and their families, and the concern went on successfully for about five or six years, when Billingsley left the concern, and it was continued by Coke, afterwards by Cutts the foreman, but altogether discontinued about 1812. The ware made here by Billingsley was of that peculiar transparent character of which the receipt was only known to himself, and which he subsequently introduced at Nantgarw; a favourite pattern was the French sprig or "Chantilly," being an imitation of the Angouleme china. We give the following examples:

Fig. 390. A flower pot, French sprig pattern; Mr. W. Bemrose, jun.

Fig. 391. Ice pail, primrose ground, with deep border of flowers by Billingsley; S. K. Museum.

Fig. 392. A sugar bowl and cover painted with landscapes, red border; Mr. John Hawkins.

Fig. 393. A jardinière, painted with views of Dove Dale and other places in Derbyshire; Mr. John Haslem.

LOWESTOFT.

Although the manufactory of porcelain at Lowestoft was one of the largest in England, yet the recollection of its existence and the productions which emanated from it have been lost sight of, and have gradually died away, although it was in active work for fifty years, and only ceased in the commencement of the present century. It is well remembered by the older inhabitants of Lowestoft, who ridicule the idea of anybody doubting it, and the houses in the vicinity are teeming with Lowestoft china; in fact, it is to be found all over England, but is usually, for want of a better and truer name, classed as "Oriental," being a sort of hybrid ware which nobody who knew what the true Chinese porcelain was, could for a moment mistake.

On the site of the old works one of the kilns still remains, and the cottages where the clay was prepared at Gunton are in existence, as also the great wheel which ground the materials of the ware.

The manufactory was established about 1756; the owner of Gunton Hall, Hewlin Luson, Esq., having discovered on his estate some fine clay, which, upon examination, was found suitable for making porcelain; hence the origin of the china manufactory at Lowestoft. Gillingwater says it met with great opposition from the china manufactories near London, who actually bribed the workmen to spoil the ware made there, and exercised every art to render the scheme abortive; but, notwithstanding this unhandsome treatment, the manufactory was permanently established by Messrs. Walker, Browne, Aldred and Richman. Several important aids were favourable to the undertaking; they had on the sea shore the finest and purest sand which could be found on the coast of England, and as silica entered largely into the composition of their china, it was essential to the proprietors.

That a very considerable trade was carried on here in the manufacture of porcelain is beyond dispute, not only in the adjacent counties but in London, where, according to Gillingwater (*History of Lowestoft*), a warehouse was kept to execute the orders received from London and the adjoining towns, and Lowestoft being on the extreme easternly point of England, the inhabitants had great intercourse with Holland, where doubtless much of the ware was sold, and it is thought a considerable amount was exported for the Turkish market. Its greatest prosperity was from 1770 to 1800.

The works were closed in 1802, and the best workmen were transferred to the Worcester works, which will account for many striking similarities between the blue wares.

The question about *hard paste* having been made at Lowestoft is placed beyond dispute upon the best authority. It was probably introduced about 1775, after Champion's failure. There are several parties now living there who can testify to the fact that nothing passed out of the factory but what was made in it, and that no Oriental porcelain ever came into it to be decorated. There is a much greater variety of Lowestoft porcelain than is generally imagined; the most frequent is *hard paste*, ornamented with pink and purple roses and minute highly-finished roses in festoons. The ornamental borders are exceedingly rich, being diapered with gold and colours. The more highly-finished services usually have the initials or coats of arms of the families for whom they were made, and are superior both in design and delicacy of pencilling and finish to most other English manufactures. A rich cobalt blue was sometimes introduced in the borders, overlaid with gold stars.

The principal painters were Powles, who painted views and landscapes; a French artist named Rose, who painted flowers; Robert Allen, Sparham, Curtis, Redgrave, &c. For a detailed account of this important manufactory, the reader is referred to *Marks and Monograms on Pottery and Porcelain*, by W. Chaffers, pages 612-640.

Examples.

Figs. 394 and 395 represent a plate, cup and cover, with views and birds, elaborately gilt, attributed to Lowestoft.

Fig. 396. Cup and saucer, with an owl, the crest of Woodley of Beccles; in Mr. Walker Joy's collection.

Figs. 397 to 401. Coffee pot and four cups, of this manufactory; in Mr. Emerson Norman's collection.

PLYMOUTH.

As early as 1758 William Cookworthy commenced his experiments to ascertain the nature of true porcelain of hard paste, and had searched with great perseverance throughout England for the materials which had been described by the Père d'Entrecolles as the constituent parts of Chinese porcelain. At length a friend of his discovered on the estate of Lord Camelford, in the parish of St. Stephen's, Cornwall, "a certain white saponaceous clay, and close by it a species of granite or moorstone, white with greenish spots, which he immediately perceived to be the two long sought-for ingredients, the one giving whiteness and body to the paste, the other vitrification and transparency." Lord Camelford says, in a letter to Mr. Polwhele—"The difficulties found in proportioning properly these materials so as to give exactly the necessary degree of vitrification and no more, and other niceties with regard to the manipulation, discouraged us from proceeding in this concern, after we had procured a patent for the use of our materials, and expended on it between £2,000. or £3,000. We then sold our interest to Mr. Champion of Bristol." The patent was dated 17th March, 1768, and the materials are described as growan stone and growan clay. They carried on the works for nearly six years, and consequently made a considerable quantity of ware. Cookworthy engaged the services of a French artist, M. Soqui, whose ornamental delineations on the articles produced here were very beautiful. Some elegant salt cellars and table ornaments in form of open conch shells resting on a bed of coral, &c., all well modelled in hard paste, were favourites for the table.

They continued to work this manufactory until 1774, when the patent right was sold and transferred to Richard Champion.

Examples.

Fig. 402. Coffee pot, blue ground, and panels of flowers; Fig. 403. Beaker and cover, painted with flowers; Fig. 404. A bird in white porcelain; these are in Lady C. Schreiber's collection.

Fig. 405. Statuette of Woodward the actor; bearing the Plymouth mark.

Fig. 406. Pair of figures, shepherd and shepherdess; Fig. 407. Sweetmeat stand of shells and rock work; Fig. 408. Centre piece, similar; these are in Mr. W. Edkins' collection.

BRISTOL.

A manufactory of English porcelain, *soft paste*, was founded at Bristol about 1772 by Richard Champion, but to this he afterwards added the manufacture of *hard paste*, having in 1774 purchased Cookworthy's patent. The ware was, however, brought to great perfection, but the large outlay prevented its being remunerative, and in three or four years he sold his interest in the patent to a company of Staffordshire potters. Horace Walpole, in his catalogue, speaks of "a cup and saucer, white, with green festoons of flowers," and this was a favourite pattern for services. In these few years a considerable quantity was made; the mark was a cross painted in grey or slate colour; but sometimes the crossed swords were adopted.

Examples.

Fig. 409. Dish, painted with flowers, presented by a descendant of Mr. Cookworthy; Figs. 410 and 411. Bowl and cover, cup and inkstand; in the Geological Museum.

Figs. 412 and 413. Two tea pots, painted with flowers; Fig. 414. Dish, painted with flowers; Fig. 415. Tripod, supported by griffins; Fig. 416. Shell salt cellar; in Lady C. Schreiber's collection.

CAUGHLEY, near Broseley, Salop. This manufactory was established in 1751 by a Mr. Brown, and afterwards carried on by Mr. Gallimore. It was not until 1772 that it rose to any importance, when Mr. Thomas Turner commenced operations. He came from the Worcester porcelain manufactory; he was an engraver, and probably learnt his art from Robert Hancock.

The excellence of Turner's porcelain gained him great patronage. In 1780 he produced the celebrated "willow pattern," which, even at the present day, is in great demand, and completed the first blue printed table service made in England. Mr. Thomas Minton of Stoke assisted in the completion of it, being articled as an engraver there.

Mr. John Rose was also in Mr. Turner's service. In 1799 Turner retired and Rose became proprietor by purchase; who altogether removed the works to Coalport about 1814 or 1815.

The Salopian porcelain had several marks, and has been frequently confounded with the Worcester; on the early ware the word "Salopian" is impressed, but sometimes the letter *S* only. The blue printed china made by Turner, of Oriental designs, are marked with Arabic numerals, with flourishes giving them an Oriental character; some of the jugs have a crescent like the Worcester mark.

Fig. 417. Jug, painted in blue, inscribed "James Kennedy,

1778"; Fig. 418. Mug, painted in blue, with birds and fruit; Fig. 419. Plate, blue landscape and figures; in the Geological Museum.

The porcelain works at COALPORT were established by Mr. John Rose about 1780 or 1790, having removed his manufactory from Jackfield. He carried on this and the Caughley works simultaneously. In 1820, having purchased both the Swansea and the Nantgarw manufactories, they were incorporated with Coalport, and Billingsley of Nantgarw (whose beautiful transparent china is well known) was engaged as mixer of the clays, and remained there until his death in 1828. His receipts for making this china are still in the possession of the firm, but it is too expensive a process to be followed to any great extent, except in special services. The "worm sprig" and the "Tournay sprig" were much made at Coalport. In porcelain and pottery the old "willow pattern" and the "blue dragon" still remained staple articles.

COLEBROOK DALE is another name for the Coalport works. The letters C D and C. B. D are frequently found upon the decorative china. A more intricate mark has been used since 1861, composed of a large cursive monogram of S and C for Coalport, Salop; within the three loops are the Roman capitals C. S and N, signifying that the works of Caughley, Swansea and Nantgarw have been added.

The mark of a red rose is found on some of Rose's early china. The ware is well known, and has much the character of the Derby.

Fig. 420 is a pattern plate (part of a service) given by Her Majesty to the Emperor of Russia; in the Geological Museum.

BOW.

The manufactory of porcelain at Stratford-le-Bow was established about 1730. Thomas Frye, an eminent painter, appears to have been instrumental in bringing the china to that perfection for which the manufactory was celebrated. He took out two patents for the improvement of porcelain;

the first in 1744 was in conjunction with Edward Heylin, the second in 1749. In these the processes are minutely described. In 1750 the works were disposed of to Messrs. Crowther and Weatherby, who also had a warehouse at St. Catherine's, near the Tower. In Aris' *Birmingham Gazette* for 1753 we find an advertisement for "painters in the blue and white potting way, and enamellers on china ware, to apply at the China House near Bow; likewise painters brought up in the snuff box way, &c., and a person who can model small figures in clay neatly." In 1763 "John Crowther of Cornhill, china man," became bankrupt, and in the following year we find gazetted "Benjamin Weatherby of St. Catherine's." Crowther recommenced business; and in 1770 we find in the *Directory* that John Crowther of the Bow China Works had a warehouse at 28, St. Paul's Church Yard, and that the firm of Weatherby and Co., potters, were still in existence, and probably were concerned with him.

The interesting bowl made at the Bow works in the year 1760, and painted by Thomas Craft (now in the British Museum), is accompanied by a short history of the works, and informs us that the names of the proprietors were known all over the world, that they employed 300 persons, about 90 painters, and 200 turners, throwers, &c., all under one roof. (See illustration, figs. 433 and 434.) In 1775 or 1776 the works were sold to Mr. Duesbury, and all the moulds and implements transferred to Derby.

In *Nollekens and his Times* we find a gossip between him and Betew, stating that Nollekens, Moser, Crisp and Bacon used occasionally to model for the Bow works; that spirited figures were produced there—"Quin in Falstaff," "Garrick in Richard," "Frederick Duke of Cumberland," &c.

Vases with flowers, painted, and with ornaments in relief, are frequently seen. A favourite pattern was Chinese daisies, birds, quails, &c.

A triangle stamped underneath the ware is supposed to be a Bow mark; but it is also found upon ware marked *Chelsea*. The well-known milk jug, of goats in relief with

a bee in front, supposed to represent B for Bow (but actually a wasp) has a triangle; one in Mr. Russell's collection, marked with a triangle, has also legibly written, "Chelsea, 1745." The salt cellars, also with crawfish in full relief and rock work, bear the same mark; but Walpole, in his *Catalogue of the Strawberry Hill Collection*, speaks of "Two white salt cellars with crawfish in relief of Chelsea china." Some of these have the triangle stamped, others have it in blue. On some china, supposed with more reason to have been made at Bow, we find a bow and arrow, but any marks upon the ware are scarce. For a more detailed account of the Bow porcelain manufactory, the reader is referred to *Marks and Monograms on Pottery and Porcelain*, by W. Chaffers, 3rd edition, pp. 676-699.

Examples.

Fig. 421. Salts (pair of), kneeling figures holding shells (see fragment found at Bow, Chaffers' *Marks and Monograms*, p. 699). Fig. 422. Statuette of Mrs. Kitty Clive, of white china; in Mr. John J. Bagshawe's collection.

Fig. 423. Milk pot, with goats and bee in relief. Fig. 424. Tea pot, flowers and insects. Fig. 425. Salt cellar, shells in relief. Fig. 426. Bowl on foot, with insects. Fig. 427. "New Canton" inkstand, 1751. Fig. 428. Plate, painted flowers and hawthorn, relief border. Figs. 429, 430. Two cups, one flowers, the other hawthorn pattern; in the Geological Museum.

Fig. 431. Tea pot, printed with the King of Prussia; fig. 332. Plate, printed with Æneas and Anchises; in Lady C. Schreiber's collection.

Figs. 433 and 434. Bowl, painted by Thomas Craft in 1760, and inscription; in the British Museum.

Fig. 435. Porcelaïn figure, a coloured model of the Farnese Flora at Naples, ascribed to John Bacon, R.A., late XVIIIth Century; in the S. K. Museum.

Fig. 436. Vase with scrolls and cover, with flowers and birds in full relief; fig. 437. Basket vase, supported by two cupids; fig. 438. Sauce boat, flowers, &c. in relief; fig. 439.

Pug dog of white china; fig. 440. A sphinx of white china; fig. 441. Bust of George II. on a pedestal, height 17 inches; in Lady C. Schreiber's collection.

Fig. 441A. A white china group of the Seasons; and Fig. 441B. A coloured group of the well-known "Tea Party" (slightly damaged); in Mr. John Sanders' collection.

CHELSEA.

The celebrated porcelain manufactory of Chelsea was established shortly after Bow, about 1740, and the early productions of the two are frequently mistaken one for the other; but, fortunately, the Chelsea wares subsequently, especially the finest pieces, were marked with an anchor in gold or red. The period of its greatest excellence was from 1750 to 1765. It has been thought that Venetian workmen were first engaged here, and this supposition is in some degree borne out by the great similarity of the two wares both in painting and gilding, added to which, the mark upon both is a red anchor, and both are of a fine soft paste.

The early ware made at Chelsea, especially the plates, have underneath three spots or blemishes, caused by the contact of the three points, on which the piece rested in the kiln, removing the glaze.

Faulkner, in his *History of Chelsea*, says, "The manufactory was set on foot by M. Sprimont, a foreigner. The original proprietor having acquired a large fortune, retired from the concern, and his successors, wanting his enterprise and spirit, did not so well succeed, but in a few years abandoned it." Who these successors were we have not been able to find out, unless the allusion is to Mr. W. Duesbury of Derby, for it passed directly from the hands of M. Sprimont to him.

The early pieces were copied principally from the Oriental, being decorated with Chinese patterns, and these were marked with an embossed anchor.

A fine set of Chelsea porcelain, which cost upwards of £1,000. was presented by the King and Queen to the Duke of Mecklenburg in 1763.

The beautiful vases in the French style, in imitation of Sèvres, with *gros bleu*, crimson, turquoise and apple-green grounds, were made from 1760 to 1765.

The Foundling Vase, 24 inches high, (one of a pair) was presented to the Hospital in 1762 by Dr. Garnier, and a pair of vases given to the British Museum, is thus recorded in the donation book:—"Two very fine porcelain jars of the Chelsea manufactory, made in the year 1762, under the direction of Mr. Sprimont, from a person unknown, through Mr. Empson." (See fig. 452.)

In 1769, by order of Mr. Sprimont, the proprietor of the Chelsea porcelain manufactory, the whole of the matchless pieces, consisting of valuable vases, urns, table and dessert services, were sold by auction, also the fine models, mills, kilns, presses, buildings, &c."

The works were purchased by Mr. W. Duesbury of Derby, and carried on by him at Chelsea until 1784. The later pieces made here under his direction are easily distinguished; these vessels are of simple elegant forms, with the frequent recurrence of gold stripes, and the same forms and style were adopted simultaneously at Derby, but they are inferior to the vases made when M. Sprimont had the works under his direction. The pieces marked with an anchor surmounted by a crown are Duesbury's productions at Chelsea.

Examples.

Fig. 442. Statuette of Marshall Conway; fig. 443. Statuette of Wilkes; fig. 444, 445. Shepherd and shepherdess; fig. 446 to 451. Six birds, some with raised anchor; in Lady C. Schreiber's collection.

Fig. 452. A large Chelsea vase; "Death of Cleopatra;" in the British Museum.

Fig. 453. Vase, supported by three caryatides; fig. 454, 455. A pair of figures, the Pedlar and his Wife; in Lady C. Schreiber's collection.

Fig. 456. Statuette of Diana with a dog; fig. 457. Vase, in imitation of wicker work, scroll stand and birds; fig. 458.

Plate, with rose bud and leaves in relief, coloured; fig. 459. Dish for fruit, painted with flowers; Miss Hartley's collection.

Fig. 460. Group of the three Maries before the cross; in Lady C. Schreiber's collection.

SWANSEA. Mr. Dillwyn retired from the concern in 1813, leaving it to his son, Mr. L. L. Dillwyn. It was in the year 1814 that the manufacture of porcelain was revived at Swansea. At that time Billingsley, or Beely (a contraction of his real name and by which he was probably best known), had commenced making his beautiful porcelain, which was much admired, at Nantgarw; it naturally attracted Mr. Dillwyn's attention, and conceiving that the kilns used by Billingsley and Walker might be considerably improved, made arrangements with them to carry out their process at Swansea; with this view, two new kilns were erected at the Cambrian pottery, and the manufacture conducted by them for some considerable time. Hence the origin of the Swansea porcelain, which obtained great repute, and it was continued for six or seven years, an excellent body having been obtained. Baxter, a clever painter of figure subjects, left Worcester and entered Mr. Dillwyn's service in 1816, and continued there for three years, returning to Worcester in 1819. In the year 1820 the manufactory was discontinued, and all the moulds and appliances purchased by Mr. John Rose, who removed them to Coalport about the same time as those of Nantgarw. The ware is usually stencilled in red 'Swansea.' The mark, sometimes impressed or in colour, is a trident, occasionally two tridents crossed, as in the margin.

SWANSEA

Figs. 461, 462, are two plates in the Geological Museum.

NANTGARW. This porcelain manufactory was established in 1813, by Billingsley, a celebrated flower painter of Derby; he served his time to Mr. Duesbury for five years, from 1774 to 1779, and probably left there about 1785. In some of the early Derby pattern books, mentioned by Mr. Binns, now at Worcester, we frequently find "to be painted with Billingsley's flowers," particularly specified, so that he was a desirable workman at that time. He was not only a first-class painter, but he thoroughly understood the manufacture of porcelain in all its branches. In 1795 he established a porcelain manufactory at Pinxton, in partnership with a Mr. John Coke; here he remained about five years, dissolving partnership in 1800, but the works were continued until 1812. In 1800 we find him superintending a small decorating establishment at Mansfield, where he remained for four years. In 1804 he was at Torksey, in Lincolnshire, engaged in a manufactory there. Mr. Marryat says he married a daughter of Mr. Landers, the banker, and for some time carried on the business of a painter on glass at Bristol; if so, it must have been between this and 1811, for in that year he was engaged by Messrs. Flight and Barr, of Worcester, in the mixing room, until 1813, when he left, probably in consequence of Mr. Barr's death. His son-in-law Walker, was also at the Worcester works, and made some great improvements; he introduced that most important invention, the *Reverberating enamel kiln*, already in use at London and Derby; the method of building this kiln was kept secret, Walker always working at night to complete it.

In 1813, Billingsley and Walker left Worcester to establish a porcelain manufactory at Nantgarw. Here they produced some very fine porcelain, of the same peculiar character as that of Pinxton, with a sort of vitreous appearance and a granulated fracture like lump sugar, which being very soft paste would not in all cases stand the heat of the kiln; some of the early pieces are consequently frequently found cracked on the glaze, or slightly warped and bent.

The Nantgarw porcelain was of remarkably fine body and texture, but its production was expensive; specimens are scarce and command high prices. About the year 1820 the manufacture was discontinued, Billingsley and Walker having disposed of their interest in the concern to Mr. J. Rose, the moulds and everything connected with the works were removed to Coalport, and they superintended them until Billingsley's death, which happened in 1828.

Examples.

Fig. 463, 464. Two plates painted with flowers; in the Geological Museum.

Fig. 465. Cup and saucer, birds and flowers; in the S. K. Museum.

Fig. 466. Vase with a band of flowers, the Welsh harp forming the handles; Fig. 467. Vase with flowers and gold scrolls; Fig. 468. Vase, painted with flowers, gilt vine ornament in relief; in the collection of Mr. W. Bemrose, jun.

THE END.

Dryden Press: J. Davy & Sons, 137, Long Acre, London.

465

Cedro

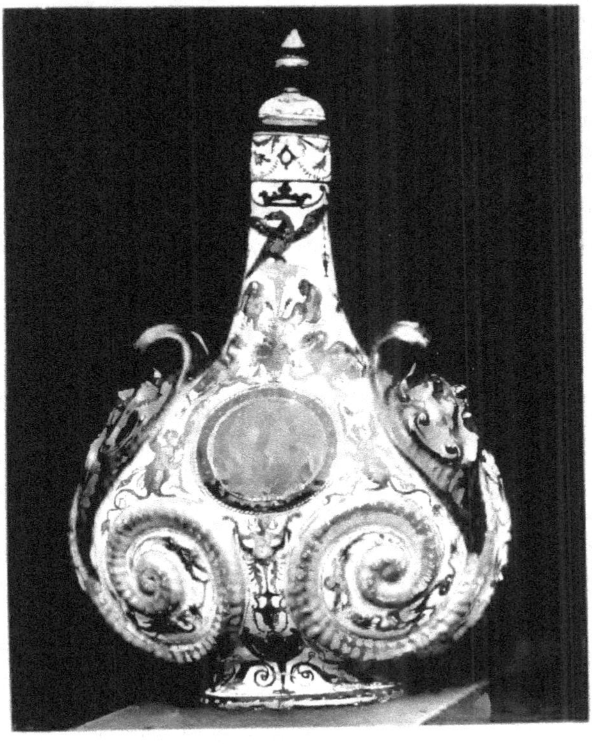

Plate XXXII

[illegible]

561. [illegible]

South Kensington Museum

MONTE [illegible] — [illegible] XXXVI

[illegible]

[illegible] 1522

LUCA DELLA ROBBIA.

[illegible]

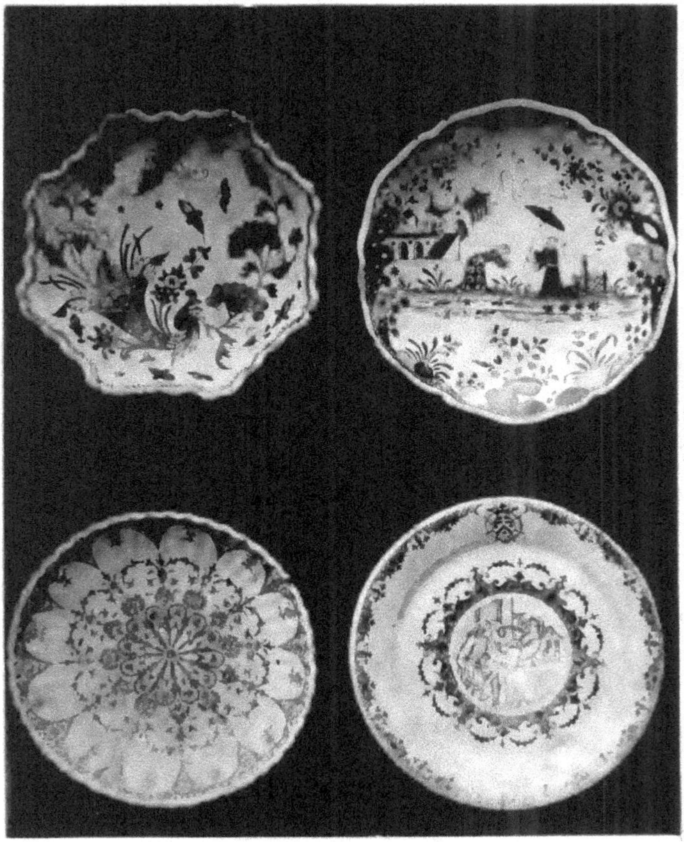

·I·1737·D

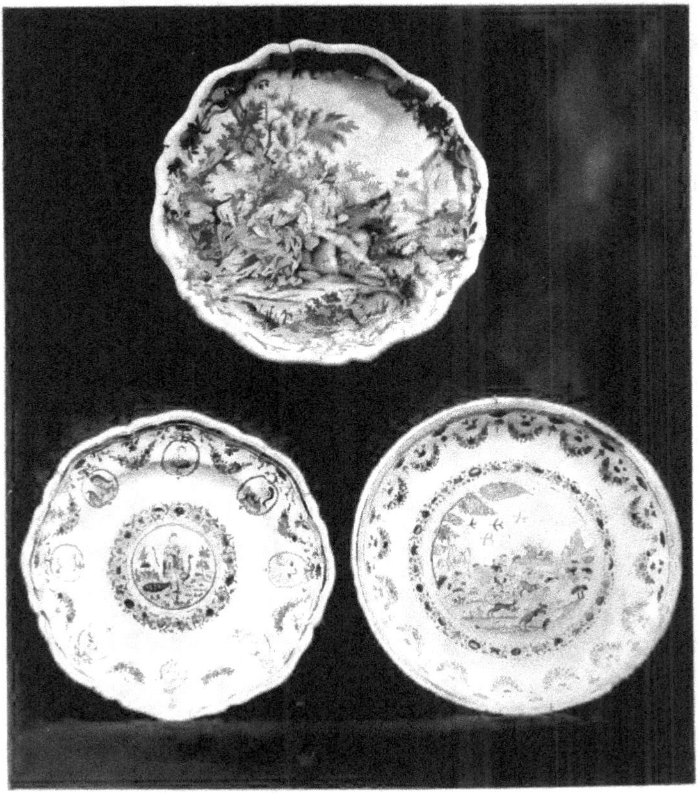

Plate LXX[illegible]

[illegible]

[illegible]

[illegible]

LXXII

COLOGNE

DRESDEN